AN ORDINARY
DECENT CRIMINAL

AN ORDINARY
DECENT CRIMINAL

Michael Van Rooy

MINOTAUR BOOKS

A THOMAS DUNNE BOOK
NEW YORK

A THOMAS DUNNE BOOK FOR MINOTAUR BOOKS.
An imprint of St. Martin's Publishing Group.

AN ORDINARY DECENT CRIMINAL. Copyright © 2005 by Michael Van Rooy. All rights reserved. Printed in the United States of America. For information, address St. Martin's Press, 175 Fifth Avenue, New York, N. Y. 10010.

www.thomasdunnebooks.com
www.minotaurbooks.com

Library of Congress Cataloging-in-Publication Data

Van Rooy, Michael, 1968–
    An ordinary decent criminal / Michael Van Rooy. — 1st U.S. ed.
        p. cm.
    "A Thomas Dunne book."
    ISBN 978-0-312-60628-2
    1. Ex-convicts—Fiction.   2. Crime—Canada—Fiction.   3. Winnipeg (Man.)—Fiction.   I. Title.
    PR9199.4.V3656O73 2010
    813'.6—dc22

                                                            2010012889

First published in Canada by Ravenstone, an imprint of Turnstone Press

First U.S. Edition: August 2010

10 9 8 7 6 5 4 3 2 1

For Laura, who taught me about love

AN ORDINARY DECENT CRIMINAL

1

had a gun I didn't want to use. It was a small, heavy thing of blue-black metal overlaid with a rainbow patina and stuffed shit-full with fattened copper bombs. It was hidden away in the right-hand pocket of my paisley dressing gown with my fingers resting gently on its butt. There were three men in my new home, one behind me with empty hands and two in front; one of those with a cheap hunting knife and the other with a piece of iron rebar as long as my arm. As far as I could tell, though, I was the only one with a gun.

"My wife is upstairs and pregnant."

All three men laughed nervously but didn't move. I was about a hundred percent certain I knew what they were thinking, but I couldn't afford mistakes because my wife and child were upstairs. The three had been caught breaking and entering and hadn't decided what to do. They could run or they could stay, and in either case they could hurt me or mine. That gave them three possible actions to choose from and two were bad, and that forced my hand.

"But . . ."

The hair on my arms went up as I made a decision. All three were wearing black woolen balaclavas with eye and mouth holes, and later I'd find out that the one behind me was also wearing a baseball hat that advertised Esso Gas.

". . . I'll give you all blow jobs if you'd like."

Time slowed for me as the one with the rebar grunted with effort and swung, but I was already falling inside the arc of the blow and twisting as I went. The crack of the iron denting the table beside me was loud as I raised the gun and pulled the trigger. In the quiet house the gun was a thunderclap and it woke my wife and my son and my dog and my mouse.

"Fuck!"

The boy cursed shrilly as the bullet entered his belly to fragment against his pelvic bone and steal the strength from his arms and legs. Shards of copper and splinters of bone briefly shared the same velocity as they scythed through meat and muscle, but, meanwhile, I was rolling towards the middle of the room and switching the gun from right hand to left. The other two boys had started to move and I fired twice more while they were stunned by the noise of the first shot. In the dimly lit room, the shots were accompanied by jets of burning gas almost a foot long, a blinding light that drove the bullets through the air.

One boy catches the round in the left eye of his mask and the second is turning when his bullet catches him under an armpit and cracks his spine. Both are dying as they fall and by the time they land, their hearts have stopped and their brains no longer spark. The echoes of the shots are fading and I can hear my son crying, my wife swearing, my dog finally waking and barking, while my mouse rustles in its dry aquarium.

Claire, my wife, comes down the stairs with a bayonet off an old rifle, held in a fencer's grip, and she is completely naked and gloriously full-breasted. She glares at the dim room and takes in the whole scene with a single glance and a narrowed mouth before moving into the kitchen with the blade held parallel to the ground at waist height, ready to stab or slash. The dog follows her but he's young and still confused by the loud noises and so he moves in a parody of solemn silence and virtue. I listen carefully to the silence for anything above the cries of my son, which have changed from terror to outrage at his inability to get anyone to bring him food.

". . . Ehak . . ."

A cough comes from the first person I'd shot and I kneel. The skin under the mask is white and his breathing is erratic and slowing even as I watch.

"She's not pregnant."

The man, no, the boy, makes it sound accusing but I pay him no attention. The dog has come over and is sniffing the boy in friendship and curiosity, only to get pushed away with a feeble hand. I check to make sure the rebar is well out of reach and smile as though to a half-heard pleasantry.

Claire moves back through the room towards the front of the house, checking the windows as she goes for signs of entry. She does not look at the bodies, but moves around them to avoid the slowly spreading stains on the carpeted floor. The dog looks up at her and trots over to join the new game, which looks like much more fun than the one I was playing.

Upstairs, I find my son Fred, holding hard to the bars of his crib. He is just ten months old and teething a little as he sobs. I pick him up and he is calmed by my smell and tries to reach the gun in my hand. Instead, I give him a rattle shaped like a black and white Christmas tree and he is satisfied and quiets down. Back downstairs, the boy on the floor hasn't moved much and I go over to watch while he dies.

"You should have taken the blow job."

I feel kind of sorrowful and kind of relieved, and Fred reaches out with a chubby hand and touches my cheek, and so I kiss his fingers, which makes him happy. I revel in that touch but I can hear sirens in the distance and my vision narrows until all I can see is the lame mask concealing the dead boy's face and the dog who's come back to sniff at the outstretched hand.

2

onty? Sam?"

Claire had come back into the room with the bayonet lowered and a dark flush fading slowly across both breasts and on her neck. Fredrick had fallen asleep in my arms and drooled peacefully on my left shoulder, and the dog had finally settled down. Claire flipped on the overhead lights and I could see the taped boxes stacked against the walls, each with a black number and letter combination drawn with a marker on the sides. She glanced at the bodies and exhaled through her nose; she'd done this kind of stuff before and hadn't liked it any more then.

"There's no one else here. What happened?"

Claire can tell when I lie, most of the time, anyway, and she put a little rawhide and steel into her voice to remind me of that.

"Would you like the truth or what we're going to tell the cops?"

My voice cracked with residual strain and I resented it, it was unprofessional. She nodded like I'd already told her something important.

"Both, I think."

"Good choice."

I handed Fredrick over and he complained a bit but fell asleep again after Claire put her knife down on the table. Right beside the knife was the dent made by the rebar club.

"These three assholes broke in to rob us. I heard them and came down with the pistol to chase them out. They tried to kill me and I shot them."

Claire's eyes narrowed when I mentioned the pistol.

"With the pistol? What pistol? Certainly not a pistol you kept? Right? Hmmm? Not after you promised."

Busted. I held up both hands.

"I kept one piece, just one. Not for work, I promise and I mean it. It was for self-defense. I'll crucify myself later."

I waited and she looked at me. She was a hair's breadth from leaving me, I could feel it. We were together on certain conditions and if she thought I was lying about this, then she was gone.

"No more, Monty. Nothing at all, ever again. Am I clear? I'll crucify you myself. Okay?"

The cold rage coming off her was palpable. I waved it off and went on.

"Between us, I gave 'em a chance and they didn't take it. I'm very sorry it happened."

The sirens were closer and I walked to the front of the house so I could see the street. Claire followed. Her mind was already working on more practical matters, like how to get away clean.

"Shouldn't you wipe the gun?"

"Hmmm?"

I glanced down at the snub-nosed gun and felt the cool, checkered walnut grips. The gun was a Smith and Wesson K Frame revolver, a Patrolman model built to handle .38 caliber special rounds, and it was pretty much untraceable. I'd done the work myself with acid and an emery wheel, grinding down the serial numbers on the outside and the set hidden inside until it was as clean as I could make it.

I hadn't even stolen it in this province.

"No. Our story is that the bad guys brought the gun with them. I came down and we wrestled."

I paced around and gestured with my hand.

"Wrestle, wrestle, wrestle. Then I took the piece away from them and had to shoot. You woke up. We don't have a phone yet so we couldn't call the cops."

I thought about it and continued. "They'll be here soon enough, anyway."

There were curtains on the front window and I could see through the gap. I'd laughed when Claire had put them up first thing, but now I appreciated them. The sirens were louder, and a blue and white Crown Victoria sedan pulled up to disgorge two Winnipeg cops, a youngish blond man and a brown woman. She yanked the shotgun out of the holder built into the dashboard and carried it at port arms up the path, but that didn't surprise me, it was that kind of neighborhood. I felt a little thrill. I hadn't dealt with cops for a while and I wondered if these were any good.

"Sound good?"

"Fine."

Claire's voice was clipped and I turned back towards the dead bodies. Already they were starting to settle as the air left the lungs and the piss and shit seeped out to mingle with the blood on the carpet. Fortunately, we were renting.

"Stall 'em a second, hon. A little panic/fear/rage would be appropriate."

Fred started to cry when the dog began to bark, which he did as soon as the cops passed into the front yard. I put the pistol on the table and then pulled a plastic baggie with extra bullets from the dressing gown pocket. The unarmed man had fallen on his back, and I opened the front pocket on his black nylon windbreaker and dumped in the six lead and copper rounds. I shredded the baggie into a half-empty box of cutlery and then came back as the cops reached the porch.

"Police. Open up."

They were doing it right, one on each side of the door and a long reach to knock and announce. Claire glanced at me and I nodded and opened the door. Before I could do anything, there was a thumb-wide shotgun barrel jammed into the hollow of my throat and a pale brown face staring down the receiver. The gun was crude, primitive, and lethal, and eminently capable of blowing my fucking head from my fucking neck so I slowly exhaled and made no movements at all.

"Police. Hands up, please. We have a report of shots."

Her voice had a West Indian lilt that sounded like music and she smelled like cinnamon mixed half and half with gun oil. Slowly my hands went past my shoulders and she smiled and nodded. Her part-ner slipped past me with a Buck Rogers-type pistol in both hands, pointed at the ceiling.

"I want to call a lawyer. My name is Samuel Parker and this is my house, my family just moved in and we have no phone yet. The woman behind me is my wife and the baby is my son. Three men broke in with guns and knives to rob us and I killed them in self-defense. I want to call a lawyer."

Out of the corner of my eye, I saw the younger cop blush furiously when he saw Claire standing there naked. Reflexively he moved to holster his piece. "Jeez," he said.

The woman with the shotgun made a gentle spitting sound like a chicken critiquing her young and her nose wrinkled in disapproval.

"No, Officer. You keep the gun out. You ignore the pretty naked lady. You check the house. Then you call for an ambulance. Ma'am? Please don't move. This has to be done a certain way to avoid un-pleasantness."

The boy cop held onto his gun and started into the dining room, staying near the wall and out of the lady's line of fire. Fred cried and the shotgun stayed steady at my throat as Claire spoke with a voice that cracked with the same cold rage. "Goddamn you. Take that gun off my husband, he didn't do anything wrong. Go do your job."

The bright eyes sighting along the shotgun didn't even twitch and the cop's cheerful voice dropped half an octave. "Be quiet, ma'am."

The other officer finished checking the first floor and came into view out of the corner of my vision. "We got three deaders back there."

He looked blank and started talking into the walkie-talkie on his belt. "We need two ambulances plus crime scene and homicide to a private home on Aikins. No sirens. Repeat: no sirens, one suspect, and needing crime scene and homicide. Reference officers Ramirez and Halley."

Our dog Renfield, a Frankenstein-mixed mongrel, ambled up to sit pretty beside me with a battered Frisbee in his mouth.

"Sorry, boy, not now."

The cop behind me grabbed my wrist and I felt the cold steel forcing my hand down to waist level before ratcheting tight, one wrist to the other. The cop with the shotgun didn't do anything until I was pulled down to my knees and then she spoke. "The gun, Officer. The one on the table, bag it. You should have done that right away."

The younger one had a whine in his voice as he answered and it grated on my nerves. "What about chain of evidence?"

The shotgun was now pointed at the floor and the cop's finger was finally outside the trigger guard. Now I could focus past it to read "Ramirez" on the name tag.

"Chain of evidence don't mean shit if the lady with the baby shoots us dead. We protect ourselves first."

She gave me a sweet half-smile at odds with disinterested cop eyes.

"Sorry, sir. We have to do things in a certain way. I am quite sure you have done nothing wrong."

Fred had finally stopped crying and I turned my head to see Claire standing about four feet away and staring at Ramirez as she asked, "What is your name?"

The cop smiled and showed beautiful teeth. They looked capped and were even, with a smudge of lipstick on one incisor. "Elena Ramirez, ma'am. That is a beautiful boy you have there."

Claire didn't say a word; she just stared with narrowed eyes and I recognized her rage, but then she smiled and chucked Fred under the chin. When he laughed, I relaxed a bit and allowed a smile as Ramirez glanced down at me with a slightly confused look and then back at Claire.

"Yes. His name is Fredrick."

The cop shifted her grip on the shotgun and I knew what she was seeing. Here she was, talking politely with a man who had just killed three people and a naked woman who looked absolutely relaxed despite having three stiffs in the same room. She was probably wondering if she had missed something because all the little cop alarms were going off in her head. She stepped back and looked me over again, and I knew she was trying to place my face. Early thirties, slightly over six feet tall, with very pale skin and lots of old scars on his arms and hands. Pale gray or blue eyes and blond hair cut short. Normal enough, except I looked comfortable despite the handcuffs and the corpses and the cops. Cops know that only psychopaths, soldiers, and cops can kill and be comfortable with it, and she was probably trying to put me in the right category.

Others had tried, so I grinned at her, "Lots of luck."

I said it out loud and Ramirez glanced at Claire and looked even more confused. My wife was mad, which made sense, but not scared, which didn't. So Claire ended up filed away in the cop memory too, five foot nine, about a hundred and forty pounds, well built, sun-browned all over except for a narrow strip around belly and crotch. She was crowned with thick, unkempt, reddish-brown hair worn long, and had dark brown eyes. I wondered if the cop would recognize the untannable stretch marks brought on by pregnancy.

The other cop was back on the walkie-talkie, deciphering the Babel of static and code with ease and answering too low for me to hear.

Ramirez said, "Perhaps, ma'am, you might get dressed. I think you might distract the paramedics when they arrive. You are also certainly confusing Officer Halley."

Claire allowed herself to be escorted upstairs and started a conversation about babies, while I waited in the doorway with a really dumb cop behind me with a pistol and a walkie-talkie. My hands weren't used to being handcuffed anymore and they ached with tension and muscle memory until I consciously relaxed. I could see out the open door past the front yard to the tree-lined street and, although it was early spring and cold, neighbors were starting to cluster in small groups on the sidewalk. The police car still had its flashers on and the harsh light threw the whole block into sharp relief.

In time Claire and Ramirez came back down with Fred but she wasn't allowed to talk to me, and soon after that, an ambulance showed with a half-dozen cop cars and a small panel truck. The first non-uniformed cop into the house was a big man with washed-out blue eyes in a cheap, gray, three-piece suit, carrying an unlit, expensive cigar. In the house I could hear Ramirez talking and then the big cop came back and stared at me while he lit the cigar with a wooden kitchen match. In front of us, the yard was filling up with cops in uniforms and paramedics in white smocks.

"Mister Parker?"

"Yes. I would like to call a lawyer."

I said it as loud as I could without yelling and some of the people in the yard flinched but the big cop paid no attention.

"My name is Detective Enzio Walsh. You are under arrest. You have . . ."

In the background Claire yelled that I was innocent and I let a smile cross my face because for the first time in a long while, I knew where I stood.

3

Sergeant Enzio Walsh burst through the steel door that kept the world out of the little interrogation room on the sixth floor of Winnipeg's Public Safety Building. The door smashed against the wall and a uniformed cop named Daniels jumped off his stool and came to attention. I sat there and yawned.

"PAR-ker?"

Walsh yelled and I nodded peacefully as his glance pinwheeled around. The room was three yards by three square, and two and a half yards high, with rivetted walls painted some colour between green and gray. It had a stool for the cop and a table built into the wall and a ledge upon which I could rest my sorry ass. Above the door was a camera mount with a security camera in a heavy-duty cage, but it hadn't moved since I'd come into the room three hours ago. During that time, my only company had been Daniels, who'd tried to talk to me about anything at all. With no fucking luck 'cause momma taught me never to talk to cops.

"Par-KER?"

I nodded again. I'd had my head down on the table, exhausted as the adrenalin from the shooting leached slowly out of my system The handcuffs still cranked tight behind my back. Claire had tossed the cops a pair of jeans and a T-shirt and about an hour ago they'd let me put them on.

"Parker?"

Walsh stood with a bundle of paper in one hand, his conservatively colored tie loose around his neck. His coat was open and I could see the checkered grip of an automatic pistol on his right hip with the butt towards the front. With a quick little gesture, he motioned Daniels out, grinning with an intensity that didn't quite touch his eyes. When Daniels was gone, he shut the door and pulled the stool up across from me.

"Parker?"

I yawned again and blinked as he went on.

"No, no, no, my lad."

He cleared his throat and read from the sheet in front of him.

"Montgomery Uller Haaviko. Also known as Sheridan Potter, Igor Worley, and Gerry Timmins. Habitual offender from way back. Arrests for assault, arson, uttering threats, theft, breaking and entry, smuggling, possession of weapons, possession of prohibited weapons, possession of controlled substances, sale of controlled substances, and seven counts of attempted murder over the years. Convictions leading to eight years of prison out of the past ten. You got off easy before but I've got you now, you prick, and in my very own province. And for murder, of all things, you finally got it right after all that fucking effort."

It had taken the cops longer than I'd figured to put my name to my face and prints.

"I would like to speak to a lawyer. It's not illegal to change your name and I did it all legal and proper. Through the courts. And I've done my time, all of it, so I'm not on parole or nothing. I ain't got no handle."

A smile split my face.

"So. I would like to speak to a lawyer, I've said that before and I'll say it again. Three men broke into my house and attacked, and I acted in self-defense with a reasonable amount of force to protect myself and my family."

"A real ODC."

I'd never heard the term. Finally, I asked, "ODC?"

He picked something pink from between his front teeth and examined it. A half-moon of bright blood appeared on his gums before he tongued it away.

"My Da used to be a prison guard . . ."

"Screw."

Walsh stopped.

"The term is 'screw.' "

He patted my shoulder roughly.

"Prison guard. In Wormwood Scrubs, in London back in the seventies."

He shuffled through the papers in his hand, examined one, and then shuffled it back.

"Back in the seventies they started to deal with all sorts, all mixed together. Paddy bomb tossers blowing up school kids. Raghead pedophiles. Nigger arsonists. Along with the regular kind of cons . . ."

He winked at me.

"The ones the screws called ODCs. Ordinary Decent Criminals."

He shuffled the papers again and then again.

"Guys like you. Burglars. Thieves. Thugs."

He picked one paper out and held it loosely between two fingers. "Just like you."

Walsh pushed the paper across to me. "Sign this."

The paper was blank and I looked it over as Walsh sat there with a pen in his left hand. His smile had finally reached his eyes and triumph glittered there until I spat a mouthful of spit onto the paper and started to laugh slowly. "Ha. Ha. Ha."

"Dumb. Dumb fucking move."

His voice was low and he kept smiling. He gathered the papers up and scraped the spit off onto the table edge, then slowly got to his feet and came around to my side of the table. I could have reached him with a kick but I never tried. The stallion design of the Colt was about six inches from the corner of my eye and it drew all my attention.

"Mister Haaviko, we can do this hard or soft, but it will get done."

I rehearsed it. Lean back. Kick Walsh's right knee into pudding with my left heel. Kneel and get the gun. Click the safety off (I tried to remember if Colt put their safeties on the left or the right side), twist sideways to aim the gun (hard to do sideways and behind your back but not impossible). Pull the trigger twice. (Cop mantra, "One to the belly, one to the head, makes a man dead.") Find the keys to the handcuffs (they're unmistakable, small, light, and with a short, hollow barrel), probably on Walsh's key ring, open the lock (I've done it before blindfolded, in the dark, with a nose full of cocaine, while being shot at). Drop the cuffs. Shoot any cops who come in (I tried to remember how many rounds a Colt carried, six at minimum, up to nine for some of the later models). Get out of the building fast, hijack a car, take a hostage as needed, if needed. Drive away.

I didn't do any of it.

Walsh's suit coat was open and it swung heavily around his body. Like there was something in his right-hand pocket, maybe. So maybe the gun in his belt wasn't his only piece. Maybe it wasn't even loaded. Maybe he would let me grab the belt piece and pop me with the one in his pocket.

I looked at his right hand and saw that maybe it was trembling just a little. And that the tendons on the back of his hand were rigid, maybe with stress. And I remembered that most cop shops had rules requiring officers not to carry their guns into interview rooms. Maybe Winnipeg was an exception but that made lots of maybes and it was a bad cop looking down at me with contempt in his eyes.

"You are a piece of shit, just like all the rest, and you are not welcome in my town."

I looked into his eyes and then I blinked and spoke softly. "Criminals are a cowardly and superstitious lot."

He nodded in agreement and I went on, "That's what Batman says. Too."

His hand trembled and two bright spots appeared on his cheeks and then he went to the door and let two men in. Both were in uniform pants and old T-shirts stained gray at the armpits, and wore Sam Browne belts with empty holsters. They were in their fifties and beefy with beer muscle and one had a fouled anchor tattoo on his forearm.

"Gentlemen, Mister Haaviko here would like to do this the hard way."

Both cops grinned and the one on the left removed his dental plate to show a gap of about four teeth in front. He dropped the plate in his empty belt holster and I took another breath.

"My name is Samuel Parker and I would like to speak with a lawyer."

And they beat me. It lasted a long time, most of which I spent screaming.

That didn't work so I tried crying and then puking. Then I pissed my pants but nothing worked. Sometimes, if you make a big mess, the beatings stop, but it didn't work this time.

It just went on.

There are rules to taking a beating, jailhouse rules, tried and true. Rule one is to scream because people who inflict pain like to know you're feeling it, so even if it doesn't hurt, scream.

Rule two is, if you decide to fight, do it right away before weakening because a good session of torture will tire you right out. Rule three is, if you do fight back, then fight to kill.

Rule four is a corollary to rule two and also the golden rule of all bad guys everywhere, and that's never kill a cop. You kill a cop, you even hurt a cop, and you're dead. You may be walking but you're still dead. Cops don't let cop killers walk around breathing.

It's a principle or something.

The cops did it right, nothing minor league about it at all. Open-hand blows hard to the top of the head and keep doing it and you get a concussion without bruises.

A phone book and an old-style billy club or the new-style tonfa riot stick, and take turns beating the book while someone holds it across the perp's ribs. Do that for long enough and you shake someone's insides loose.

Slap an open hand into someone's kidneys and eventually you get blood in the urine; keep going and you can kill someone.

It went on until all three of us were covered in sweat and the room reeked of testosterone, piss, and vomit, and then Walsh came back into the room and showed the paper to me again, only now there was a neatly typed confession.

"What say? We can go on. We're not tired."

The panting of all of us filled the room with echoes and I spoke in a voice raw from screaming. "I want a lawyer."

Walsh went rigid and the cop with the tattoo grabbed me and held my head immobile.

"Wait, wait."

When I spoke the grip on me loosened a little. I knew it was crazy as soon as I opened my mouth. Then I yelled. "Give ME the KEYS, you fuzzy sock SUCKER."

It was the punch line from an old joke, the edited dialogue from *The Usual Suspects,* and I'd seen it in prison the year before with a whole range of maybe eighty cons howling laughter until the screws had shut down the power and killed the water. The line didn't go over well with the cops, though, and the one with the missing teeth pulled a couple of cotton swabs from a belt pouch along with a can of pepper spray. It was the cop stuff, not as strong as that sold to civilians. Citizens, however, are only supposed to use pepper spray on bears and dogs and those rules don't apply to cops.

"This will hurt."

It was a promise. Walsh braced his back against the door and he

17

watched as the swabs got sprayed with the clear solution and then brandished close enough to make my nose run and my eyes ache.

"Last chance."

I didn't do or say anything. The cop behind me pried open my eyelids one at a time and the other one swabbed the naked jelly and I went blind. About a second after that, the shock hit and everything was pulled out of my brain, sucked along by a scream that deafened even me.

4

Mr. Haaviko? Can you hear me?"

I nodded to the invisible voice and looked out into fog. There were shades of color there, and dim shapes, but the room looked neater than the one I'd been in. Did they move me or clean up the mess? How long had I been out? The figure across from me was thin and wearing dark clothes, including an overcoat. Not a cop, unless it was a detective. I was thirsty, my muscles ached and burned, and I was still handcuffed, but the clothes were new and clean and that was a plus.

When I spoke, my voice was ragged with pain. "It's Parker, actually, I've given up Haaviko. Too many memories."

The shape bobbed its head and I went on.

"I want to see a lawyer."

"I am a lawyer. Your lawyer if you want me to be. My name is Lester Thompson and my office sent me."

It took me a while to think that through. When it finally sank in, I wanted to cry but instead I asked a question. "Are you honest?"

It came out as a croak and Mr. Thompson thought for a while before answering, which I felt was a good sign. "Yes."

He didn't sound too sure and I smiled to myself. "Fine. You're hired. Could you please get me a drink of water and get these handcuffs off? I can't feel my hands."

He nodded (I think) and went to the door, where I could hear him talking quietly to someone outside. After a few moments, someone came in with a Styrofoam cup of lukewarm water and the keys to the cuffs. After freeing me, he put his keys away and paused as if he was going to say something before walking out. My hands ached as I tried to retrieve some sensation beyond pain by massaging the swollen meat. It was only with difficulty that I avoided rubbing my eyes.

"Okay, Mr. Haaviko, um, Parker, there's not a lot that I can do. The police have your confession and I've seen a copy of it. I don't think the Crown will deal down past murder two but it could happen. You really shouldn't have said anything."

I ignored him and picked up the cup. The water went into my cupped hand and then I bathed each eye and let the water run onto the floor to avoid re-contaminating myself. Water on oleosporin hurts as the capsicum oils are reactivated but there was nothing else I could use. In a few moments they felt better and when I was done with that, I drank the spoonful I had saved and went back to manipulating the pinched and puckered flesh on my wrists.

"Sorry. Pepper spray. I could use more water or ye old Seattle Face Wash but neither seems to be available."

"Mr. Parker!"

My lawyer was angry but I kept talking, squeaking away, as the pain spiked and swelled.

"Yep. Don't know if the wash would work here, not in the eyes. It's a handy little kit, first a bottle with a mixture of vegetable or mineral oil, water, and dish soap, followed by a rinse bottle of water and clean cloth. But it's gotta be clean."

"Are you listening, Mr. Parker? Do you understand what I'm saying?"

With my eyes relatively clear, I could see Thompson. He was a skinny man in his mid-twenties with thin lips and pale brown eyes. He was wearing a chocolate brown wool suit with a bright blue power tie and the clothes looked out of place and almost new. On the table in front of him was a thin manilla folder with my name printed on it and on the floor beside him was an expensive aluminum briefcase with a complicated combination lock. He looked excited and ran his fingers through already thinning brown-blond hair and tried not to smile. My stomach turned as I smelled some kind of musky, cheap cologne radiating off him.

"Yes, I heard. Murder two times three, maybe. The police have a confession, kind of. No Crown deals, probably. Is that about it?"

He moved abruptly and awkwardly like a nervous animal and drummed his fingers on the metal tabletop. "Yes."

I carefully put my weight on my feet and fought more nausea to stretch and rotate my hips and then my shoulders. My whole body ached from the beating but I doubted there'd be any bruising. A professional hijacker I knew briefly in Millhaven Penitentiary had heard it called a "soft tissue workout," cop and con slang for the new third degree.

"The confession isn't signed, right?"

"No. But it really doesn't need to be, there are witnesses who heard you admit that you murdered the three men after an argument."

Bracing myself against the wall, I started doing isometrics, pushing muscles against tendons and stretching through the pain, beating it into submission. I realized I was wearing orange detention overalls and I briefly wondered where my clothes were and then I put that out of my mind. Vaguely I remembered Walsh playing with my hands and bagging the confession afterwards, which meant the cops would have fingerprints to show I'd read the damn thing if they needed that.

"Yeah. But a signature would've been nice. Now we're going to have to work."

"What are you talking about?"

Thompson spoke without passion, doodling on a pad of yellow paper with a black and silver Montblanc pen.

"I didn't make any confession."

He snorted. "I've heard that one before. Three witnesses, though, three statements, all cops, you a felon . . ."

I was offended and stretched some more as shooting pains spiked through my back and sides. I gagged on bile and water and finally spoke. "Ex-felon."

"All right, an ex-felon. Who's the judge going to believe?"

At that point I looked up and saw a video camera above the door. I grinned and covered with a cough before walking over to look at the unit from underneath. My lawyer cleared his throat as I checked out the thick-gauge wire basket around it and the armored cable feeding into the wall. He was staring at me with curiosity and something like fear when I came back.

"May I? Thanks."

I took the pen from his hand and braced my wrist. Two steps and a hard thrust and I burst the lens amidst a shower of sparks and the smell of ozone. Thompson recoiled as I handed the pen back.

"Are you crazy? That pen was from my mother. That camera was off, it's never turned on when there's an interview."

"Sure. The cops'll be in right away so I'll talk fast. I didn't make the confession and I can prove it but if the cops find out how, then they'll fix it."

I was lying (a little) and praying (a lot) at the same time, which didn't matter to Thompson, who was just quietly furious. He remained on his stool and shook his head while gathering his stuff together to leave. It was interesting to watch as tiny flakes of dandruff rained down onto his shoulders and the pad of paper in front of him.

"You're dreaming. The cops aren't watching, the camera's standard equipment and it's never turned on during interviews. They'd be breaking client/lawyer confidentiality rules."

Walsh came in with his hand on the butt of his Colt. "Any problems?"

Thompson's lips whitened and he looked at me through slitted eyes. I smiled and addressed myself to him. "All right, how'd they know the camera got broke unless it was on in the first place?"

"Any problems?" Walsh repeated himself, looking everywhere but at the camera.

Thompson stood up and exhaled through his nose. "Officer Walsh, do you have a room where I can do an interview? One without a camera?"

Walsh rolled his eyes. "Well, they all have cameras. It's SOP these days. You should know that, Mr. Thompson. Sorry."

He didn't sound sorry.

I waited and watched the man but my adrenals didn't kick in, I guessed they were empty. I wanted to kill Walsh with my bare hands or some kind of tool but I was tired and sore and old. And then the pain started again.

"What about the bathroom?" I asked.

"The bathroom . . . you've got to be kidding."

"No. I've got to go."

"Well, sure, I'll take you. Least we can do."

Thompson was livid now, his thin face pinched with rage. "Hasn't my client been allowed to go to the bathroom yet?"

Walsh didn't move his hand from the gun. "He was busy confessing. He got all caught up in unburdening his soul and time just flew."

Thompson stepped a little closer to Walsh and his knuckles whitened around the pen.

"My client is also looking a little battered. That didn't happen when he was in your custody, did it? That would be unfortunate for you."

"That kind of shit just breaks my heart. Don't worry, your client was treated like gold here. Pure gold."

"Fine. After this I want to see whomever's in charge."

Walsh was acquiring an audience as cops in uniforms and plainclothes showed up along with clerks to peer in like spectators at a zoo. The smells of fresh coffee and tobacco smoke filled the interrogation room and made my stomach knot and I realized I was real close to pissing my pants. Elena Ramirez, the cop from the house, was in the front row and watching blank-faced.

"That'd be Lieutenant Ross. He just got in. He's reading Haaviko's statement in his office. I'm sure he'd love to speak with you. Let me set it up."

The pain was growing worse and my head was aching. My voice slurred when I spoke and my tongue felt fat and thick, like an uninked stamp pad. "Can I please use the bathroom?"

"Sure."

Daniels stepped forward at Walsh's gesture and started to usher me off to the left. My eyes were tearing and I wondered if I was going to throw up again. I stopped worrying when I realized there was probably nothing left in my stomach to throw up, even if I wanted to.

"Mr. Thompson, come with me, please," I said.

I blinked back the tears and looked directly at Walsh.

"Please, I just don't want to get beaten again."

Everyone flinched and then slipped back to work and a twitch started under Walsh's right eye, but he remained silent as Daniels led me and Thompson to the bathroom. We passed through a big room full of desks with glass-walled offices on two walls and interview rooms along the third. The fourth wall was covered in corkboard tiles holding notices and pictures and that held doors to the bathrooms.

Daniels looked at me impassively. "Leave the stall open."

The cop leaned back against the sinks and watched me with his arms crossed while Thompson turned around to wash his face. I used one hand to brace myself while manipulating the soft, plastic zipper down the front of the overalls. The overalls were one piece and it was a practiced humiliation that made it necessary to remove your clothes all the way down to the ankles to use a toilet. I did it without thinking and pissed a weak, pain-filled arc.

I stared and puzzled out loud. "Red?"

The bowl filled as I watched but my brain didn't register at first. "Red means blood."

It came out in a trickle, diluted with urine, and the pain spiked and I doubled over as Thompson and the cop rushed over.

"Oh shit."

Suddenly the cop was trying to hold me up and then I heard Thompson dialing his cell phone and asking for an ambulance and then I passed out.

5

The hospital bed was a deeply comfortable nest of crisp white cotton and I was out, out, out.

The five milligrams of generic Valium the nurse had forced on me hadn't been necessary and I tongued it out once she'd left the room, but I had to keep it in my mouth because of the lady cop across the room from me. They'd let Claire and Fred in to visit and my wife squeezed my right hand, as it was closest. Each hand was handcuffed to the bed frame and the contact of flesh to flesh made me smile. From her arms, Fred looked solemnly down.

"You want it?"

I'd told her about the pill in my cheek and she shook her head. The cop raised her eyes at my whisper but nothing happened and she went back to reading an old issue of *Guns and Ammo* magazine.

"Keep it, just in case. You look like shit. Consider it your kryptonite crucifix." That made me smile something weak and tenuous. It was a line stolen from late-night TV and pleasant because it was shared. She went on, "Vampires and Superman both."

Claire's eyes were alight with pleasure and twinkled with humour but her mouth was grim and she held herself rigidly between me and the cop. She was spoiling for a fight and I couldn't and wouldn't argue with her.

"Yeah."

The pill went into the top of my cheek, where it was dry and cool, and I could feel it nestled there, a bitter and metallic memento. My body ached with the memory of the drug, the sweet forgetfulness that lay therein and the surcease from the pain and the altered state it would bring. Claire squeezed my hand again and brought me quickly away from that line of thinking. I was intellectualizing the addiction and that was a bad sign.

She said, "You're stronger than that."

She was right and wrong at the same time. I was stronger than the pills with her and Fred there, but the pills were stronger than me if I was alone. I nodded anyway. "So you called the lawyer?"

Claire switched Fred to her left arm and snorted.

"It took a while. The cops didn't let me go until past one and Ramirez called a cab, which got me to a hotel. I took the file case with your papers after the cops looked through it and phoned from the hotel. I reached your old lawyer in Calgary and he gave me a name here in town. He sounded happy to hear from you."

I couldn't nod, there was a monitoring tube up my nose and a brace across my neck, but I rolled my eyes. "I always paid on time."

She shrugged and switched Fred to the other arm. "Yeah, he's a vulture, but a good vulture."

"True."

She shifted Fred again and a frown creased her forehead. "How we gonna afford the shyster?"

It was almost a whisper and I motioned her close. The cop shifted a little in her chair, but didn't do anything. "Legal aid. It's a good case, lots of publicity. The money will come from the province and so will the lawyer."

She leaned back and her eyes narrowed at the sight of the restraints on my wrists. "You've changed. I know that. Isn't it obvious? Can't all the cops and all the cons and all the rest see? You've gone straight."

It was a plea, a demand, a complaint, and there was no answer I could make. She leaned down and kissed me gently but the effect was ruined when Fred tried to pull the tube out of my nose. She raised her head and patted my shoulder.

"They just don't realize that I'll pull your lungs out if you fuck up again. Oh, well. I'll see you tomorrow, so behave. Tomorrow we'll roast 'em. But for now, sleep."

And I did, but it took a long time to forget about the pill slowly dissolving and numbing my whole mouth and reminding me of what I had been. It's not like I ever really stopped being addicted, I just stopped doing the drugs.

Something pinched my foot gently through the sheet and I woke up slick with sweat and trembling with remembered pain. The room was dark and there were low snores coming from the cop's chair.

"Claire?"

Someone had drawn the curtain around the bed, shutting out all the lights except for the watch lights down low on the walls to stop people from tripping on obstacles.

"No, not Claire."

The voice was unfamiliar and I adjusted my left hand into a striking surface before I remembered the handcuffs. Then I stopped and waited.

"Monty, my man. Remember me?"

I didn't and he flipped on a penlight with a piece of electrician's tape over the lens. The tape was pierced with a pinhole and I could see a vaguely familiar face in the silken thread of light.

"No."

On second thought, he was still no one I knew, and my heart drummed tightly. He waited for a second and then shut off the light, but his image floated there, a sharp-planed face, a Canadian mixture of Scot and Cree with wide nostrils and a thin nose. He was wearing loose-fitting hospital greens and looked toned and lean.

I remembered what e.e. cummings said about Buffalo Bill: "Christ, he was a handsome man." And I wondered if I was looking at my executioner.

"C'mon. You must remember. Teddy Stiles, the one and only."

He took my hand gently in the dark and squeezed it.

"We were in Drumheller on the same range. 'Bout four years back. Ted Stiles. In for arm-ed robbery."

He separated the first word into two parts and the fact he said "armed" told me a lot. Serious cons don't say "armed robbery," that's for social workers. Serious cons assume the armed.

"No. Sorry."

He sounded hurt. "You sure? I had a house with Benjamin Capito? Played blackjack with you a few times?"

"Sorry. Been in lots of jails with lots of guys."

"Oh. Well."

He thought about it and changed the subject. "How bad off are you?"

His tone was conversational, casual, and I matched it. "Two, maybe three days in here but I can walk or even run right now. Nothing permanent, bruised kidneys and general contusions, nothing broken."

He pushed my legs over and settled in next to me with his knees resting on the rail around the bed. When he was comfortable, he lit up a cigarette.

"Good."

The lady cop let out a massive snore from outside the curtain.

"What about the cop?" I asked

"Ropena, Rophena, Ropellis, shit. I can't remember."

He fished out his light again and turned it on to look at a brown vial half full of oblong white pills. "Aha. Rohypnol. Not just for rape anymore. She was dozing when I got here, you were all the way out. I just brought her some fresh coffee on my way by with a laundry cart. I gotta remember that, no one looks at someone pushing a cart of dirty sheets. She'll be out for five or six hours, depending on weight, and she's a big heifer. Or is it sow, considering all things? She won't remember much, either, which is handy."

He shifted his weight and the bed creaked. "Got some left over from a badger game."

I wasn't tracking too well. Badger games were cons done with a girl who plays the hooker, a guy who plays the irate boyfriend/brother/ father/husband, and the john who doesn't know he's even playing anything at all. Easy money in a resort town or working a convention. Rohypnol would make sure the john didn't remember anything but what the girl wanted to tell him. Actually, it was a nice touch.

"Ted, right? Not to break up old home week but what'cha doing here?"

He blew smoke towards the ceiling. "In Winnipeg? Working, favours for friends, little games of this and that."

"No. What are you doing here—here? With me."

The cigarette glowed as he inhaled. "Checking up on you and delivering a message from an acquaintance named Robillard. He runs some action in town and one of the boys you capped last night was a cousin or some such shit."

In the dark the words floated and I could taste them.

"The message is . . . ?"

He lit another cigarette from the stub of the first and drew deeply. "The boys in your house weren't heavy. Not with guns, anyway. They were break-and-enter artists feeding their veins. It is generally accepted by the bad guys around these parts that those boys were too dumb to use guns. If they ever got a hold of iron, they'd sell it. So Mr. Robillard figures you set them up and knocked them down."

He took another hit off the cigarette and the smoke swirled around my face as he exhaled. "Now, Mr. Robillard doesn't really care, family ties just aren't that strong. But the whole thing shows a certain disrespect. So he figures that you and your family . . ."

My face felt very cold. His hand was still on mine and the hand-cuff gave me maybe six inches of motion and I decided not to let him finish.

"...ew..."

It takes about ten pounds of pressure to break a joint, about fifteen to break a bone. I twisted my wrist and grabbed his thumb and three fingers and broke them. That much pain was disabling, paralyzing, and he squeaked but I didn't let go.

"...ew..."

The coal of the cigarette gave me something to aim for as his free hand groped towards my face. The nurse had left a thin cotton sheet over me and I kicked it loose and brought my shin up hard to mash the cigarette into his face. While I was doing that, I twisted his broken fingers and ground the torn-open nerves against each other. His hand closed on my face weakly and I brought my left leg past my right one and kicked his face again, this time connecting with my toes.

My left big toe broke on his forehead so I kicked him twice more with my right foot and twisted his hand down until I felt his fingers break some more.

"...ew..."

He was leaning down towards me to get away from the kicks but moving really slowly. His breath was stale and full of cigarette smoke and sandwich meat. I locked my legs around his throat and chest and twisted his body down onto the bed.

"...ew...ew...ew..."

His left hand stopped grabbing my face and flopped over to the other side of me, where I grabbed it with my left, also handcuffed, hand. Merrily I started to break those fingers too.

Stiles spasmed with the pain and tried to raise his head and I tightened my legs and turned out his lights. An LA cop could do it in twenty seconds with a billy club but it took me twice that long. Even after he stopped struggling, I held my legs in place around his neck, but I did relax them a little finally and waited.

After a while he shuddered and took a deep breath and I could feel his muscles tense.

"Ted. Listen to me. I can choke you out. I can break your neck. I can crush your fingers. Can you understand me?"

It took a few moments.

". . . ew . . . I understand."

"Good. You packing?"

". . . a knife."

"Where is it?" He took another breath. "Right-hand front pocket."

" 'Kay. I'm gonna tell you what happens next. In a bit the nurse will come in and I'll turn you over to the cops. I won't press charges but the cops will. Feeding a mickey to a cop is assault. You cool with that?"

"Do I got a choice?"

I took a deep breath. "Yeah. If you don't wanna do the time, I can break your neck."

He thought about it before answering. "Cops."

"Now tell me about Robillard."

He thought about it. "Or?"

"I break your fingers some more."

"Yeah, you would. Okay, Robillard runs ten or twenty guys. Grows and sells hydro-weed, fences some, smuggles crank from out west, guns from the south, heroin from the east. He's connected to the Angels in Quebec, Christian Identity freaks in Idaho, some Native gangs."

"So he sent you to take me out."

It wasn't a question.

"Yeah."

"What did he pay?"

"Nothing. A favour for a favour."

"Even though I'm probably going down on murder?"

Stiles groaned. "You are? Shit, I didn't know . . ."

Amateur night. I thought about breaking his neck anyway but the urge passed.

"So far, Ted, I'm regretting keeping you above the ground. Make yourself useful. Tell me more."

"I'm thinking, I'm thinking. He's a big guy, like three hundred and fifty pounds and maybe five foot ten. Brown and gray hair worn long. His wife is smarter than him, she used to be a whore, a tough chick named Sandra. Had some of that when she was working and a sweet little snatch she's got."

My toe was throbbing. I must have really broken it well and thoroughly. "Why's he so pissed?"

"Like I said; you killed his cousin. It's some kind of personal insult . . ."

His voice had been getting weaker and it finally trailed off and shock took him away. I lay in the dark with my legs wrapped around the idiot's neck. Finally the nurse came in and the shit hit the fan.

6

The nurse came in at a grotesquely early hour, saw the drugged cop (who had vomited into her lap during the night), the unconscious felon lying across the bed, and me. Then she fled out the door like rabid dogs were after her and a few minutes later the room filled with cops, security guards, doctors, nurses, and candystripers. Or is it strippers?

"Raise your hands. Now. Don't think about it, just do it."

The cop had good crowd control and his Glock clone pistol pointed at the bridge of my nose. I rattled my handcuffs and he looked sheepish.

"Oh."

Gradually the room cleared and finally I was wheeled out into an examination room, after they'd pulled Stiles off my legs. Later, the original nurse came in, followed by a nasty-looking cop who wore a ballistic vest over his shirt and stood at the foot of the bed. The nurse came over and patted my forearm.

"So how are we feeling?"

She was a bright-faced and cheerful woman with hair the color of a deer mouse's fur and mild hazel eyes set far too close together. She leaned over me to adjust the pillow and I was exquisitely aware of the gentle heft of her breast on my forearm. Her breath smelled of strong spearmint, chewing gum or maybe schnapps, I couldn't tell which.

"I'm sore."

"Of course. Of course."

"And exhausted."

"Of course." She said it absently and stood with her back to me, staring at the cop, who had crossed massive arms across an equally massive chest, and I wondered how long he had been doing steroids. The door to the hallway was open and the noise of the hospital staff changing to the day shift was steady and soothing. No matter what happened to me, the hospital was saying, what the hospital does will go on. The sick will pass or perhaps not but sickness itself remains and never changes.

In the hallway a slope-shouldered black man walked by, wearing a dark blue quilted jacket. Over one arm was slung a tiny backpack extolling the virtue of Queen Amidala. I wondered who Queen Amidala was.

Thompson walked in and ignored the nurse and the cop. "Good morning."

I smiled but otherwise didn't move. My legs and hands ached from hard use and my whole body was parched. I was stupid and weak with exhaustion and charmed by the big, bright lie of addiction that kept popping into my head. The ego buzz of amphetamines, the promise that the meth-enhanced user can take care of anything. That word, "enhanced," danced through my head and that was its very own lie, in and of itself promising more and more and more.

That lie grew even bigger and showed me the memories of the prismatic flicker of my mind on crystal meth and the tidal surge that came via PCP. I wanted/needed/desired the drugs, any drugs, and so I stopped smiling and closed my eyes. Up, down, sideways, anywhere just as long as I was altered and changed and no longer fucking here.

Thompson cleared his throat and spoke. "How's it going?"

He looked seriously out of place, standing there in his overcoat.

"Fine."

He waited and I realized he wasn't going to talk. Instead, he toyed with his briefcase.

"Nice case."

He yawned and I could suddenly smell his breath from two yards away. It muted the smells of the cop and the peppermint nurse. The nurse left but nothing else happened and finally Thompson got pissed and addressed the cop directly. "You can leave."

The cop's mouth turned down at the edges. "I am assigned . . ."

"Talk to your sergeant. Talk to your lieutenant. Talk to your chief or the Crown, because I am this man's attorney of record and I need to interview him."

The cop was unimpressed and stubborn. "I have a job to do."

Thompson tried a new tack. "I will lay charges."

The cop sneered. "For what?"

"I'll come up with something. Civil. Criminal. Procedural. Try me."

The cop tightened his mouth and started to leave.

"Oh. Take one handcuff off. I might need a signature."

He took the cuffs off my right hand only and put them away. "I'll be right outside. The door will be open. Am I understood, Mr. Haaviko?"

I ignored him. When he left, Thompson rubbed his forehead. "Okay, let's start fresh. Mr. Haaviko . . ." He sat down in a chair near where the cop had been standing and pulled out a pad of canary yellow paper.

"It's Sam now, Mr. Thompson, Sam Parker."

"Legally?"

"Court-ordered and everything. Legal as legal can be."

"Okay. So, how are you today? Able to talk?"

"I'm in rough shape. I've been trapped and beaten. But able to talk."

"You've had some time to think since yesterday, I hope. Do you want to change your mind? Do you really want to take this to trial?"

Translation, did I want to deal? I thought about it, the Crown might go for three manslaughters. Maybe four years for each. No way I'd get out in a sixth of the time with my record, so I'd be looking at a third, minimum. That meant four to six and closer to six years, maybe nine, depending on how the judge phrased himself during the sentencing. Probably the full stretch, twelve years, maybe more.

"Mr. Parker?"

Claire wouldn't wait, she'd divorce me and vanish, she'd wasted enough time while I played my games. Fred would be grown up before I was out, a real person and everything. Renfield would be dead, so would the mouse. No house, no home, no nothing.

"No. No deals." I'd have nothing to go back to. "Definitely not. I'll take my chances."

Thompson coughed and recited in a monotone, "You're risking a quarter century up to life, and closer to life."

Yeah, the worst-case scenario. He stared until he was sure that I shook my head. Then he beamed.

"Fine. Just perfect. As I understand it, three armed men broke into your house, a fight ensued, and you killed them, that right?"

I made some kind of noise in my throat.

"Right, and last night another man broke into your hospital room, I assume he broke in, right?"

Another noise.

"A man armed with a knife, pills, bad intentions. He drugs the cop and tries to off you. But you fight him off, disarm him, knock him unconscious, and hold him until the next morning."

"Where are you going with this?"

"There's no way we're going to be able to convince a jury or a judge that an unarmed man killed three armed men and didn't get a scratch. Then we've gotta convince them you disarmed and held an armed man when you were handcuffed to a hospital bed."

I deadpanned. "You're looking at Superman. The Elvis of crime. Best thief in western Canada once upon a time." I thought about it and then modified. "Well, second best. Third, if you count a guy who lives here but works Mexico and the southwestern US."

He was unimpressed and made a couple of quick notes on his pad. "Let's consider the three dead men, that's the worst situation. As I see it, they've got you on toast. Confession, past history, witnesses, an airtight case. You're gone."

He sounded happy.

"Of course, those kind of cases encourage prosecutors to make mistakes. They don't know where the defense will come from. Airtight cases can be a bitch."

"There's also no such thing. What's the strongest thing they've got?"

"The confession."

I shook my head very slowly. "I don't think so. There's no way I made a confession. I was a professional bad guy for all my adult life and those habits stay, no matter what else happens. Pros do not give confessions. Shit, no one gives confessions these days, not without a lawyer. Mark my words, within your lifetime the judges will toss any confession unless it's done with a lawyer for the defense on hand or a camera in the room."

Thompson got up and started to pace. "Okay. So we've got an unsigned confession."

Thompson had his pad in hand and kept doodling with his scratched pen. Apparently it still worked. Montblanc made good pens, I'd have to remember that. He continued, "So how do we get the confession thrown out? Assuming you never made it."

"I never made it. The cops got nasty. There was a Detective Walsh and two other cops, one with bridgework in the front of his gob and the other with an anchor and a cable tattooed on his arm. They beat me, swabbed pepper spray in my eyes, shit like that. I told you that last night."

Thompson looked a little sick. He swallowed it. "Great. Prove it."

He doodled some more before speaking again. "Chemical tests for pepper spray?"

"Good. However, it would take two or three days to get it set up with a qualified lab. By then the evidence would have been washed out. Next."

"What about bruises?"

"No good. Maybe they happened before I was arrested. Who can tell?"

Thompson scratched the top of his head with the blunt end of his pen. "What about damage to your kidneys? Yours were pretty badly bruised, from what the nurses are saying."

We were both quiet and then I spoke up. "Could you get the doctor in here?"

Thompson left and I closed my eyes until he came back, dragging a young Chinese man wearing a knee-length white coat and holding a clipboard. He looked about eighteen and I realized with a sinking feeling that he probably was a doctor and that just made me feel old and tired. The doctor stared at me peacefully while listening to Thompson, who said, "So I am the lawyer for Mr. Parker here. He was beaten by the police last night. We need a medical opinion and you are his physician, correct?"

"Yes, but . . ."

It was a lawyer trick to end statements with questions. It was supposed to force participation but, in this case, it just seemed to irritate the doctor. He turned to address me.

"Mr. Parker. I am Dr. Leung. Good morning. You caused a considerable disruption."

"Sorry about that."

"Well. Do you remember me, Mr. Parker? You were delirious when you came in."

He went to the foot of the bed and held his clipboard in front of his groin.

"Not very well. Thank you, by the way."

Leung showed very bad teeth in a vague smile and tapped his clip-board with his forefinger. "How are you doing?"

"I'm in a lot of pain."

He made a note. "I will ask the nurse to bring you something."

"No. Thank you, though."

He hissed loudly and read the notes at the foot of the bed. "You are very stubborn. Okay, Mr. Haaviko, or is it Parker?"

Thompson answered him before I could. "His name is Parker and we would like to know about his health."

"Okay, Mr. Parker. I can answer some questions, but I am not an expert in . . . forensics, I suppose. For this reason, my value in a court would be minimal. You are not in danger but you will be in pain for quite some time. Your kidneys are bruised, practically ruptured, and we will probably have to put you on dialysis for a period of time. Do you understand?"

He was lecturing me, which was fine, so I nodded and answered. "It's a mechanical means of cleaning blood when the kidneys don't work."

Leung put the records back and walked around to where he could hold my wrist. His lips moved as he counted off the pulse and then he listened to my heart with a stethoscope. "You seem to be in extremely poor physical condition. May I ask why?"

My first instinct was to tell him to fuck off but I swallowed it. "No secret. I was hooked on crystal meth, coke, and other stimulants up to about nineteen months ago. I popped 'em in the skin, injected them in the vein, snorted 'em, smoked 'em. I was also a casual abuser of morphine, heroin, other downers, but that was never as serious. I managed to kick but it's taken a toll."

He sat there and blinked quickly like he was sending some kind of message. "So that explains your general aversion to drugs."

He looked me over and flashed bad teeth and worse gums, and then turned to look at Thompson. "Well, what is it that you wish to know?"

Thompson spoke up. "Could he have hurt his kidneys himself?"

"No. The bruising is considerable and he would have become unconscious long before the required amount of damage was done."

"Could it have happened before the arrest?"

"Of course, it's hard to tell exactly when a wound occurred unless it killed the patient. If death results, then there are physical processes that stop and that allows a determination of the time of death to be made. The injuries could have happened yesterday, maybe earlier if Mr. Parker took it easy. After the injuries were caused, he would have remained conscious for only a little while before collapsing."

Thompson doodled some more before speaking. "So there's no way to prove that the damage was done while he was in the custody of the police?"

That tickled a memory so I coughed to attract Thompson's attention. I asked, "Excuse me, Doctor, but could I have lifted anything heavy while injured, done any kind of serious physical labour before collapsing?"

"No. The injury is much too severe. There was much bruising in the kidneys, torn muscles around them. In truth, I'm surprised you survived, especially now that I've learned your history. Street drugs do tremendous amounts of damage to kidneys. They're notoriously impure and toxic."

Thompson looked at me pointedly. "So? What's the deal with the heavy labour?"

"I wasn't very popular in Edmonton before I left. The cops thought I was running some kind of scam before I left, so did most of my bad-guy friends."

"I repeat, so?"

"The cops had me under surveillance, possibly filmed, hell, probably filmed. They were looking to bust me back inside on any kind of violation once I was out of the halfway house. Probably their Major Crimes division. There's a guy named Theophillus who arrested me the last time and thought I should do lots more time. He would've run anything they had going."

The doctor looked mildly interested and I went on. "So, if you act fast and call Edmonton, maybe you can get a copy of the report, maybe even the film."

My lawyer was looking intrigued. "I repeat, again, so?"

"I loaded the truck in Edmonton. By myself."

He got the point right away.

"So, we might get film from the cops showing you weren't injured before you came to Winnipeg."

He ticked it off on his fingers.

"And the cops say you weren't injured in their custody but you are injured now."

I went on. "And, according to the physical evidence, I shot the three men in my house, which meant I was fairly active. To nail that we'll need to get me a paraffin wax test, which will prove I fired a gun that night. You should also be able to find some neighbors who saw me unload. Plus there might be testimony from the guy at the U-Haul station who took the moving van back. That's another person who saw me up and about before the arrest. Which means?"

Thompson finished it. "The only place a judge will be able to place the injury is in the custody of the cops. There's physical evidence showing no injury at any other time. If Dr. Leung will testify."

The doctor exhaled softly and adjusted the sheet around my feet. "I can testify that someone with Mr. Parker's injuries could not have lifted any great weight. That I can do." Then he addressed me directly. "However, couldn't the police simply state that you had received the injuries during your . . . altercation?"

"Yes. But if that had been true, then they would have, should have, taken me to the hospital or offered me first aid. They would have records for that. Neither happened."

Leung looked at me steadily with very calm eyes that seemed to have seen a great deal of pain and approved of little of it. "Gentlemen, if you will excuse me, I now have rounds to do."

He reached for my wrist again and put his forefinger gently against the underside where the big veins and arteries were, and stared placidly at the space between my eyes. "Mr. Parker, did you poison the young lady who was watching you during the night?"

I could feel my pulse and so could he and I wondered about the possible consequences if the doctor decided I was lying. However, I could answer the question, I could even answer it honestly.

"No."

He stared at me with happier eyes and I could see tiny crow's feet in the corners. "Of course not. The young lady will be all right, by the way. The other gentleman should be fine as well. He has a serious concussion, though."

Dr. Leung tilted his head to the side and I answered.

"He could be dead."

"There is that. I will check on you later. Were you really beaten by the police?"

"Yes."

Gee, two questions in a row I could answer honestly, must be a red-letter day. He let my wrist fall to the bed.

"Well, they did a fine job. I'll talk to you soon. Eat very little. Drink less. Try to rest."

"How long will I be here?"

Leung smiled. "A week, maybe two. It depends entirely on how well you follow directions."

After he was gone, Thompson picked up his briefcase and slid the pad of paper into it.

"We've got a lot to do, Monty—I mean, Sam. Rest, like the doctor said. I'll call the Crown right away and she'll pull the cops back a little if she's even half bright. The situation last night might put a different spin on matters. I'll try to put a rush on the court date. Do you need anything, anything at all?"

"Something to read."

He tossed me a magazine someone had left on a shelf and went on. "You know, we're probably not going to win."

He was watching me to see how I felt about it.

"And I wasn't supposed to live to thirty. And I wasn't supposed to be able to kick my various bad habits. And there was no way my marriage was going to last."

"Right. Just so you know."

He snapped his fingers. "What about your neighbors? Would they have seen anything?"

I could have kicked myself. "Yes. I yelled out that I wanted a lawyer when Walsh arrested me. The cops heard, so did the paramedics and about thirty of my neighbors. It might be worth getting statements, if they'll give 'em."

He waited for more but I was tired, so he left. I found I couldn't sleep, even when they brought me back to my room. I was still thirsty but I ignored it and started to read *Bowhunter's Digest*. A new cop, a uniformed one, came in and sat in a chair they brought and ignored me. A few hours later, Claire and Fredrick showed up to visit and after that the hospital finally gave me something to eat. It was barely edible but Fred seemed to like it. Claire held my hand and she talked about moving furniture around in the house. Then she broke off on a new subject.

"You know, this is a pretty dumb way for you to spend the third day in our new home town. It's suspicious, even."

Fred grabbed the handcuffs on my left hand and rattled them.

"You think I did this to avoid unpacking?"

She nodded solemnly and we both smiled.

7

The Winnipeg Law Courts were downtown near the provincial legislative building and were an unattractive pile, a mixture of old and new buildings. Half were built of pale Tyndall limestone blocks and half were made entirely of steel and tinted glass, both with tall, narrow windows. Inside, Thompson told me, there were lots of steel barricades, bars, bulletproof glass, metal detectors. I'd been given a temporary release from the Health Sciences Centre with police escort and had been dropped off on the corner with a leg chain hooked through the frame of the wheelchair. Claire and Fred were already at the court and so it was just me in the chair with Thompson pushing and a sparse scatter of pedestrians. Well, actually, it was us two plus six cops in civilian clothes making sure I didn't make a break for it, and to top it off the sun was out and Thompson was singing Gilbert and Sullivan. Badly.

"... felonious employment, lonious employment ..."

He was struggling with an obvious hangover and seemed determined to ride it out.

"Must you?" I had a lap full of three briefcases and was busy keeping them from falling to the ground.

"Could be worse. I could be singing 'Sympathy for the Devil.' "

He belched and paused to adjust a shoe and then looked up. "We must hurry, though. We have a date with justice. A date with destiny. A date with . . . shit."

He muttered to himself just loudly enough for the cops around us to hear. "Too much for some, too little for others, too late for all."

I looked up and saw a crowd of about thirty people with microphones, TV cameras, and still cameras coming towards us from the court entrance. Three of the cops from behind moved to intercept the crowd while the other three stayed close to me. One of them put his hand on my arm and my lawyer looked at him in disgust, and said, "Like he's gonna run."

He turned back and his lips moved as he counted. "We've got print, radio, and TV bringing up the rear. Not bad. Mr. Parker, let me do the talking."

In the front of the pack were reporters with micro cassettes; the ones behind had big belt units of recording gear and collapsing poles, while the ones with the TV cameras were far at the back. Cables draped across from battery to microphone and back, and the poles probed up and over to catch every nuance. Thompson, looking grayer, spoke in a loud and booming voice that obviously hurt him. "Ladies and gentlemen. Please, excuse us."

The crowd shouted him down as the camera beings caught up and we tried to keep moving. A man with greased hair and a severe overbite wagged a long microphone marked Station C43FM in my face and spoke over my head. "Is your client going to plead?"

Thompson went on with his hands outspread and the microphones started to reach towards him. The cameras focused on him and everyone seemed to take a deep breath as he concentrated on the man in front of him. "Plead? What? No. Who told you that? That's actionable, you know, the kind of thing that can prevent someone from getting a fair trial. What's your name? Who told you a lie like that?"

That was good strategy. Deal with one person at a time. Separate them. Don't let them gang up. Just like dealing with a bank full of people during a robbery or paying a bribe, deal with a crowd one at a time. There was silence for a half-second and then a bleach-bottled blonde with old eyes and immense breasts cut in. She was holding a microphone that looked like a latex penis and right behind her was a fat guy wearing overalls and carrying a really big camera.

"Mr. Haaviko? Mr. Haaviko? Did you murder those men during a drug transaction?"

Thompson kept shredding the radio guy, who was backing out of the crowd, looking prim and claiming various amendment rights and privileges. I looked idly at the woman and Thompson stopped and leaned down to whisper. "Her name's Mildred Penny-something. She does provincial news and sports, mostly light stuff, and people trust her. She gets sourced big time from lots of cops. Don't talk to her."

"Thanks. But I must, I must."

And then I spoke up loudly and directed it at her. "Mildred? Good morning."

Thompson was watching and trying to look amused and confident.

"You really should check your sources and you shouldn't believe everything people tell you. I will answer that question, though."

Everyone was quiet and stopped pushing. Thompson glanced at his watch and I talked faster.

"I killed three men who broke into my house and tried to rape my wife. The police know this. I am going to talk to the Crown attorney right now so justice can be done. I am very sorry the men are dead but they gave me no choice at all. That's it."

More cops and a few sheriffs in brown uniforms showed up and we made it through to the courthouse steps without answering any other questions. Thompson relinquished the chair to a deputy and walked beside me so I could see his face.

I asked, "What do you think?"

He looked pissed and sour and angry. He had been that way since he'd arrived at the hospital. I'd expected to meet him at the courthouse and he'd tried twice to talk with me in private at the hospital and in the prison van, but the cops had been adamantly on some time-table all their own. He'd finally put his foot down when they'd tried to slip me in the back prisoner's entrance to the courthouse, but we still hadn't had a chance to talk.

"Very good. No way anyone can put too big a spin on what you gave 'em and there were too many people recording to not get out at least one or two accurate versions. I wonder how they found out we were coming this morning, though?"

Somebody opened the doors to the courthouse and we went into the big foyer.

"Last night I asked Claire to call in exclusive tips to all the stations in town," I said.

He looked at me with respect mixed with his hangover. "I never would have thought of that."

I tried to look bashful and failed. "Well, that's the difference be-tween being a shit-kicker ex-thief and a big-time lawyer."

Thompson grunted and we went on.

The Crown prosecuting attorney we'd drawn had an office on the third floor of the older court building. Her name was Nancy McMillan-Fowler and that was all Thompson could tell me as we waited in the hall. He kept looking at me and opening his mouth to talk, but the cops were thick around us and the reporters were not far off.

Finally, she opened the door and ushered us in. She was plain, almost ugly, thinly built with good bones and fine skin. She was wearing a simple, gray, tailored suit that emphasized her shoulders and mini-mized her ass and she'd splurged for some makeup, maybe because she expected to have to talk to the press later. Behind her the intercom buzzed and she turned and picked up the headset. "Yes?"

She had a good voice and she could use it well, bringing it from a tenor to an alto and back again, and probably capable of filling it with disbelief, passion, or contempt as needed. "No. No. Yes. No. Never. Fine."

Then there was a long pause.

"I said okay."

She pressed the disconnect bar on the phone and reached someone new. "Please bring your recorder with you. We'll need a record of this."

She leaned over the big steel desk in the middle of the room and squared her files before finally coming around to shake Thompson's hand. I held mine out but she ignored it and went back to the desk to sit down.

"Good morning, I am Thompson and I am the counsel for Mr. Parker."

"And this is . . . ?"

"Samuel Parker."

She looked at me and her eyes turned to slits. "You mean Montgomery Haaviko."

I grinned. "It was Haaviko, it's not anymore. Pleased to meet you."

I held out my hand again and she ignored it again. Then she drummed her fingers briefly as a woman in a plain black dress came in with a stenograph machine.

"All right, gentlemen. I trust you don't mind if I keep a record of this meeting?"

Thompson sat down in a really cheap chair that creaked like an old man farting and nodded as he opened his briefcase on his lap. "Oh no. We're going to tape this as well."

He looked very confident and the prosecutor shuffled the files on her desk from pile to pile until her confidence came back, "So you're going to plead?"

I answered, "No."

Thompson interrupted and talked fast. "Oh no. No plea, let's go to trial. Quickly, too. How's next week? Maybe the week after?"

She focused on me and reshuffled her files. "Do you know what you're doing? Three murders in the commission of a felony? You've been in prison before but do you really know what you're doing?"

Thompson started looking through his briefcase. "How about the week after? That's good too."

She raised her voice until it was almost a shout. "Is this some kind of joke?"

Thompson slid a file across to her. "No joke. Look at this."

She held the manilla file and scanned it quickly. "A doctor's report from a Dr. Leung stating that Mr. Haaviko/Parker has bruised kidneys and assorted other injuries."

Thompson handed over another file from his case and she took it.

"A report from the Edmonton Major Crimes Division detailing surveillance on Haaviko/Parker. So?"

"One of my associates in an Edmonton firm has filed a court order for the video tapes before the cops could destroy them. They're coming. Look at the dates."

"Thirteen to ten days ago. Video surveillance of your client?"

"Right. Shows Mr. Parker loading a truck full of furniture in Edmonton prior to moving here. There's also a statement from the halfway house where Parker was living up to two weeks ago, it's just a fax but it includes a medical report from an attending physician. He was recovering from various addictions and there are references to thirty weeks of weekly drug tests, all negative, all administered by the parole board and Corrections Canada."

He pulled a little plastic vial with a flat top and bottom out of his case and set it on the desk. It contained a murky yellow solution full of particles. "Urine sample." He covered it with a piece of paper and made a face.

I said, "That's a signed deposition by a nurse who drained the catheter coming out of me. The particles in it are blood, but ignore that. Mr. Thompson asked the nurse to keep the sample and sign across the seal. It's also dated."

McMillan-Fowler raised her voice. "What is this all about? I have a signed and witnessed confession."

Thompson smiled. "Bear with me. The police version is that my client killed three men, was injured during the fight, was overcome by guilt, confessed to the police, went to the hospital. Right?"

She nodded and he went on.

"Our version is that three men broke in, our client killed them, was arrested by police, was beaten by police, confession was extracted by police, went to hospital."

She was tight-lipped. "Do you really think a jury's going to believe that kind of garbage?"

"Maybe not. But forget that for a moment. Police videotape showing our client in good shape prior to arrest and medical records showing a bad shape after. That's one element that leads to the second question. If the police knew our client was injured during the fight, why wasn't an ambulance called?"

"Maybe the police didn't know."

"Sure. They searched him, stripped him, and didn't find the bruises, or anything wrong at all, and my client just started pissing blood and screaming. After eight hours of interrogation."

She didn't even blink and Thompson went on. "We have pictures taken at the hospital, plus X-rays and lots of statements that are evidence. Evidence that shows extensive internal bruising and disabling abuse, which would mean that the police tortured my client by not providing medical attention, perhaps due to ignorance. That's option one, but there's a second option."

She was flicking through the files and the image of card games stayed with me. "And that would be?"

"The police tortured my client while he was in custody. Supporting this is the fact that the interview room camera was turned off for more than eight hours. Look for the tape if you want, but it doesn't exist."

I smiled and she quickly turned away while Thompson went on. "In either case, the confession is invalid. In one case, stopping my client from getting medical attention, the counter-charge will be civil. In the second case, the beating, the counter-charge will be criminal and civil. You pick which version you want."

The Crown looked at me again out of the corner of her eye while Thompson kept talking.

"Time of the shootings is listed at 11:07 p.m. Monday. Time of arrest is listed at 1:35 a.m. Tuesday. My office was called by Mr. Parker's wife at slightly past 3:00 a.m. and the authorities didn't let me see my client until 9:40 a.m. on that Tuesday."

She shuffled her files. "Maybe Mr. Haaviko wanted to confess."

"Parker. Mr. Parker. Not Haaviko, not anymore."

Thompson handed over another file. "This is a notarized statement made four years ago regarding another . . . um, legal matter. In it Mr. Haaviko is advised by his lawyer of record in Edmonton never to make a statement to the police or anyone without either himself or another legal representative being present. He knew his rights."

She shrugged. "This'll never make it to court. Maybe Mr. Haaviko was suddenly overcome by guilt and remorse."

"You gonna sell that to a jury? Guilt-wrought? After the first half of the trial details what a cunning, ruthless, professional criminal Mr. Haaviko was?"

"I never said he was a cunning— Oh. You will."

"Right. I'll also bring up the fact that it took the police eight hours to extract a 308-word confession from my client, which he then didn't sign. That's 28,800 seconds in total, which translates to one word every minute and a half. Hell, maybe I'll read the statement out to the jury, one word every ninety-three seconds. That might convince them."

The Crown prosecutor picked up a cheap yellow pencil and tapped it against her teeth to make an unpleasant, tinny noise. "This case can get convoluted, I admit that, but I'll win anyway."

"Ah yes, but it will get worse. First, my client's not gonna press criminal charges against the police, he's going after the City of Winnipeg in the civil courts for not providing health care while he was in custody. The pictures and medical evidence will prove that he was unharmed before the arrest and injured afterwards."

Thompson finally put his briefcase down and stretched out his feet. "Now, that's gonna be open and shut. The city police will lose credibility if they try to force the issue of the confession there and it'll tie up the confession in the criminal courts until the whole thing is dealt with."

The Crown attorney smiled. "You're forgetting. We have LERA in this province. The Law Enforcement Review Agency, all charges against members of the police have to go through that agency first."

My lawyer just shook his head. "No. We're suing the city, not the police as an organization and not a single officer. LERA isn't involved, not now. You think it's confusing now, just wait."

"You can't be serious."

I spoke up for the second time. "Yes. We're serious. We're also willing to talk."

McMillan-Fowler didn't seem to want to, but she found herself responding. "You mean a deal? There's no deal that I can see. We have your fingerprints on the gun, tests that show you fired the gun, a confession you shot the men. We have everything."

Thompson adjusted his tie as he spoke. "We have a gun that doesn't tie anywhere to my client. It was brought by the men breaking in. That contradicts the police. The men who broke in had a history of similar offenses and that contradicts the police. We have a jimmied door showing where the men came in and that contradicts the police. We have evidence of a fight that supports my client's story and contradicts the police. We have statements by citizens that my client asked for a lawyer immediately upon arrest and that contradicts the police. We have evidence that my client knew his rights and wanted a lawyer and that contradicts the police. We have evidence that police procedure wasn't followed in extracting the confession and that contradicts the police."

He mopped his brow with a red silk handkerchief that looked seriously out of place and continued. "We have two separate scenarios that describe how the confession wasn't entered into voluntarily. We also have two scenarios that show either criminal behavior or stupidity on the part of the police."

I spoke up again. "Pick one."

She stared at me and I went on. "I can explain the gun, the paraffin test, and the bodies. The police cannot explain any of these things."

Thompson shushed me with two fingers and handed over another file. "Ms. McMillan-Fowler, I'll cut to the chase. Here's a copy of our complaint to LERA about the fact my client was not given access to a lawyer immediately. That's despite past advice he's been given by his attorneys of record. Here's a copy of the charge I'm going to be laying in civil court for mistreatment of my client by the city. Here's a copy of my client's real statement, given to me the morning after the incident. And . . . can we talk privately now?"

The Crown was looking tired. This wasn't going to be simple and all of a sudden she couldn't see the end of it. She nodded and the secretary folded up her equipment and left. When she was gone, the Crown gestured to Thompson. "Go on."

Thompson spoke softly. "I've given my client written advice this morning. It's on record, mine and his, and I state that I believe he should wait until after the criminal trial is resolved before proceeding with any charges against the police. I have given him this advice because I believe evidence will be manufactured by the police in order to discredit him, should he proceed at this time."

She stuck out her lower lip and snorted, "That's been tried before. It's never worked before and won't work this time."

Thompson nodded, "It's an indirect challenge to LERA's constitutional viability. A lawyer has just advised his client that his federal civil rights might be violated if he goes forward with a complaint to a provincial board."

He closed his briefcase and glanced at me.

"I'm also going to be leaking some of what I've told you to the mayor and the city council, so get ready. More will be going to the local MLAs, MPs, and so on. You should make up your mind very quickly on how you want to proceed because it'll be going to the press. Amnesty International. Society for the Wrongly Convicted. Anyone else we can think of."

The Crown was now looking angry and frustrated and I was feeling bone tired, so I tried to wrap it up. "You'll notice that we're giving you more than we have to. Think about that. Consider it a sign of good faith insofar as I want this to end quickly."

We started to leave and she kept tapping her pencil against her teeth. I knew what she was feeling. She had thought she was playing poker when she had actually been playing fifty-two pick-up.

In the hall Thompson's confidence faded like steam. He asked, "Think she'll buy it?"

"Sure. It just turned political. She'll talk to her boss and her boss will talk to his boss. The buck will be passed. Each person will make it more complex and in the end I think they'll take what we offer."

Thompson pushed me towards the elevator and, after a minute, he reluctantly agreed. "It's a weak case without the confession."

"Right."

He kept speaking as though he hadn't heard me. "Lots of risks for them."

"In this biziness there is much risiko."

"What?"

"James Bond. Actually, some candy-assed villain speaking to Bond."

"Right."

He looked sick and preoccupied.

"How about faint heart never won fair maid?"

He didn't seem to hear me. Ahead of us and down the marble hall, the cops were still keeping the reporters at bay.

"That's poetry. There's also the SAS motto, 'Who Dares, Wins.' "

He was pushing me erratically down the hallway, weaving from side to side in preoccupation.

"Or 'Carpe Diem,' seize the fish. Never understood that one, though."

Thompson stopped and came around to face me over the briefcases. He looked drained and exhausted.

"I have something I have to talk about."

"Go ahead."

Thompson wheeled us over to a bench, where he sat and accepted the briefcases off my lap. He stroked his chin for a moment and then pointed a finger right at my face. "Last night I got a phone call at home. It was Walsh. He had found my private phone number and all your records."

"And . . ."

He leaned against the back of the bench. "He was pretty direct, pretty vivid. You wanna tell me your side?"

"Sure. I used to be bad. Now I'm not."

"Bad?"

His bloodshot eyes shifted to the side and back again.

"When I was sixteen, I robbed a pharmacy for product and cash. When the owner wouldn't open the poison box, where the narcotics are stored, I shattered his collarbone with the flat of a hatchet."

Thompson nodded.

"A year later I was dealing ecstasy to an undercover cop out of a hotel room in Banff. She pulled her piece and tried to cuff me. By the time the other cops had broken the door down, I had stabbed her three times with a filed-down screwdriver I'd hidden in my sock."

Thompson swallowed audibly.

"There's more. Got caught with a duffle bag of sawed-down shotguns. Assault, goes without saying. Dangerous driving. Resisting arrest. Attempted murder. Smuggling. Fraud. Drugs. Shit like that."

"I see."

"Been addicted to cocaine, methamphetamines, crank, heroin, and

PCP. Alcohol too. Abused and used acid, grass, ether, peyote. You name it."

"You making excuses?"

"Nope. Don't care what you think of me."

He thought about that and I tapped his knee to get his attention. "I've lied. Cheated. Stole. Killed. Dishonored my parents. Worshipped false idols. Coveted. Committed adultery."

The cops were still keeping the reporters away and I smiled bitterly. "Now, I've got a wife. A son. Pets. A home. It's a long way from everything I knew before. And I'd like to keep that distance."

"I see. Was it really that bad? Being a crook, I mean?"

"Yes, it was that bad." I opened up a little. "You do the math. If you're a bad guy, you don't have a job, no bank account, no apartment. You live in hotels, move around a lot, eat in restaurants. But not expensive hotels because you might be noticed in those and you'll need ID."

He was riveted on me.

"You need maybe sixty bucks a day for food and a little more than that for the hotel and maybe another thirty to fifty for incidentals. That's every day."

I tried to find a comfortable spot in the chair but my whole lower back ached where a band of red and blue bruises still circled my kidneys. The rainbow of pain filled every moment.

"That's about one-eighty each day. Life gets stressful, though, so you start doing a little something to deal with the stress. If you drink or do grass to level you out, that's another twenty or forty per day. But you can't be level all the time, you might have to move fast so that means keeping cocaine or crank or meth handy, and that's another fifty to one hundred a day and that's if you don't have friends. That's a total of about three Cs per day. Every day. That means two grand one per week, or eight grand four per month, and that means one hundred and nine thousand, two hundred dollars per year. Period."

Thompson's eyes were staring into the middle distance.

"It's fun to do for a week, a month, even a year. But do it for year after year after year and it gets stale. I'm not depressing you, am I?"

He had no answer, no comment.

"The lifestyle means nothing is permanent. You can't even do laundry. You can't bring anything with you. You can't even follow a TV series you like. You're too busy."

I breathed deeply. "No friends and no love, either. You can buy tail, though, and that'll add to your bill. And there's always the chance that the drug dealer or the hooker or someone else is going to rat you out."

Thompson was waiting for me to finish.

"Your other option is to build a fake life. That takes money and time. A few hundred hours and dollars for the driver's licence, the same for a birth certificate, social insurance card, banking history, it can all be built but it takes weeks and months to do it right. Anyhow, you put in six months and maybe ten grand and then you can buy a car, rent an apartment, do whatever, just like a civilian."

He brushed his hair from his eyes and a fine rain of dandruff came down.

"Of course, anyone, and I mean anyone, who knows just a little bit about you can crack the whole thing open and you're back on the run again at twenty-one hundred per week."

Thompson was only half listening to me. The rest of his attention was focused somewhere far away and I wished I knew where.

"To pay for your two choices of lifestyle, you steal, you hustle, you deal. The math there is rough too. An average bank by a solo operator nets between one and three grand, a good bank nets up to twelve. An armored car is worth thirty plus but it's almost impossible to do it by yourself, which means partners, which means someone's going to rat you out. You also have to split the take. Dealing drugs requires capital and the profit for a gram dealer is maybe only ten dollars per unit, and when you're dealing in bulk, that brings its own problems like bodyguards and bribes and other shit. If you deal grass, it's not so bad and not so profitable but coke dealers deal with cokeheads and those guys are just shit. They also call you at all hours asking for a taste on credit."

I was getting tired and yawned. "Pimping is fine but requires a fine touch and a fair number of women and they are hard to keep under control. Smuggling is okay too but you've got to develop routes, which means you become a stationary target. Professional killers exist only in books and it doesn't pay that well, anyway. It goes on like that."

Thompson finally snapped out of it and started to laugh. "So what you're saying is that you stopped being a crook because it was too much work."

I had closed my eyes but at that I opened one and grinned widely. "That and I fell in love with my wife."

He was silent so I pointed straight ahead down the hall. "Home, James."

8

Officially it took the Crown three days to decide. I knew it was coming; I could tell when the cops pulled the handcuffs off the day after the meeting with McMillan-Fowler. They left one guard on duty at the foot of my bed but that didn't bother me as much, it certainly guaranteed me a private room.

Every eight hours a new cop came but I just focused on breathing through the pain without whimpering. If I made noise, the cops called the nurse and she brought the blessed-hated pill and that brought surcease. That I counted as a loss.

On the third day the new cop in the morning was the woman that Stiles had drugged. I hadn't had a good night, maybe thirty minutes of shallow sleep, and when she came in, I spoke up. "Morning. How you feeling?"

She gave me a hard look and then came over right beside the bed. Her eyes were bright with caffeine and her skin was grayish and taut. She watched the corridor and spoke very quietly. "Hello, killer, I've been told I have you to thank for dealing with the asshole who drugged me."

If she thought I was going to say anything, I disappointed her. "So. Thanks."

I still didn't say anything so she stared some more and then sat down and opened a copy of the *Winnipeg Sun* newspaper. In the bed I squirmed and felt my bladder cut painfully loose. They'd put in a catheter and I was still pissing blood and it hurt but so did breathing, eating, sleeping, and being awake. My teeth caught my tongue and held it while a brilliant noise only I could hear started and peaked. When the noise was gone and I was emptied, I exhaled through my nose and trembled a bit as the shock cut out.

"What about you, killer, how you doing?"

The pain had preoccupied me and the cop was back, leaning over me with her crossed arms inches from my head. She looked pleased.

"Peachy."

My voice cracked and Thompson came in. Apparently, the cops had been given orders about his presence so she just started past him to her chair without a word. When he raised a hand, though, she paused in mid-stride and looked at him incuriously with her right hand on her holstered pistol.

"Hold it. Officer, you can go. Sam, the Crown's dropping the charges so you're free."

Free, I almost laughed. My kidneys were ground round, I had a fever of a hundred and change, and I had a plastic tube running into my dick, but I was free. Capitalize that sucker, FREE!

The cop sounded petulant, though. "Sorry. I have to be relieved by a superior. Until then your client is in my custody."

He fumbled out his cell phone and handed it over. "Call your boss."

She went to her chair and Thompson sat down. His overcoat flapped open as he yawned and I turned my head away from his breath.

"Did you call Claire?"

"First thing. Now, the shooting is still up in the air, but the Crown has dropped the murder charges and pitched the confession. You might still do some time for discharging a firearm within the bound-aries of the city, something like that. I'm not sure about that."

The cop still had the phone.

"What about Stiles?"

"The felon you stopped from assaulting a cop? They just want to forget about that entirely. It's a bitch of a thing to try to explain to a jury."

"Um, Thompson? That's the cop who got drugged behind you."

"Oh."

He turned and looked at her and then back at me. "Did she say thanks?"

The cop blushed and focused on talking to someone on the other end of the line.

"Yes. So how long I am looking at for the shooting?"

He made a big deal about thinking about it. "A month. Like that."

"Nah. I don't think so, it's in their best interests to let it slide. All or nothing."

The cop came over and dropped the phone on the bed. Then she removed the restraints and slapped them against her leg. "It's true. See you around, killer."

My lawyer watched her go and yawned again. "I don't think she likes you."

"Breaks my heart. So you're still representing me?"

"Yes. I thought about you. You're a pretty reprehensible human being."

"Yep."

"Not gonna try to defend yourself to me?"

I grinned and shook my head. "Fuck you. I'm not responsible for your morals. That's your problem. I have enough trouble with my own."

Thompson patted my arm. "Right. Anyhow, the reason I'm still here is because I hate being forced to do anything. I hate being conned. I hate being manipulated. I hate being threatened."

"Which is what Walsh was doing? Is doing?"

"Right."

He stared at me. "Plus, I believe you. Part of the way, at least."

"Thanks."

He left and I turned on the TV at the end of the bed. I'd been watching it a lot, not enjoying it but watching it. The local stations, the morning shows, the afternoon talk shows, the early afternoon news, the soap operas, the kids' shows. At first the cops had monitored what I'd watched, but soon their interest had waned and they'd started to ignore both it and I. Or is it I and it? Me and it?

In their minds I had become meat they had to watch. Nothing more.

I'd watched the TV but hadn't paid attention to anything but the credits at the end of the shows. Producers, directors, writers, researchers, the faces in front of the cameras, and the people behind the machines, proper spellings, names, titles. Those I had remembered, repeating them endlessly and silently until they became my mantra.

When the nurses had given me newspapers, I'd memorized more names. Not the crime reporters, those guys had to be in the pockets of the cops in order to do their work effectively. So I concentrated on the political reporters, the guys doing the town hall work, not the guys doing the editorials or the opinion pieces. Opinions I could get anywhere. They were like tits and balls, everybody had two, and I needed facts.

A very shy nurse-in-training came in and froze when she saw no cop.

I said, "C'mon in. Charges have been dropped."

She was pretty and olive, a Filipino girl with a beautiful complexion and the movements of a dancer. She blushed and changed the plastic bag that the catheter fed and then she danced out on the tips of her toes.

Winnipeg had two daily papers and four local TV stations. By the time the cops decided to let me go, I had the names of five people who might know something and who might talk to me. That was when the TV caught my attention again.

"The police are not releasing the name of a local businessman who was rescued from a bizarre situation this morning . . ."

It was a local news show, the noon report.

"According to confidential sources, the businessman was found in the living room of his house after he had failed to show up to open his store. He had been tied into a chair and surrounded by more than a dozen containers of gasoline, which were wired to explode a device strapped to his own body. Although the police managed to rescue the man, he has so far refused to offer any explanation or indeed to help the police with their inquiries."

I shut the TV off. With criminals it's always about money or power. With amateurs it's about revenge or sex. Wiring a businessman to go boom was what? Whatever it was, wasn't my problem, though, so I stopped thinking about it and tried to sleep.

9

The things you do to avoid real work."

Claire held my arm tightly until my balance returned and I could move again in the big park area near the hospital. From where we were, we could see the women's hospital across the street, but I was concentrating on not falling and didn't have time for sightseeing. Fred was rolling in the grass and trying to eat a black and white moth, all the while kicking the hell out of his stroller.

I said, "I hate that stroller, you know that, don't you?"

Claire squeezed my arm. The stroller had been a gift from her parents, a very deliberate insult to me about the things I couldn't afford for my family and for that reason I hated it. I focused on that hate until I was on level ground and Claire could let me go.

"I know, but it does transform into four separate, useful shapes."

I swayed and nodded and that hurt. Actually, everything hurt. Behind me was a rolling IV stand carrying glucose that dumped into a vein buried in my right arm. I would have preferred to use my left arm but the veins there had long since been scarred into leathery armor by heroin and crystal meth and cocaine injections.

Dr. Leung had advised against my little walk but Claire had promised I'd behave and so she watched and waited while I stood there. Fred wanted more stuff and he proceeded to look for other things he shouldn't eat.

"You just gonna stand there?"

Claire grinned to take the sting out and I stuck my tongue out at her. "Nope. Watch."

It was a cross between a deep knee bend and a controlled collapse and then I raised back up.

She clapped loudly and Fred rolled over to look for the cause of all the excitement.

"Bravo. And for an encore?"

"I may pee without aid or assistance."

She made a face at me as I sagged down again and sweat poured out to stain my gown at the throat and crotch. After I'd done six of the bends, I sat down on the ground and started to lean back and forth, covering maybe six inches of an arc per time. After ten of these, I had to stop and rest, and Claire kissed me.

"My hero. How does it feel?"

"Hurts."

My breath was coming in short gasps and there were spots in front of my eyes.

"How?" Her voice was low and soft so I rolled myself onto a nearby bench and she kissed me again.

"It's knives in the small of my back. Short ones with wide blades. Never enough to kill, just to wound. They go peck-peck-peck."

Fred was eating a dandelion and Claire rescued the bright yellow flower and then sat back to listen. She listened brilliantly and understood and when she didn't understand, she'd ask about specifics. When she didn't agree, she'd wait and make her point afterwards.

"The knives come with each breath. With each inhalation and exhalation and movement. They peck when I even think about moving but that's not real. That's just psychology."

I got up and did the whole routine all over again. Claire watched and wrestled with Fred for a bit and the sun just shone down.

When we were back in my room, Claire saw an audio tape on the bed and handed it to me along with a note that read "LISTEN TO ME." When asked nicely, the peppermint nurse lent me someone's portable stereo and I listened to a conversation caught in the middle.

"Be it ever so humble."

It was Claire speaking dryly and politely and it was a good recording.

"Could be worse."

That was Thompson and then he grunted and repeated, "Could be worse."

Sounds of glasses and ice and liquid coming through very clear and then Claire spoke up. "Here, I'm not gonna drink alone."

Clinking sound like a toast and then Thompson, "Lawyers' lunch."

The sound of another drink, maybe two being filled.

"How bad is it?"

"Seen worse, seen better. The Crown should know something's bush about it all and, well, maybe they'll do the right thing."

"And . . . ?"

"Then they'll drop the charges. Or they'll come on hard, depending on local politics, and then we'll go to appeals and the Crown will continue to press hard or let us go. If they press hard, then we go to the provincial Court of Appeal. Beyond that there's the Supreme Court, where I've never been."

Thompson kept speaking and I could hear him drinking. "That's simplified but basically true. The Crown can drop the case now, or during the preliminary hearings, or in the court during the case, or during appeals, or during re-appeals or anywhere else that seems good to them."

There was a long pause and then he went on, with his voice

sounding progressively slurred. "We've only got to win once. They've got to win every single time."

She spoke up, still dryly, still without passion. "Monty used to say the whole system was like a starfish. Once it started eating you, it couldn't stop, it was built to start eating and its very nature prevented it from stopping. The whole thing was to avoid getting tasted in the first place."

"Yeah. The system can't afford to stop once it starts, they can't afford to admit they make mistakes. My dad was in the army and he used to say, 'Never complain, never explain.' It applies to the law too."

More drinking.

"Been hearing some stuff about Sam. Rough stuff. Bad stuff. Doesn't match what seems to be happening. Married, straight, and respectable. He even has a baby son, who is where by the way?"

"I left him with a friend."

"I thought you had just come into town, you found a friend that quick? Did you know someone here before?"

"No. A woman called Ramirez is watching Fred. She's one of the cops who arrested Sam. We both have kids and started talking when I tried to go down to the station house and Sam was on his way to the hospital. She thinks I'm okay. Just making some bad choices."

"Well, shave my ass, a cop. See, this is a nice town, lived here all my life and I can definitely say it's a nice town. So which one is the real Sam? Married? Straight and true? Respectable? Thief? Killer? Drug addict? Tinker, tailor, soldier, spy?"

Claire laughed. "He was one and now he's the other. I've got to go. Thanks for the drinks."

There was a gasp, a female one. Then the sound of kissing and the sound of cloth on cloth, then skin on skin.

I looked across at Claire, who was sitting on the chair at the end of the bed and bouncing Fred on her knee.

The sound of skin on skin kept coming, then the sounds of more kissing, then gasps and the creaking of a bed, moans, sighs, gasps.

Across the room, Claire was chucking Fred under the chin and making him laugh. On the tape, the noises petered out and then I heard Claire again. "Well, keep in touch. Anything you need, just give me a call."

Thompson, his voice completely slurring. "Sure."

"Do you want me to call a cab?"

"Nah, I'll be fine."

Sound of a door shutting and a lock closing, then she laughed. "I never will understand . . ."

When the tape was over, I handed it over to her.

"Ummm. Sweetheart?"

She was putting the headphones on and trying to stop Fred from biting his own toes. "Yes?"

"Did you sleep with Thompson?"

"No. Why? Should I?"

I looked out the window but there were no answers there.

"Then we have a problem. Someone really doesn't like us."

Claire listened to the tape and rewound it to the start before answering slowly. "I think you're right."

She said it calmly enough but I could see that she was angry. Her brows were drawn together and her lips were tight and narrow. She exhaled and spoke. "What are we going to do about it?"

I thought about breaking the tape into small pieces but I reconsidered. "I don't know yet."

Two tiny red spots appeared on her cheeks, signs of strong emotion. "When you're done with him or her, then they're mine."

She exhaled through her nose and listened to the tape for a second time. "Okay. Some of it seems to be part of a conversation that Thompson and I had at my hotel room the night after you were arrested. He came by to introduce himself and ask me some questions."

I looked at her quizzically. "To your hotel room? He came to your hotel room?"

She laughed but it sounded brittle. "Yes. Very un-lawyer-like. He called before he came and asked a few questions, and he could have asked the rest of them over the phone but he came over instead. Actually, I thought he was going to dump you."

Claire patted Fred down and checked his diaper.

"When he got up to the room, though, he was flushed and angry. Sort of scared and smelling of booze and cigarettes. Does he smoke?"

I had to think about that and a series of images of my lawyer flashed through my mind's eye. Smokers have tells, twitches, just like any other addict, but there are also a bunch of physical signs that hadn't been there.

"No. His hands are clean, his breath is okay, his teeth are pearly white-ish. And I've never seen him light up. He does drink, though."

"Does he ever, he drank about half a bottle of Stolichnaya. He asked a bunch of questions about your past, mine too, for that matter."

"What did you tell him?"

She smiled sweetly. "The truth, of course. Don't you remember the rule?"

I smiled back. "Yeah. Always tell your own lawyer the truth and always tell the other guy's lawyer the lies."

Another golden rule of thieves. I thought it through and then spoke slowly. "Walsh put some pressure on him. I think he went to you to try to deal with it."

"Fine. Is he going to fold?"

"I doubt it. He's too angry. He'll be even angrier if I let him hear the tape."

"Yes, he will."

Claire and I looked at each other across the bed and smiled and the tape sat there in the space between and steamed its poison.

10

They made us take a taxi when they finally let me out of the hospital. I argued until Dr. Leung told me I would be staying if I didn't get a cab and at that point I agreed. Claire had a bag with my clothes over one shoulder and pushed the stroller with Fred while Leung pushed me in a wheelchair. One tire wasn't straight and kept grinding as he lectured in a dry, flat voice.

". . . so take it easy. No stress, no strain, and no exercise beyond the stretching we've talked about. No alcohol, no coffee, nothing caffeinated. Those things would strain your system. What little is left, that is."

The nurses and orderlies paid us no attention as we passed and finally we made it to the main entrance.

"No red meat. Fish and chicken, though, wouldn't hurt. Just a little."

"Doc?"

He leaned over until I could see his nose.

"Yes?"

"You've got a lousy bedside manner."

He smiled and kept on pushing.

The peppermint nurse caught up with us and pushed something into my hands. "Mr. Haaviko? You forgot this . . ."

This was a vase half full of dandelions that Claire and Fred had picked for me. The nurse exhaled loudly, wiped her brow theatrically, and left.

Claire stifled a laugh. "She likes you."

She sounded entertained as Leung pushed the chair up to the bench outside the doors and motioned for her to go on. My wife smiled on one side of her face and folded the stroller up while ignoring both of us. With effort I got my ass to the bench and sat down, but Claire didn't add anything and I had to ask.

"Okay, I'll bite, why do you say that?"

Claire had the stroller in a small, compact bundle under one arm and Fred in a larger, squirming bundle under the other. "She had three buttons undone and then did this."

She inhaled and her breasts rode up under a pale lavender silk blouse. Something tingled inside and I recognized the first real, concrete urge for sex since I'd been beaten. Claire noticed and winked while Leung helped me to my feet and thought about what Claire had said. Then he added, "I'll talk to her."

The cab was waiting and a red-headed kid in his late teens opened the door and I let my family get in first.

Leung held out his hand. "Well, Mr. Haaviko, or Parker, or whatever. It's been a pleasure and I hope never to see you again."

I shook the strangely limp and lifeless hand.

"Ditto. There's a book out called *How to Win Friends and Influence People*. I'll send you a copy."

That made him smile and he bowed slightly at the waist. "Good luck."

Leung nodded to the driver and we left. Maybe ten blocks away we were long out of sight of the hospital so I kissed Claire and Fred and relaxed a little.

"Can we get out here?"

"Why? It's another, what? Six blocks? Something like that 'til home."

"I need the exercise."

We got out at the corner and she paid off the cabbie while I assembled the stroller and inserted Fred. Main Street ran parallel to the Red River and there was a wide park with trees from the edge of the street down to the water. Some people were fishing and others walking and the shops along the way were mostly small with not a single chain store or national brand in sight. Cars were parked up against the curb and people said hello and good day. The sun was bright and not too warm and we walked very slowly towards the river. As we went, we looked around at everything.

"Look, over there, a coffee shop with an attached diner. No Starbucks that I can see, no premium Colombian brew with extra caffeine for the added addiction factor, no smog, fewish panhandlers, low street crime. Too many cell phones, though. Not as bad as Toronto, thank God."

Claire was quiet and let me push Fred for a while before linking her arm through mine and taking over. "You do it all wrong. Let me."

We walked in silence and turned into the park past an empty baseball diamond and a small sandbox.

"I'm sorry but I have to tell you. I borrowed some money from my parents."

She wasn't sorry, not really, she was just being polite and I let it lie there between us as we passed a hot dog cart and another one selling French fries. There were yells from down on the river as someone fishing caught something big, so we turned to watch the battle as a six-year-old boy wrestled a silvery fat-bodied carp into the air. There was a bench so we sat down and Fred started to snore loudly.

"Sam, c'mon, tell me, how do you feel about me borrowing the money?"

My first instinct was to lie, my second was to get angry but, instead,

I just let it go. "Bad. Like I'm a failure. But there's nothing I can do about it. How much have we got in the kitty now?"

"The rent's paid for this month and one more plus grocery money for three weeks. Four or five if we go for welfare cooking, which is both hot and brown."

Long pause.

"Ground beef and macaroni."

"And liver and potatoes."

"Blech."

She pressed the side of her butt into my hip.

I changed the subject. "It's a nice town."

Claire patted my knee and then squeezed my shoulder. Fred rolled over awkwardly and humped his butt up until it was pointing at the sky. She stared at him and then spoke. "You sound wistful."

"Well, we're not going to stay, are we? Which means I can be wistful as I want in consideration of all the things that could have happened for us here."

I could see far away across Main where an elderly man in a white coat was sweeping the sidewalk in front of a barbershop. He used a corn broom and stopped as I watched to talk to a passerby. I started to say something and Fred farted loudly and startled us both into quickly hushed laughter.

When I could breathe again, I said, "Remember what they say in the Maritimes?"

"What?"

I put on my worst Newfie accent and did an impression. "Well, now, me boyo, your cough sure sounds better."

Claire snorted once and tucked Fred back under the light blanket. The old man across the street went back to work and then cleaned a spot on the display window with the edge of his sleeve and some spit. I talked as I watched the man. "You know, you'd never see that in Edmonton."

Claire nodded agreement. "Or in Calgary, or Vancouver, and certainly not in the big, bad, old Toronto. No one in any of those cities would ever sweep their own sidewalk. They'd wait until the city did it or the wind picked up."

"Yep. It's really a very nice town, all things considered. Friendly, clean, and we've got no past here. That's nice in a lot of ways. It gives some leeway just to be here."

Fred woke up and whined until I gave him my finger to bite. Then he settled down and went back to chewing on me and I thought about how many times I'd used that finger to hurt someone or to threaten pain, to extort or to steal. Fred's puckered face didn't care, though, he didn't know and he didn't care and I couldn't feel much else but love at that moment. Claire sat back and I could feel the tension leaving her body. Like always, she knew before I did. When she spoke, her voice was husky. "And you're clean here, so am I."

"Right. No one's looking for me that hard. And I've never had a real job and I'd kind of like to know what it's like."

She got up and helped me to my feet as Fred looked from face to face and blew spit bubbles.

"Right, well then, that's decided, so let's get home. I'm sure your damned dog has ripped the place to shit by now."

As we walked down the road, I linked my arm back in hers. "Why is he my dog when he does something bad and your dog when he does something good?"

She laughed and refused to answer, which I felt was extremely unfair.

11

S o, how do I look?"

Claire moved around in front of me and adjusted the tie.

"Like an ex-con looking for work."

I was wearing an expensive, pale gray suit with a pale blue cotton shirt and a pair of oxfords with steel toes, fairly useful remnants from a life of crime. They were good for kicking a door in or crunching up a kneecap without breaking a toe.

"But an attractive, reliable, honest ex-con looking for work, right?"

"Oh, yes. Gently changing the subject, she says, this tie. Have you ever untied it or did you just make a knot sometime last decade and leave it?"

"Yes. How can you tell?"

She pulled at the knot, which did nothing, so she stepped back to pick at it with her teeth.

"I was kidding. I was only kidding."

The clothes made me feel like a loser. These clothes were not me, these clothes were the ones I wore when I talked to the judges and the prosecuting attorneys. These were the clothes that translated into a badge of failure. Fred crawled over and bit my knee and I cheered up.

"You still love me, don't you, Fred?"

He kept chewing and I sat down and started to wrestle with him, which he seemed to like. Fred had my blond hair and Claire's chocolate brown eyes and a belligerent personality that he got from God-knows-where. He was ten months old and we'd conceived him in prison just after Claire and I had decided it was maybe perhaps time for me to go straight. The dog came over and licked us both, which made Fred grunt.

"Owf, owf."

"Claire, he said 'Daddy,' plain as day!"

She talked around a mouthful of silk or rayon or whatever the stupid tie was made from. "He said 'Owf,' which means 'dog.' More specifically, it means 'our dog.' Other dogs are 'Owwffa.' I don't know if it's plural or not. You really have to pay attention to what's going on. Changing the subject again, she says, this is a really ugly tie, but then you know that, right?"

I ignored her with dignity, the tie was eight years old and I'd wanted a black leather one but they had been out of style at the time. Fred grabbed Renfield and hugged him hard and I had to rescue him before someone ended up being seriously bitten. The baby kept squirming until I put him down and he started to crawl off into the dining room, looking for something new to destroy.

"Stand up." Claire retied the tie and stood back to admire her handiwork before handing me a leather carrying case marked N.S.T. in ornate gold script. It was old-fashioned and Claire had bought it at a garage sale in Edmonton before we'd left and now it held a copy of my resume, which was mostly lies. So far, neither of us could agree what N.S.T. stood for and we were getting increasingly wild in our guesses.

"Maybe it's from an atom bomb testing area and stands for 'No one Stands There.'"

Claire shook her head. "Maybe. But I doubt it. Maybe it's for a whale recovery program, 'Narwhales Sans-Teeth.' "

"That's worse than mine."

"Not by much. Go forth and gain gainful employment. I have a house to clean."

She kissed me and I kissed her and then out I went. Before I'd reached the end of the walkway, she had started up the vacuum cleaner and Renfield had started to bark at the thing invading his space. At the end of the walk, I turned back to look at the two-storey house we were renting and shook my head. It still didn't feel like home. I really wasn't sure what home was, but this place wasn't. It wasn't quite comfortable or friendly and nothing was quite where it was supposed to be, although Claire had unpacked most of the boxes. She came to the window and made a shooing gesture, so I kept walking towards Main Street, enjoying the feeling of the weak sun on my neck.

As I walked, I looked at the houses on either side of the road. They were nice, two or three storeys high with poorly kept yards, most of which had toys scattered in the grass. A few houses were less well-kept. There the grass had been grubbed down until only bare dirt showed and the paint was flaking off the siding. Alongside those, neighbors had put up good fences to hide the eyesores. Everywhere were fragile elm trees, vibrant and only now starting to come into leaf. As I walked, I could hear the small mouths of caterpillars starting to eat in the trees and the flutter of young birds as they tried to eat the bitter green worms.

At Main I turned right and headed in the general direction of downtown. I was already starting to get tired but I needed to find a photocopying place. Claire had managed to type up an uncheckable resume, working on a second-hand Underwood, but there was only one copy. She'd claimed that working on the resume had given her something to do while waiting for me to be released from hospital. I finally found a place and had fifty copies made and asked the girl behind the counter where I could go for coffee.

"Um, I dunno. There's a 7-11 on the corner. Does that help?"

The copies of the resume went into my case along with a box of paper clips from a rack near the door, which I remembered in time to pay for.

"Actually, is there somewhere I could sit down for a cup of coffee? A restaurant, or bar, or hotel, something like that. Not a Starbucks, though."

Her brows unclenched and she aimed me towards a commercial bakery a block away with five round tables under an awning around the side. There were four other patrons, two old men sitting by themselves and drinking small cups of coffee, and a pair of middle-aged women in pantsuits eating pastries and drinking designer bottled water. I sat down and a minute later a young man with dark, curly hair, blue eyes, and a gold earring came out, holding a menu. He was wearing a set of white overalls and an apron, and crushed into his pocket was a chef's hat.

"Good morning, can I get you something?" His voice rolled over the consonants.

"Sure. Could I see the menu?"

He handed it over grudgingly and I noticed the flour on his hands and shoulders. I also noticed a great deal of black body hair that stuck out of the ends of his sleeves and out the top of his shirt.

"Do you work in the bakery as well?"

"Yes. With my brothers and father. We take turns taking care of the customers out here."

"That's fine. Could I get a large coffee with cream and sugar and whatever pastry you recommend?"

He started to smile and then recovered his game face. As he headed back to fill the order, I realized that maybe he was smiling because not many people asked his opinion. Smiley, a bad guy I'd known, had the idea that people like it when you defer to their opinion and they like it when you're polite and ask questions. That had led him to one of his mottos: "Be nice. Nice is good. Nice sets a standard. Then, when you get mean, the shock is strongest." So here I was, trying to be nice (without the mean at the end), and it seemed to be working.

The baker came out with my coffee and a Danish with a dirty yellow filling. Before he could go away, I gestured to get his attention.

"Is this a cheese Danish?"

He nodded.

"A real cheese Danish? Never frozen, no preservatives, no, God help me, additives? A real, honest to God, fresh cheese Danish? I haven't had one since Chicago years and years ago."

"Yes, it's real and it's very bad for you. Enjoy."

I did. When I was finished, I sat back and licked the tips of my fingers and then I drank some coffee. That was good but not in the same category as the Danish. When the baker came back, I accepted a refill for the coffee and motioned him close. "Do you guys do bagels too?"

He showed bad teeth in a broad smile and nodded.

"Then I'll be back."

Over the second coffee I clipped the copies of my resume together and then put them back into the case. Then I tipped half of the total bill and went on. I figured I could cover five or six blocks today and the same tomorrow, stopping for more resumes as needed.

When I reached home after three, I found Claire in the kitchen on her hands and knees with her head in the oven. I admired her butt and listened to Fred sleeping on a pillow under the table in the dining room.

"My favourite end."

She didn't turn around but a hand snaked between her legs and gave me the finger. "How'd it go?"

There was a small table under the only window in the kitchen and I sat at it and picked up an apple from the wicker bowl. "They were polite. No one refused to take a resume but no one promised me the stars and the moon. Family businesses and mom-and-pop shops."

She pulled her head out and breathed deeply. There were spots of grease on her forearms and chin and the smell of oven cleaner was strong. "What the hell did you expect?"

She dropped the rag she was holding and came over and jumped into my lap. I shrugged and rested a hand above the comforting swell of her hip.

"I don't know, baby. I've never had a job before."

She pushed herself back a bit and looked into my face. "Are you serious?"

"Yes. Really. I've either stolen or been in jail. I've never had a job-job."

She laughed softly and then took my hand and put it down the top of her shirt. "Well, you know what will make you feel better?"

I didn't but she did. We would have done it a second time there on the kitchen table if Fred hadn't woken up and started to cry.

12

The next day I was up at 7:00 and headed down Main and hit thirty more businesses before taking a break around noon to go back to the bakery for a bagel. It was almost, but not quite, as good as the Danish, and the cream cheese was a little too bland to be really top notch. The baker lent me a copy of the local Yellow Pages so I wasted time in the cool spring sun with a second cup of coffee and made notes on the back of one of the resumes.

"More coffee?"

"Please."

The baker stood there for a few seconds and read over my shoulder. "Looking for a job?"

"Yes."

He waited, I guess for me to add more but I didn't, and he sniffed loudly. "It's a good time of year."

He glanced at the clouds but when I still didn't say anything, he sniffed again and walked back into the building.

In a few seconds the anger faded. It was odd, in prison you wouldn't think of prying into someone else's personal space, they might kick the shit out of you, shiv you, or fuck you. In the real world the interference seemed like a fairly common occurrence, and no one seemed to care or give it much thought. I also suspected that kicking the shit out of someone for reading over your damned shoulder would be frowned upon. The wind shifted a little and brought a dirty smell off the river and I realized that going straight was going to be hard. There were no referents, no signposts, no maps to how to behave.

There were lots of businesses listed nearby in the Yellow Pages: garages, groceries, convenience stores, five-and-dimes transformed into dollar bargain stores, bars, restaurants, and so on. All those needed untrained workers and I certainly qualified for that category but they also paid very little, about $7.25 an hour for minimum wage, according to the call I'd made to the labor board. I did the math on the corner of the resume and came to a total before taxes that would leave us with four hundred a month to live on (after rent). That's if I could get forty hours a week.

"That's not right."

I did the figures again and then looked around. There were two old men sitting solo at the counter and one turned slowly and looked at me so I stared back. He was small, just over five feet tall, with long arms and a shock of white hair that swept down and blended into gray eyebrows. He was wearing khaki pants and a white button-down shirt about three sizes too big for him. His skin was deeply tanned and his eyes were small and brown with very fine lashes, like those of a young girl.

"Can I help you?"

"Depends. You looking for work?"

I folded the resume up and took a sip of the coffee. The old man didn't look like he had a job of his own, much less that he could hire anybody, but I could be wrong.

"Sure."

"I don't need a lot of help but I need some. Maybe an hour's work once a week and I'll pay you ten under the table."

He carried his coffee over to my table and sat down before going on. "I own an archery shop down the street and I'm getting a delivery in. I have to watch the door while someone else brings in the boxes. I'm also too old. The fucking driver won't touch anything once the truck stops. What do you say?"

Ten bucks would cover yesterday's coffee and today's, so I agreed.

The old man's shop was called The Buttes and I tried to make a joke of it.

"It's an old English term for where you shoot a bow."

"Oh."

"Bet ya feel pretty stupid."

I ignored him and he showed me where the truck was going to come up behind his place and where I should stack the boxes. Then he led me around to the front of the place and let us both in with a big ring of keys. Once inside, he took down a laminated sign hanging in the door and put it on a post with several others. As he went to turn on the lights, I read the signs. One said "Deer Season!," another said "Gone Fishing," and the last two said "Coffee at the Greek's, be back soon" and "Lunch, be back later," respectively.

"Ya gotta tell your customers straight what's going on."

I hung my coat and vest on a circular rack of odd-looking bows in the middle of the room and looked around at an incredible mess. Along one wall were racks of bows for rent, along another were more for sale, and several large machines full of rollers and counterweights sat near the cash register. Shelves in the middle of the room held racks of camouflage clothing, bags, accessories, quivers, and a bewildering variety of arrows and other equipment. The back end of the room was given over to two ranges about twenty yards long that ended in a wall lined with several hundred sheets of pressboard stacked on top of each other and held down by industrial-sized clamps attached to the ceiling and floor braces.

"Nice place, huh?"

"I do not have the words. Is there really this much need for archery supplies?"

The old man was checking the answering machine and making notes on a clipboard attached to the wall. "Yep. I get hunters, Olympic wannabes, target freaks, schools, and clubs. Hell, these days I even get couples coming out on dates. I do fine."

He scratched his nose and then continued. "Now, don't get me wrong. Business could be better. It could always be better, betcha even Izzy Asper said that. Before he died. Here, I'll open the back door for you."

He walked down the lane to where an old, pocked target was still pinned to the wall. Inset near one corner was a steel door with a complicated latch, which he opened and then propped into place with a stop carved from a piece of two-by-four.

"The truck should be here any time. My name's Frank, by the by, yours is . . . ?"

"Oh. Sam Parker. Glad to meet you."

We shook hands and then he scratched his nose again. "Well, when he comes, unload the stuff into the middle of this range here and then we're square and I'll pay you. Okay?"

The bell that announced customers rang in the front of the store so Frank headed off while I waited for the delivery. In twenty minutes the driver showed up, pulling a five-ton diesel truck into the back lane and scraping the buildings on both sides. The driver hopped out, bringing with him a cloud of smells, dried urine and testosterone, flatus and halitosis, and coming towards me with a rolling gait like a sailor. He was a short man with a big belly and a wart right at the corner of his left eye.

"Where's the old man?"

I could hear archers talking inside along with the regular thud of the arrows into the target. I pointed over my shoulder. "He's in the front. Does he have to sign for something?"

The driver pushed a battered clipboard into my hands and belched. "Yeah."

As I took the delivery sheets back to Frank, I idly flipped the forms back to reveal that the driver had taped a centerfold to the clipboard itself. The picture was of a fat, ugly woman with bad teeth who had both hands locked into her vagina and was pulling it apart with what looked to be satisfaction at a job well done. I shuddered and flipped the pages back into place and let Frank sign.

"You look spooked."

"Never mind."

"You looked at the picture, didn't ya?"

"I said never mind. I meant never mind."

Frank scratched his nose with the tip of a broad-headed arrow. "Actually, I think it might be his wife."

I started to walk back and he shouted at my back. "Or his sister."

When the driver had his papers back, he opened up the side doors and stood back.

"There you fucking go. First two fucking pallets and don't leave any fucking wrap behind. Fuck."

The pallets were maybe two yards square at the base and three yards high, and consisted of brightly colored boxes of archery and outdoors equipment, tents, bags, and camouflage clothing. They were all wrapped in thick plastic that looked like Saran Wrap on steroids. I jumped up and looked at the pile.

"C'mon, I ain't got all fucking day."

There was no way around this. I grabbed hold of the edge of the plastic and started to tear it.

When I had the top layer exposed, I took the first box and looked for a place to put it. Finally I had to climb down and put it by the door. While I was doing this, the driver had retrieved a small cooler from the cab and was drinking a can of beer and eating a foot-long submarine sandwich loaded with meatballs and dripping a semi-translucent red sludge onto the ground in front of him. He saw me looking and waved the bottle around.

"Don't worry, it's only fucking American beer. It's like piss."

It took me almost an hour to unload both pallets onto the ground. When I was done, the driver slammed the door shut and nearly took my fingers off.

"Took you fucking long enough."

He was a small man, shorter than I by maybe a foot and a whole lot heavier, but he dwindled when I got in close. I smiled into his face and he reached for his belt, where a multi-purpose tool or folding knife was holstered in a leatherette case.

"You know . . ."

He squared his shoulders and undid the clasp on the case. He was using his right hand with his left to hold the case and it was on his left hip, which meant he'd draw it across his body before he could use it. That gave me possibilities, which made me smile widely.

". . . I could show you how to wear a Colombian Necktie. It'd look good on you. First I cut your throat, just a little, right under your chin. Then I pull your tongue out really hard until it sticks all the way down the outside of your throat. You don't bleed to death, you suffocate. It's been a while since I've done it but we can try, it'll come back to me."

He froze and broke and the next thing I knew, he had jumped into his truck and taken off, so I turned and went back to loading the boxes into the shop. Frank watched me from the front for a while and then came back to see how I was doing.

"What's wrong?"

"Hurt my back a while ago. I've got to take it slow, hope you don't mind."

Frank scratched his nose some more and thought about it. He was holding a big fiberglass-and-aluminum bow painted in camouflage colors. There were big pulleys at both ends of the arms and the line went back and forth over and over again. He changed the subject.

"You ever shoot?" Frank looked at me down the arm of the bow.

I answered, "Bows? No."

"You should, it's very relaxing. Peaceful, even."

I put down the last box and stretched to loosen my back. "Is it hard?"

"Not at all. Take this one. It's got a fifty-pound pull but you only hold twenty-five at the apex. It's legal for deer, elk, bear, anything you can find in Canada or the States. With one arrow you can take a rabbit, change the arrowhead and you can put a two-inch-wide hole right through the chest of a grizzly, change the arrow again and you can take fish. Bows are versatile, which guns ain't."

"Well . . ."

I picked up the last packing case from the truck.

"Let me put this stuff away and we'll talk."

Frank added. "And shoot."

"Long as it's free."

"First time always is."

I kept working. First taste is always free in both worlds.

13

Claire held me at arm's length when I got back home that afternoon and sniffed the air loudly on either side of my head.

"Ye gods, sweat, I do believe the boy has sweated."

Any retort I might have made was silenced when she thrust an odiferous Fred into my arms and turned to walk back towards the kitchen.

"This is not fair! Fred's crapped himself."

Fred nodded in serious agreement and tried to throw himself to the floor. After I changed him, I went upstairs for a shower, carefully putting the baby gate into place in Fred's room and locking it despite his squalls of outrage. I had to raise my voice to be heard downstairs over the baby.

"I'm showering!"

Claire came up and idly dusted flour off the front of her sweatshirt.

"You have no idea how glad I am. Dinner will be in ten minutes."

Upstairs the taps ran cold, then hot, then warm and finally they stuttered along at that temperature for just long enough. I changed into a pair of black dress pants cut down to shorts and a sleeveless white dress shirt and then came down to find the dining room lit by candles, with Fred dozing in his high chair.

"Monsieur." Claire made a broad gesture with her arm and showed me to my seat at the rickety old card table we were using since the cops had taken away our dining room table. God knows why. Probably to test it for blood or other crucial evidence. This despite the fact they had at least two confessions, both of them mine, plus whatever other theories they might have come up with. From past experience I knew we might maybe get the damn table back in a year. That was a big maybe and odds were we'd never see it again unless we visited a cop's house or went to a police auction.

I sat down and Claire brought out a cracked and chipped blue china plate, holding it at the bottom with the towel. On it was a very large, very bloody piece of meat with numerous score marks across it and a great number of peppercorns floating in a blood sauce. Beside the meat was a single baked potato steaming in a jacket of aluminum foil, and beside that was a small cup full of spinach with vinegar already added.

Claire gave a truly regal nod and wink and I burst out, "You are trying to kill me. Do you remember what the doctor said? 'No meat, maybe just a little chicken.' Help, help, my wife's trying to kill me!"

I picked up a mismatched steak knife and fork and prodded the meat, only to have Claire pull the plate away.

"Well, if you don't want it . . ."

When I growled at her, she put the food down and went to get her own. By the time she came back, I was on the fourth bite.

"Oh, God! This is better than sex."

She looked at me and arched an eyebrow so I covered. "Um, er, with anyone but the present company, of course."

She put real butter, chives, and sour cream on her potato, and then passed them.

"Good. Nice recovery. I guess my mama was wrong. You can be taught."

I ate some more. "Not to look a gift cow in the mouth, my sweet, but this is hardly welfare dining."

She waved a small chunk of meat in the air and I saw Renfield follow it with his muzzle while a thin line of drool broke free from his lower lip and fell to the floor.

"This, my virtuous little ex-con, is a reward. While you were out sweating and doing God knows what (although I do hope it was legal), I took a message. Apparently your charm has managed to convince one Steven Marquez to hire you to work in his convenience store. You start tomorrow at 7:00 a.m. sharp."

I went over and gave her a kiss on the cheek, which she accepted as her due. On my way back I stole a tiny bite of her steak and she waited until I was sitting before continuing. "As for the steak, it was cheap, cheap, cheap. No one knows how to cut meat any more and no one actually likes to eat it, either, and so this poor little well-marbled steak sat there naked and battered for three days past its due date until only I could see the essential goodness within."

She cut off a nice-sized bite and examined it. "So I got it, nicely rotted, for a song."

She ate and I felt my stomach churn. Claire's father had been a butcher with his own shop in Banff and she had learned from him while growing up. If she said the meat was good, then it was good, so I took another bite and she went on. "Tell me about your day."

So I did and frankly it was kind of boring but she listened and she asked questions and we talked. After a while we spent some good time staring into each other's eyes and eating in an easy silence that filled the whole house. Outside it became darker and cooler and quieter.

When it came, the knock on the door was shockingly loud and I jumped in my seat. Renfield barked twice and looked around as though wondering where the noise had come from. Claire looked at me bleakly and lifted a mouthful of spinach to her lips. "Ignore it."

Her voice was dead. Premonition? Fear? Knowledge? The knock was not repeated, although I waited. Finally I stood up and picked up the crowbar I'd put in the umbrella stand.

"I just got to know."

I stood to one side and gently pushed open the door with the straight edge of the bar, but there was no one there. Claire had come up behind me and held the bayonet behind her back as she stayed near the front window.

"What's there?" she asked.

My voice cracked as I answered. "A bottle of whiskey and a shot glass."

My knuckles were white on the crowbar as I leaned down and picked up the note. In pencil on the sheet of foolscap was the command "DRINK ME."

I crumpled the note, then thought better of it and smoothed it out before handing it to Claire, who read it without comment. I looked up and down the street and saw nothing and when I spoke again my fury was under control.

"Someone has a nasty sense of humor."

The bottle gurgled as I picked it up and I held it up to the light so I could see the dark browns, the almost-reds of the liquor within.

"Sam? Just let it go."

Claire was talking fast and nervous. It wasn't that easy to just dump the stuff. A failed dancer in an after-hours club had introduced me to Jack Daniel's Kentucky Bourbon and vice versa.

I'd been sixteen and I'd drunk it pretty much all the time for most of my life. I'd drunk it to wash down cocaine residue and to smooth acid paranoia. I'd drunk it first thing in the morning and the last thing in the evening. I'd drunk it from the hollow just above a pretty girl's ass and out of the bottle and just about every other way there was. I'd drunk it straight with a gun in my other hand while an imaginative young woman did expensive things to my partner after robbing a jewelry store. I'd choked it down as a veterinary hospital dropout had dug police-issue buckshot out of my hip. For me it had been a sign of the times.

"Yep, someone has a very nasty sense of humor." My voice broke as I looked at the bottle and then I shuddered and threw it high into the air. My rage carried it far out to smash into shards on the road in front of the house, where the lights from the streetlights glinted on the glass and the liquor and made a kaleidoscope of rainbows appear.

Claire took my arm as I shut the door. "Let's go finish dinner."

She led me to the table and on the way I put the crowbar where it belonged. I thought about neighbors and cops and bad guys and good guys and tried to think past the alcohol.

"The booze. It could be any one of a hundred people."

She sat me down at my spot and went back to hers before speaking pensively. "True. Well, whoever it is, I guess we'll have to deal with him or her or them, right?"

I looked at her and smiled and then she went on.

"But let's do it honestly, honestly and gently. I like having you here on the outside looking in instead of vice versa."

Pressure. I could feel it building, coming from all sides and increasing. Popping my eardrums, bruising my skin, distorting my life. Claire smiled at me and I smiled back.

But pressure from where? From whom? The classic bits of information needed were who, what, where, when, and why, but all I needed was who. Then I could stop it. Fuck the rest.

Claire raised her glass of water and I raised mine and we toasted each other.

That night I slept badly. The memories of the liquor had swallowed me and were unwilling to let go. Finally I woke up before five and went down to the kitchen. I got out some scrap paper and started to put phone numbers and addresses to all the names I'd remembered from the hospital. It didn't take long until there was a list of people and titles, and beside each name was listed a TV station or a newspaper or a radio station.

When I was done, I leaned back and waited for dawn.

14

arquez was a thin man with brown hair, brown skin, and brown eyes, and it was 6:55 when he drove up to the front of his store and parked just to the left of the main doors. I was standing there with my suit on and an overcoat jacket draped over one arm and trying to look casual. The store behind me was a brick-fronted, single-storey building with too many big windows and heavy bars across most of them. Where there weren't bars, there were signs and advertisements and pictures of snack foods like Astro Bars, Bubble Tea, and Musk Ox jerky.

Okay, I was kidding about the jerky, but still.

Marquez locked the doors of his Cadillac Eldorado and then turned to face me. "Sam Parker?"

I took two steps forward and smiled to show my teeth as he reached out to shake my hand.

"Yes. You're Mr. Marquez?"

Marquez ignored the proffered hand and stared at me like he was trying to memorize something. I wondered what he was seeing, pale skin drawn tight like I'd been sick for a long time, but, overall, pretty big. Was he wondering about whether he should keep looking for staff? I was wearing my best and only loser suit, which made me stand out in the neighborhood, and I was probably a lot older than anyone else who had applied for the job. Those were probably pluses. Finally he made up his mind who he was and nodded.

"Yes, I'm Marquez, come in."

The doors were of thick Plexiglas reinforced with alarm wires and the display windows had bars on the inside as well. He caught me looking at the security arrangements and chuckled.

"Not a lot of crime 'round here, if that's what you're thinking. I bought the building from the city, they'd taken possession of it after a gang was caught smuggling booze and cigarettes out of here. The gang had made the place into a fortress and the cops busted it up good when they came knocking so I got it for a song. And a lot of renovations."

Inside Marquez gestured at the walls and racks of equipment. "I'll be honest, we sell mostly crap. Fried pork rinds, nachos, dips, chocolate milk, overly carbonated drinks, cigarettes, dirty magazines, things like that."

He motioned for me to walk ahead of him to where the cash register sat in an island formed by a wide linoleum counter. "For example, we are the only store in a ten-block radius that sells *Hustler*. I'm not sure if that's a good claim to fame."

He opened up the cash register and pulled the drawer onto the counter. Then he began to empty small baggies of change and bills from his pockets into the compartments, talking all the while. "I bring the money home at night and count it in the morning, before work. It's a lousy idea to try to balance your books at the end of a shift. Each day the till starts out with two hundred dollars and we open the doors at 7:30 and close them at 11:00. I take the shift from 3:00 to 11:00 and I need someone to cover the 7:00 till 3:00. I pay seven dollars and a quarter an hour and you can have all the fountain drinks and coffee you want. Interested?"

I smiled and made a noncommittal gesture.

"I need someone honest and hard-working and clean. You'll be working alone, selling to the customers, dealing with complaints, and making sure everything works. You'll also have to keep the place clean. I don't schedule lunch breaks, you can get a rush at any time, so you'll have to make your own as you get a chance."

Someone tried the door and Marquez looked over and shook his head violently from side to side and then motioned at his wrist. With an audible curse, the old man stamped away.

"Like it makes a difference if he gets his lottery tickets five minutes later. That's one of my regulars."

Marquez had shut the till and rung up No Sale, and was busy unlocking a deep drawer with steel plates reinforcing the sides and bottom. It was full of brightly painted bits of pasteboard, scratch-and-win lottery tickets with themes like "Trains of the World," "Great Music," and "Astronomy Jackpots." He shuffled through them and slid them into a display case over his head, then he reached over and turned on the computer that linked him with the Manitoba Lottery Corporation.

"Stupidity tax, anyway. Could you turn on the coffee maker? It's an old one."

I walked over and hung the jacket on a rack of oddly named generic and knock-off brands of potato chips, and then unscrewed the top of a big percolator beside a sink. Marquez was watching me as I looked into the big drum and whistled quietly.

"Not a problem."

The machine was exactly the same as the kind they had in every prison and halfway house I'd ever been in. I'd worked in the cafeteria out in Drumheller for a few months over the years and I'd nursed the same kind of machine through good days and bad. It had been a job with an interesting motivational base. If cons don't get their coffee, they'll kill someone, generally the person who's supposed to make the coffee in the first place. Marquez watched as I poured the water in and checked the stainless steel filter. It was filthy so I cleaned it before adding fresh grounds from a pre-measured foil envelope.

"Do you have any salt?"

Marquez was still watching me and I was feeling kind of nervous about being stared at.

"No. Don't worry, they won't care about bitter as long as you make it strong."

I flipped the switch and let the machine start. The red light came on and I turned around.

"All right, Mr. Parker. Do you have any experience in convenience stores?"

"It's Sam and, no, I've never worked in a convenience store."

The back of my head added, "But I have robbed many of them over the years." I ignored the voice and waited.

"You're hired. I'll work with you today until you've got the hang of it. Let's go open the doors."

And that was the start of my first day on my very first job, and that made for a lame curriculum vitae for a thirty-two-year-old man.

When I was finished work, I bought three dollars' worth of quarters from Marquez and headed west until I hit the next major street, which was Salter. A block along I found a phone booth, where I made my calls and double-checked each name and number of the news people I wanted to talk with.

I was right on the money for six out of eight and two receptionists also gave me the extension numbers. Those I marked down.

15

On my way home, a young woman stopped me in the park beside the church near my house.

"Mr. Robillard wants to talk."

She was about ten feet away in the park, standing in the shadow of a big elm. Somewhere between eighteen and twenty-five, a dangerous age, a reckless age. She was slimly built with narrow hips and shoulders, a darkly tanned complexion, large green eyes, and straight black hair worn down to below her chin.

"Shit, lady. Don't do that. You scared me."

"Like I said, Robillard wants to talk."

Without thinking I looked both ways and stepped into the park and the concealing shadows. She was wearing gloves, a leather Stetson, olive-green overalls fastened with black buttons, dark blue, high-topped runners, and a loosely fitting leather jacket. I recognized them as working clothes and my heart started to beat faster.

"Followed you this morning and saw you schlepping coffee and Snickers bars to the great unwashed."

Was this a hit? Was she going to kill me here? The overalls were a couple of sizes too big so she could have different clothes on underneath, and the jacket had room for the tools of the trade.

"I mean, really."

Her hands were visible, held loosely at her sides, and if she was intending to kill me, then I was pretty much dead, so I figured to wait until the hands moved and then dive forward to take her apart.

She'd still kill me but at least I'd be doing something. The woman smiled like she was reading my mind. "Relax, I'm not killing you today. Just taking you for a ride."

I didn't relax. "Chicago rules?"

She lit a cigarette with a small, red, steel lighter. "Don't know those."

"A ride is one way."

"Oh. No. The car's around behind the church. Robillard wants to talk at you."

"You said that. Don't you mean to me?"

She was silent.

"Even with me. But at me?"

She grunted and led me out of the park and around the church. "I meant what I said."

Getting into the car, I finished the sentence. "And I said what I meant. One hundred percent."

While she drove, the woman talked. Robillard had set up the meeting in an empty Northern Chinese restaurant downtown that he had points in. It made me feel oddly uncomfortable, like he was trying to impress me. Like he was showing his connections and power. And pride and insecurity had never been a good combination in anyone I'd ever had to deal with.

We ended up in a neighborhood of redbrick buildings five or six storeys high with old woodwork and big pieces of wrought iron framing filthy panes of starred and cracked glass. Shards of paper blew across the sidewalks and gathered in eddies with leaves, empty paper cups, and cigarette butts raped of any shred of tobacco.

"This looks familiar."

She lit another cigarette, this time with the car's lighter. "Yeah. It should. This chunk of the city's been filmed like twenty million times."

I looked out the window and tapped the glass. "Sure."

"*Framed* with Sam Neill. *Twilight of the Ice Nymphs. Acceptable Risk. The Adventures of Shirley Holmes.*"

I turned in my seat and looked at her quizzically. "*Adventures of Shirley Holmes?*"

"It was good."

I let it lie for a while but circled back to it. "*Adventures of Shirley Holmes?*"

"Drop it. Here we are."

She pulled into a tunnel in the middle of a block and drove halfway down until the walls opened up on either side and we could get out of the car. The woman took a big drag on the cigarette and snapped it away to bounce off the bricks, trailing sparks like the tail off a comet.

She asked casually, "You carrying?"

"No."

She looked at me indifferently as though she didn't believe me but let it pass anyway. Then I added, "Do I know you?"

"I used to be a hooker and you might have fucked me. But I don't remember you."

"What's your name?"

"Sandra. Now, there's no need to be nervous here. Robillard just wants to talk."

"Right. *Adventures of Shirley Holmes.* Shit."

She narrowed her eyes and pursed her lips disapprovingly. "You ever watch it?"

"Well, no."

"So shut your mouth. It was good."

There was a heavy-gauge steel door set into the wall and Sandra knocked on it six times slowly before it was opened by a sullen teenage boy.

"Hiya, Sandy. Thank fuck you're here, your husband's being a knob."

"Good afternoon, Tom, you're looking lovely today."

She looked at him and smiled at the corner of her mouth. The boy glanced at me and I saw he was carrying a thin-bodied, long-barreled Colt pistol level with his crotch. He tightened the grip on the pistol with one hand. I tried to break the ice.

"Hey, nice gun. Colt thirty-eight Super, right?"

The kid nodded half-heartedly.

"Great gun and a nice round. Good and fast. Especially for the thirties, when they started making it. Not so fast these days. Kinda old-fashioned."

The kid didn't cut me slack, just stared, so I tried again.

"Where's Robillard?"

Sandra turned halfway around to face me. "My husband's downstairs."

She walked in front of me down narrow stairs into the basement underneath the building. I followed, then the kid. Halfway down the stairs I sneezed and it echoed loudly. "Stupid allergy."

Sandra led us into a large kitchen floored with industrial gray tiles and full of stainless steel tables, counters, and equipment. In the center of the room was a perforated metal lid over a drain and I knew that this place could be a killing room just as easy as not. The drain could carry away my blood as easy as anything else.

Looking up from the drain, I saw a fattish white man. He wore a maroon silk shirt over khaki pants and held a tall can of Olympic Ale in one meaty hand. He waved the can around when he talked and some slopped into the air and fell like molten gold to the tiled floor.

"Good afternoon, Mr. Haaviko, is it? Or do you prefer Parker?"

"Parker."

"Excellent. Do you know who I am?"

He sounded reasonable. I took two steps into the room and waited while the kid with the Colt closed the door and leaned up against it. Sandra took three steps to the right and hitched herself up onto a platform beside a heavy cutting block.

"Robillard. You're a crook."

He nodded, like I was a good student. "Excellent. Yes, I am. I own parts of three or four restaurants, two garages, a pool hall, some other businesses. I smuggle, I fence, I grow and distribute weed, I lend money, I arrange for people to get hurt. I am telling you all this as a courtesy so we know where we're at."

My eyes went to Sandra and then back to him. "You a pimp too?"

His smile flickered like a neon light. A tremor ran through his face and subsided and his voice got louder. "No."

He drank some beer and I saw his hand tremble a little until some beer splashed out. For a second the drops were suspended in the air and then they hit the ground.

"Sandra's my wife. You should apologize."

Emphasis on *my*. I nodded to her and spoke very softly. "Sorry."

Robillard paused for a moment and then ran his free hand through his hair. "I am not the worst man in the city, nor am I the best. I am not a shark amongst minnows. I am a shark amongst other sharks. We all have sharp teeth and I am not to be fucked with."

The tremors in his hands came again, stronger this time, and he took a deep breath and slowly they stopped. "Yet you are fucking with me."

The way he spoke, the obscenity was in brackets and sounded like a preacher telling a dirty joke. It sounded out of place.

"This is about your cousin, I suppose?"

"You suppose right. Your actions show contempt."

The kid with the Colt shifted around a little and Sandra stared at a point on the wall above my head. Robillard went on, his voice smooth now. "And if you show me contempt, then it makes it harder for me to follow my chosen profession. I will appear weak. Some other shark will try me out. Which would lead to violence. Which would lead to bloodshed. Which no one wants."

He waited for me to say something but I didn't.

"So I really should kill you. To prove that I am not weak."

"That's an option."

His eye twitched and the tremors came back for a second. I could swear I saw Sandra hide a grin.

"What do you mean?" Robillard's voice was throaty now, full of anger.

"I'm hard to kill. Find another option."

Without making a big deal about it, I moved to the right and turned so I could see the door and the kid with the Colt out of the corner of my eye. The woman tilted her head to the side like this whole thing was amusing her and now the smile was in the open. Robillard went on, this time talking to me and then switching to Sandra. While he talked, he opened another beer from a six-pack on the counter.

"I've decided I do not want to talk to you."

She sneezed.

"I want this man dead . . ."

I interrupted. " 'Kay. Before we do that, hear my side. Your cousin broke into my home with his friends and they were killed."

Robillard took a swig of beer and a trail of translucent snot ran out his nose into the foam on his upper lip. He was trembling openly now, big, hard slabs of fat shaking with strong emotion and something else, an upper like cocaine or speed fanning his flames. His right hand rested right beside his front pocket, which bulged like it would if it was holding a gun. Of course, he could be holding a cell phone or a wallet but my money was on a gun.

I continued, "You would have done the same thing."

Click-click. The kid with the Colt moved the safety on and off again and again. The woman watched what was going on and Robillard raised his voice to a yell. "Fuck that and fuck you. You killed him for no good goddamned reason."

Sandra sneezed again.

Click-click. The kid, it was getting annoying.

"Sorry."

Could that be what he wanted, an apology? I tried that. "Look, I'm sorry he's dead."

Robillard screamed, any semblance of patience gone. "That's not fucking important!"

"Then what is?"

"Respect. You don't show me no fucking respect."

I had shifted weight and was looking over Robillard's head to examine my reflection in a hanging rack of stainless steel frying pans.

Click-click. The kid had a real nervous twitch going on.

"Fuck this." I said it out loud and everyone stared. The kid had come slightly closer and was surprised when I pivoted with my weight on my right foot with my left foot guiding. I had brought my right hand in close to my chest and drove it out open-handed to turn his nose into jelly. At the same time, I grabbed the Colt by the barrel with my left hand and then reversed the motion and handed the gun to my right hand. I thumbed the hammer back and checked the safety blindly with the same thumb. Then I pointed it in the general direction of Robillard.

"Don't!" I said it mildly and Robillard stopped. Drinking. Talking. Even breathing.

"You too." That was directed at Sandra, who had drawn a slim pistol out from somewhere and she froze as well. She laid the pistol down on the counter and I relaxed a little before going on like nothing had happened.

"So did I kill your guy back there or is he just fucked up?"

Robillard's eyes were focused on the barrel of the gun. His beer fell to the ground and bounced once and the fluid boiled out.

"I said, is he dead?"

Stepping back a little, I found I could see the boy in my peripheral vision. He was collapsed against the door with his left hand pressed hard against where his nose had been. From around his fingers I could see pink meat and white bone and the healthy red of arterial blood. His nose, though, was gone. Shock had taken him away and Sandra finally answered. "Bad but not dead."

"Oh well."

I backed up to the boy and patted him down to find two extra magazines and a cheap folding knife. As I was doing that Sandra flexed her fingers and Robillard reached down towards his pocket. Both stopped moving when I shook my head.

"Neither of you is nearly fast enough. You got a good boy here, you know that?"

They didn't respond and I walked over to the woman and took her gun. Up close I was struck by how much prettier she was than I'd originally thought. She was also eerily calm. Her gun was a Colt Woodsman in .22 with a six-inch barrel and the front sight filed off. A killer's gun. Something for someone who liked working up close and who had confidence. Normally, a .22 is a useless round, you have to be really arrogant to use it. Or you have to hate the noise and recoil of a bigger gun. Or you have to have read too many detective novels.

As I took her gun I told her, "Nothing personal."

She nodded and I got out of her space and moved over to Robillard and took his piece too before moving back. He had been packing a big Smith and Wesson revolver in .41 magnum with the barrel cut down to the cylinder and the handle wrapped in black electrician's tape. Inaccurate. Loud. Destructive.

I went back to where I'd been and covered them both with her piece and the kid's Colt. Robillard's gun went into my back pocket just in case I wanted to kill a whale later on.

"Now," I reached Robillard in two steps, "our discussion is over."

He looked hard and drug-fueled rage opened and closed his mouth until I pressed the barrel of the Colt .22 into his eye and he backed up, and then pressed some more until he backed and finally stopped when he hit the institutional gray wall.

"Stay out of my way or you die. Stay away from my family or you die. If you interfere with me, you die. You try to do anything that affects me personally in even the smallest way and you die."

With each word I jabbed a little harder into Robillard's eye and then I stopped and headed up the stairs. At the top I booked it down the alley, stopping for a second to open the hood and tear a handful of wires loose from Sandra's car. A few alleys over, I wiped down the three guns on a piece of canvas sticking out of a garbage can and dropped them one at a time into trash cans and down sewer gratings.

On the bus home I wondered about Shirley Holmes.

16

When I walked into the house both my knees were immediately bruised black by a charging dog's head. After I had untangled a very happy Renfield from my lower torso and stopped him from loving me to death, I called out, "Hi, honey, I'm home. What's for dinner?"

"Very funny and very original."

Claire came around the corner from the dining room on her hands and knees with Fred balanced precariously on her back. He looked somewhere between amazed and terrified as he clung to her shirt. She paused and Fred dug his heels into her ribs and chortled.

"And how was your day?"

Before I opened my mouth, I decided to omit any reference to the kid, Robillard, or his ex-whore wife with the very professional .22. "Boring and kind of fun, how about yours?"

She motioned so I knelt down to hear her whisper while Renfield took the opportunity to lick my ear with considerable force and enthusiasm. "The bastards are grinding me down."

Fred switched to my back without too much fuss and the three of us headed into the kitchen, me crawling and Claire finally getting to walk.

"I've been doing that for too long. Dinner will be ready in about two hours. I've made lasagna, I hope it's good. I've never made lasagna before, so even if it's bad, pretend it's not. So, what about your job?"

I dumped Fred in his playpen in the dining room and poured a glass of water.

"It's a convenience store about six blocks away. The customers are mostly jerks, local assholes mixed with a few lost tourist-type assholes. On the plus side, the work is easy and the owner's medium smart. The cash register's a bitch, though, very old and crotchety."

"Much like you. When do you work again?"

"Tomorrow, same time."

Claire checked the oven and adjusted the temperature. "So, would it be okay if I went out tomorrow night?"

That made me feel odd and I answered with artificial bonhomie. "Of course."

She sighed and wiped her hands on her jeans. "It bothers you, doesn't it?"

First rule of interpersonal relationships, when in doubt, lie. "No, of course not."

She just sighed again and rested against the counter. "It won't work, you know, I can tell when you lie."

Second rule of interpersonal relationships, when caught in a lie, lie again. "No, really."

She stared at me silently until I wilted. "Oh. Well. Maybe it bothers me somewhat. I'm feeling insecure right now."

She smiled. "Don't worry. I'll come back. It's just that Elena invited me out for a coffee and I'd like to go."

"Elena? The cop?"

"Yes."

"By all means, go. Fred and I will have a fine time, we don't need you, just see if we don't."

She shook her head and bit her lower lip. "There is one other thing. I didn't want to tell you but now I'm not sure."

"What?"

"I've been getting threats, very vivid notes. Apparently the three guys had friends."

Renfield had come in with his Frisbee and I rubbed his ears until he began to twitch and spasm in canine ecstasy.

"Everyone has friends. Even I have friends. Did you keep the notes?"

"Yes."

"How many?"

"Four. They've been coming in since you were in the hospital."

They were in a jar on top of the fridge and I laid them out on the kitchen table and read them. They were all similar, butcher's paper or sheets cut from a brown lunch bag and crayon with the words spelled out in capitals with no space between the letters. Out of curiosity, I went up to our room and retrieved the notes that had come with the liquor bottle and the tape and laid them out beside the ones in the kitchen. Claire read over my shoulder and I read them out loud.

"LEAVE, BABY KILLER." "STAY AWAY." "MURDERER." "GO BACK WHERE YOU CAME FROM." "DRINK ME." "LISTEN TO ME."

I said, "Two different people, at least."

"How can you tell?"

"The last note and the one before that, the second-last one especially. The paper is different in those two cases and a pen is used instead of crayons. It's also not smudged or marked up in any way. That indicates two people and maybe more."

I yawned and Claire patted my hand. "You should have been a cop."

I yawned again and stretched.

"No. Even with the bribes, the pay isn't enough. Can I have a nap? After supper I'll go around and make sure the house is sealed tight. Maybe I'll even find our note-wielding maniac."

She patted my hand and sent me off.

"Oh, can you turn on the radio?"

We had put an old AM/FM radio with a cassette player on a shelf near the door and I flipped it to a local station that played old rock from the fifties and sixties, the only kind of music we could agree on.

". . . this just in; a local man has barricaded himself into his home on Ridge Road and fired several shots. Winnipeg police are on the scene and are currently waiting for the Emergency Response Team. Neighbors are unsure whether the man has hostages although he does live with his wife and two teenaged daughters. Just a minute . . ."

Claire looked at me and then I went back to my chair and sat down to listen to the breathless announcer.

". . . a black panel truck has just driven up and heavily armed police officers are debarking . . ."

Claire looked at me and mouthed "debarking?"

". . . prominent among them is Detective Sergeant Enzio Walsh, the commander of the ERT . . ."

I looked at Claire and shook my head.

"More news to come."

So we waited, my nap forgotten. We waited and we listened to light music, scanning the dial occasionally for more news. The incident was being covered by all the local stations to one degree or another. Claire listened and shook her head. "I never will understand that."

"Hmmm?"

She had poured a glass of water and sipped it idly while I sat beside the radio and tried to make sense out of what was happening.

"Suicide by police. Kill your wife or kids and then get shot by the cops. Why? You're a man, you tell me why."

"Just because I have testicles doesn't mean I understand all men."

She smiled. Fred was crawling around, awake and rambunctious, getting underfoot and chasing the dog with single-minded attention.

"You must have an opinion, you always have an opinion."

The news came back on and she waved me to silence.

"And in breaking news, the barricaded man on Ridge Road has surrendered to police. During the tense half-hour standoff, a police robot was used to enter the house and locate the man. Although several shots were fired, no one was hurt. We have Simon Maniuk on the scene and he is trying to get a few words with the arresting officer. Simon?"

"Thank you. I am currently talking to Detective Sergeant Enzio Walsh, a decorated police veteran and member of the Major Crimes Unit and the Emergency Response Team. Now, Detective, can you tell me what happened?"

"Certainly. Responding to a call of shots fired, police units arrived and sealed off the area while we determined if there were any hostages. We used 'Baby,' a remote-controlled armored robot, which has infrared, sonic, and telescopic sensors, to enter the home."

There was a pause.

"When we determined that there were no hostages, we used the robot to begin a dialogue with the suspect. The suspect opened fire on 'Baby' so we resorted to non-lethal force to disable the suspect and allow uniformed officers to carry out the arrest."

"Officer, by non-lethal force, what do you mean?"

Claire glanced at me and I silently repeated the sentence in all its awkwardness and she stifled her laughter.

"'Baby' is capable of delivering various munitions such as flares, pepper spray, and non-lethal 'beanbags,' soft plastic projectiles designed to temporarily disable an offender. There is minimal risk of permanent injury and we only resorted to this when the suspect opened fire with a large-caliber rifle, putting police officers and others in the neighborhood at risk."

"I see."

"Now, I have to go. Please tell your listeners that they're safe. The Winnipeg police force is on the job."

"Thank you officer. This is Simon Maniuk, signing off."

Claire flipped the radio off. "Comments?"

"Hmmm? Cops here have a toy and they like using it, that's no big surprise, cops always have toys. Walsh is used to being interviewed and likes it. Anything else?"

"Right. Actually I was talking about the whole suicide by police sniper. Any ideas?"

"Yep. They're cowards. They want to die and they don't want to pull their own trigger."

She grabbed Fred and hugged him tightly and I hesitated. "There's more. There was an old man in Millhaven, eyes black as pieces of graphite from a pencil, face always slack, hair like fine wire, bad skin, grainy and gray. He killed his kids with a hatchet after he got divorced."

"Why?"

"Claimed his wife would be ruined without him and he couldn't do that to the kids. It wouldn't be fair for them to watch her fall apart."

"What happened?"

"To the old man? He was on serious tranquilizers, real zombie time. They screwed up on his meds schedule one night and he cut the big vein in his groin with a pop-top off a can of Diet Coke. Or was it Pepsi? Bled out, anyway."

Claire was silent and her brow was furrowed in thought before it suddenly cleared. "Aha, the magic penis theory."

Despite myself, I started to laugh. "The what?"

"The magic penis. Poke the woman with it and she'll be changed forever. All men are convinced. The guy in Millhaven believed that and acted."

I couldn't help myself, I looked down. "You mean it's not magic?"

She hugged Fred some more and he squealed.

"It's good, it's not that good."

She stood up and kissed me before whispering in my ear. "Don't tell the penis that, though."

"I won't. I'm going for a walk, I'll be back soon."

She nodded. "I'll put your dinner in the oven."

"Shit, I forgot . . ."

Claire stuck her tongue out at me. "I know, lots to think about. Go."

So I went, my pockets full of quarters, looking for a pay phone a long way from the house and with my head full of various ideas. Most of them unpleasant and some of them downright evil.

17

As far as walks go, it was productive. Once I found a pay phone, I made sure a few more reporters were still working. I also got to know my neighborhood a little better, checked out ways into it and ways out. Criminal habits, know your routes of escape, just in case you have to use them. Learn the lay of the land, how the area is put together, how the patterns of foot and vehicle traffic interact, where the bottlenecks are. Learn what was there and what was not. I'd been home ten minutes only when the phone rang and I was closest, so I answered. When I put the phone down and turned to Claire, she was drinking a cup of reheated coffee by the sink.

"I'm fired."

She put her cup down. "Why?"

"Marquez didn't say. He just said he didn't need some piece of shit like me and don't come in tomorrow."

I let it sink in. "I've never been fired before."

Her eyes went opaque for a moment and then she took another sip. "Go talk to Marquez."

"Why?"

She grunted in an unladylike fashion and poured the rest of the cup into the sink. "Why not? It beats sitting around and not knowing."

I looked at the phone and started to pick it up, when she stopped me. "Go in person."

I nodded and turned to get my windbreaker again.

"I didn't mean that you should do it now."

"No time like the present."

Outside, it had started to drizzle and I raised the collar of my jacket and wished it was a little warmer. It took me ten minutes to walk the distance and when I was near, I paused and checked the store out. I could see two shoppers through the window so I waited 'til they left before going in.

"Hello, Mr. Marquez."

He looked up when the door closed and his hand flashed down and came up with a length of pool cue. I raised my hands and let my back touch the door while his voice trembled with rage and fear.

"Get-the-fuck-OUT!"

He ran his words together and they rose to a scream.

When I answered, my voice was calm and level. This level of aggression was something I understood. It made me feel comfortable. "Sure. Right away. Immediately."

I just stood there and didn't move. When Marquez's hand stopped shaking, I went on. "Why am I being fired?"

"Why? You're a fucking thief, *un meutrier, un apache!*"

French was not my strong suit. I could order a beer, a hooker, and tell someone to open a safe, but that was about my limit.

"Well, I understand thief and murderer but what's the last one?"

The pool cue trembled with his pulse as he answered. "A gangster. I found out you belonged to a motorcycle gang."

I didn't say a word and he went on. "So it's true, right?"

My eyes were loosely focused on the cue as I answered. "Most of it. I never belonged to a gang, though. Not much of a joiner, I guess."

Marquez's fingers whitened and I knew he was about to start swinging. If he did, I'd take his shots and then move around into the register area and tear him apart. I'd been hit before and just thinking about the pain and release made me feel better. He must have seen something in my face because he flinched and lowered the stick a bit. "But the rest was real?"

The whole discussion was pointless and I turned to leave. For some reason, though, I stopped and answered.

"Yes. It happened, I did time. Now I'm just trying to get by."

His brows furrowed in thought. "But, you were a criminal, right?"

His voice cracked like he wanted to believe something and my head throbbed. All of a sudden I wished for about eight lines of good coke and twenty ounces of Grand Marnier, and that scared the living shit out of me.

"Fuck you. Here, tell you what, I remove from you the necessity of ever believing anything can ever change."

Marquez didn't say a word and I went on in a gentler tone. "Never mind. You owe me for two days. Mail it tomorrow."

And I left. The rain had let up and I could see for miles in all directions. There were no tall buildings nearby and the rain had cleaned the pollution out of the air. The prairie sky stretched out all around and shrank the city and my problems down to nothing at all. For a second I longed for a fight, someone to swing at and someone to swing at me. Bones to break, people to hurt, blood to spill. Then that feeling faded too.

At random I chose a direction and began to walk. The showers began again and the rain splashed hard on the concrete and bounced up past my ankles. Out of curiosity, I reached out with the tip of my tongue and tasted some of the rain and it was sweet and clean, like tears. When I started to get angry again, I walked on a little farther. When I was done thinking about fire and blood and razor blades, I turned back on my path and walked home.

18

Claire got angrier than I had ever been. She ended up in a mood more suited to an employee of the Spanish Inquisition. "Fucking asshole. I'll skin his dick and use it as a cape."

And I'm the one with the reputation and sheet.

"What a colossal jerk-off."

She was in the same kind of mood as one of those giants from fairy tales. You know, "I'll break his bones to make my bread." I was still smiling about it when she glared at me. "Why are you smiling? Why aren't you pissed?"

"Nothing I can do about it. Also, I was pissed on the walk home. I got over it and now I'm just curious."

She paused and sat down on the floor. Renfield took this as a sign and came over for a belly scratch. When she didn't understand exactly what he wanted, he responded by rolling over and waving his legs about until she understood the message. As she scratched, I sat down and she relaxed, dogs are good for that.

"Curious about what?"

Renfield moved towards me and I started to scratch him behind his ears as his doggy smile grew wider and wider.

"Mostly about who told Marquez about me."

"Whoever sent the notes, that's obvious."

"Right. But I still think more than one person sent the notes. Also, there's the tape, which requires skill and equipment. And a vulgar imagination."

"All right. Let's think about this."

We both sat there and mauled the dog and then she went on.

"The possibilities. Someone from your past, the cops, and friends of the guys you killed. Am I forgetting anything?"

"No."

"Now for motive. Someone from your past acting for revenge or profit (how they'd get profit out of this, I don't know), friends of the guys you killed for revenge, and the cops to discredit you."

"Skip profit. There's no way to make money here that jumps to mind. That leaves us with revenge and discrediting me. Revenge is self-explanatory and I'll look into that."

I thought about it all and continued. "Now, the cops have a good motive. If I leave town for whatever reason or get discredited, then the cops go scot-free."

Renfield rolled onto his belly and I continued scratching while Claire went and found a dog brush. She brushed for a few moments and then yawned.

"Where did the term 'scot-free' come from?"

"Huh?"

I looked up stupidly and she repeated the question.

"Oh. It's Old English. A bill in a tavern used to be called a 'scot' and if the keeper forgot to charge you, then you didn't have to pay."

"How do you know that?"

"Tons of time in jail to read. What did you think I did with all that time in there?"

She rolled the dog onto his side and then pulled the clumps of gray and white inner coat hair from the brush.

"I figured you masturbated, tried to escape, smuggled dope, cooked shine, messed with the screws, got into fights . . ."

I interrupted her before she could go on. "Yes, all that, but there was time for the finer things. So we have three possible suspects."

"Tell me what Marquez said."

I did, as close to word for word as I could.

"So Marquez knew about the things you went to jail for, is that it?"

I realized that my past had become a sore spot, then I pushed on.

"Right. He called me a killer, a thief, and a gang banger. Now I killed here, in self-defense, and in other places for other reasons, but I was never nailed for those. A thief, well, most of my time inside was for that. Bad guys know both. But a gangster? I danced around the edges but never wore a patch, never wore colors. People from my past wouldn't call me that. Some of them could do everything, the notes, the booze, and the bugging."

"Okay."

She pursed her lips and I thought about kisses but she was still working.

"It's pretty safe to say that Marquez was not visited by friends of the dead kids. They wouldn't know about your past, it was a long time ago, and in a far-off land. Friends of the deceased might have the ability to leave the notes and the booze. And maybe bug a hotel room and do some editing."

Claire looked at my face and patted my knee before leaning across the dog to kiss me.

"I shouldn't call those thieves 'kids.' Think about it this way, if the you of today found the you at sixteen years of age, breaking into the house, what would the today you do?"

"Lousy grammar."

"You're avoiding the question."

"Yep. I'd shoot me. I guess. I'd still feel guilty about it."

Claire patted me on the knee again. "Right. I'm bloody-minded, though. I would have killed those guys if I had had the chance. I just don't think I would have had a chance."

"Thanks. I think I was just damned with faint praise. Still, our note dropper and bugger is probably not a friend of the dead kids. It's probably not someone from my past, because all my criminal friends think I'm going to fuck up on my own and don't need any help. Changing the subject gently, he asks, what about your family?"

Claire chose not to respond immediately. Instead, she went back to brushing the dog before speaking. "My family loves me, period, and through me they tolerate you. Right now I'm concerned with your old friends, the ones who hate you. I think they'd shoot you if they were mad at you and this whole thing seems awfully complicated. Making you lose a job is kind of pointless."

"Right. Okay, now we're on to the cops. The Crown will be watching them carefully and they won't want to do anything too stupid. They'd have access to my record and could do the rest with no problem. The records mention gang-related activity, from way back but it's there, sales of this and that to gangsters. Buying this and that."

"Wanna be more vague?"

She was grinning and I rolled my eyes.

"In Edmonton I was selling hash oil, LSD, grass, and crystal meth. With the cash I was buying guns, paper, and jewelry, which I'd move east or west and take a profit. In Vancouver I was moving grass south to assorted independents and picking up guns to move back for sale in Edmonton. A nice three-way trade. Happy?"

"Ecstatic. Then we come to the cops who are in trouble. They could have access to the records and a need to use them. Discredit you and they go free. They could also do the booze, the notes, and maybe the bugging."

She thought it through. "The booze. I knew I wasn't thinking about this right. Whoever left the booze knew you had problems. Who knew about you and the booze?"

I laughed but it sounded kind of shaky, even to me. "Well, every-one from my past."

"Right. But didn't you say most of them think you're faking going straight?"

Then it clicked. "Yeah. They all think I'm still drinking. For them, leaving the booze would mean nothing. Whoever left the booze knew I wasn't drinking and knew it would hurt me."

"Right. Now, the cops knew that, right?"

She went on. "But. Friends of the dead kids and people from your past wouldn't know about your problems with booze."

She finished it briskly. "That means that the cops are the ones who are doing this shit."

"Why do you figure that? I'm not arguing, but why?"

Claire patted my arm gently as though to say, you're not really dumb, just slow.

"The simplest solution is always the right one. Except when it isn't. The cops are the simplest solution."

"Well. Cops, in general, are pretty simple." I thought about it and finally nodded. "The idea makes sense."

"Of course it does." She paused. "Maybe not plural, maybe singu-lar. One person could do all the stuff we've been talking about. So, it could be one cop."

"Gee. You're good. Logical, even."

She accepted the praise modestly and I stood up and took her hand in mine.

"And, as a reward, I hereby award you with an hour of oral sex."

She followed me upstairs to the bedroom and watched while I took my clothes off. "Two things. What about Fred?"

I grinned and she started to unzip her pants. "Let him get his own date. What's the second thing?"

She covered her breasts with one arm and blinked wide eyes at me.

"Well, sir, am I getting or giving that hour of head?"

* * *

Later Claire kissed my forehead and patted my back.

"Not too bad for an old man."

"Thanks."

"A question. Why didn't you have Thompson lay charges against Walsh as well as the two other cops?"

"That's complicated. Basically because it's easier to prove a case against cops of a lower rank. Walsh has a reputation in town as a hero and that's a hard card to play with a local jury. It'll be easier for a jury to believe he ordered it or that it happened without his knowledge."

I wished I had a cigarette, or even a pipe or chewing tobacco. When you've stopped smoking, it's hard to find something to do right after making love. Except sleep, and women hate it when you fall asleep right away, which I think is patently unfair, they should take it as a compliment. 'She was so good, she took all my energy.' Claire disagrees, however. She nudged me and I went on.

"I wasn't asleep. A jury wants cops to be hard on crooks. It appeals to their sense of community outrage. Therefore, they always start with a bias favoring the police. In this case we might be able to convince them that Walsh had nothing to do with the actual beating and then they might end up being mad at him for not reporting it in the first place. Or he might toss the other cops to the wolves and claim he tried to stop them."

She waited.

"Before it goes to the jury, though, the claim has to go through LERA. Gods knows what they'll do. From what I can tell, it's a rat's nest of political infighting, union favoritism, and bureaucratic favoritism. It's in the province's best interests to champion Walsh as a cop who didn't resort to violence but tried to stop it. In order to do that successfully, though, they have to admit that the beating took place in the first place."

"You're right. That's confusing. So what exactly is LERA?"

"The Law Enforcement Review Agency. Any complaints against cops have to be proved to their satisfaction first. Before it can go to trial."

"Sounds like double jeopardy."

"It is. You have to prove a case against the cops before you can try to prove a case against the cops."

"Shitty. But you're letting Walsh go, that's what it sounds like."

"No. Not really, but I can't prove he hit me, on top of which, it's also the truth. Walsh didn't hit me. Not much, anyway. He convinced Fitzpatrick and Cairns to do the heavy work."

Fred started to cry downstairs but we both ignored it for a minute.

"You also realize that it's going to make every other cop hate Walsh by leaving him off the indictment. They're gonna wonder if he cut a deal somewhere along the way."

I held her close for a too-brief moment and then went to get Fred.

"The thought never even crossed my mind."

She kissed me and laughed.

19

The next day we cleaned the house, read the latest note taped to our front door (which read, "RAPIST!"), and talked things through. We agreed we had to find out more about Walsh, Cairns, Fitzpatrick, and the three dead boys before I could talk to anyone or ask the right questions. Midway through the day, I sent Claire off to find a phone booth and call the archives of the *Winnipeg Free Press*. She came back an hour later, grinning like a teenager. "Mission accomplished, *mon capitaine*."

"What happened?"

She curtsied. "I was walking by the fire hall and some of the boys were playing volleyball. They stopped and whistled. Very good for morale."

"I see."

"They were sweet. Very encouraging."

"Hmmm. I don't keep you busy enough."

"Yep. Now about the *Free Press*: you can't get into the archives, but copies of back issues are kept in the main library downtown. Both hard copies and stuff on microfilm."

My face fell. It would take me years to go through back issues without an index of some kind.

"What's wrong?"

I told her.

"You're right. That's probably why I asked for this two-page list of articles involving assorted ne'er-do-wells."

"For that you get a kiss."

She accepted and we went back to more mundane household tasks.

By that evening I was feeling more and more nervous about Claire and her date with Elena. It ended with Fred and me following her upstairs as she prepared to go out.

"No, no, you go. Fred and I will be fine."

Claire had pulled on black stockings and was busy smoothing out a pale gray skirt. I watched her breasts sway and thought dirty thoughts as she looked around for her bra. She smoothed down her hair and glanced around. "Where's my bra?"

"I don't know but don't even think about the hardships we'll be put through."

Fred crawled from the closet with the bra held in his gums. It caught momentarily on a loose floorboard and he pulled until it snapped back. Claire took it and handed him off.

"Nice try."

Fred gurgled and we both sat down to watch Claire get dressed. I changed tack and scratched Fred's back through his cotton shirt. With the body contact, he sighed and groaned and gurgled.

"So, where you going?"

"Out. Elena didn't know. I suggested coffee. Anyplace you recommend?"

"Sure. There's a Greek-run bakery on Main but I don't know how late it stays open. Good coffee and great pastries."

She finished dressing and kissed us both. "Don't wait up for me."

Fred had crawled off my lap and was wrestling with a ferocious pillow. As I watched, the pillow began to gain the upper hand and I had to push them both back onto the futon. Outside, Renfield howled in despair. We'd chained him in the yard to remind him that he was, in fact, a dog and not a person, and he bitterly resented the whole thing. I kissed Claire again.

"Have fun."

Claire came home when the sun was coming up and I met her at the top of the stairs. She hiccupped loudly and held her stomach with both hands.

"Oh my God."

I took her arm and led her into the bedroom, where she stood and swayed as I pulled her clothes off.

"That was fun."

She smelled like cigarette smoke and beer and rye whisky. When she was naked, I put her down on the clean sheets and covered her up. There was a fan in the corner of the room and I turned it on for white noise and to get rid of some of the smell, and then I kissed her on the lips, which also tasted of smoke, rye whisky, and beer.

"Hiccup."

She had already started to snore as I left the room. Downstairs, the sun was shining in brightly through the living room window and I stood and listened intently to the silence. Then I picked up the crow-bar from the umbrella rack and took a short grip on it before letting Renfield in from the back porch. When he came in, he wagged at me ferociously and jumped up to stick his blunt head into my crotch.

"Dumb dog."

He sat down at my hand gesture and I gave him a commercial dog treat made out of rice and dried meat by-products, which he chomped up with much pleasure. He followed me as I turned on the coffee maker and then went to the front of the house. There, pinned to the wall under the mailbox with a cheap, no-spring switchblade, was the expected note. I pulled both down and went inside to read.

"LEAVE, KILLER!"

Again it was red crayon on brown paper and I folded it up and put it with the others in the kitchen. Then I looked at the knife. It was brand new and the edge of the switchblade had recently been sharpened, but cheap steel is cheap steel, so I broke it in two and dumped it into the garbage.

In the kitchen I flipped on the radio and caught two good songs, Dean Martin's up-tempo "Ain't That a Kick in the Head" and The Who's "Boris the Spider." Then a puerile announcer came on and announced that the Winnipeg Police were looking for some fugitive from Vancouver who was believed to be "in the city and armed and dangerous." The station had a description of him, right down to the car he was driving, and I listened through the rest of the news and into the next set of songs, then poured myself some coffee and waited for Fred to wake up.

20

laire woke up some time past 1:00 when Fred and I were in the front room watching the thunderclouds and listening to the rain fall. Every now and then the thunder would crash and Renfield would come galloping in and try to tuck his head under my arm. The baby and I loved the noise and we clapped with each bright flash of light and each peal of thunder. We were busy clapping rhythmically when Claire came down in her dressing gown and grimly tottered over to where we sat on the rug.

"Good morning."

Fred made a happy noise and received a kiss. I made a similar noise and was gifted with one too. The dog kept whimpering and tried to force his head right through the floor under the coffee table.

"Good afternoon. Here, sit. I'll get you coffee."

She sat down and Fred climbed into her lap and started to point outside as the rain redoubled in force. In the kitchen I turned on the coffee maker and put some bread in to burn. By the time the toast was buttered, a half-pot had finished brewing and I balanced a cup and the toast and went back out to the two of them. Outside, the rain continued to fall.

"Oh, thank you."

She sounded very pathetic and took tiny bites out of the toast. I sat down behind her and started to rub her shoulders through her dressing gown. One sleeve slipped down and I could see the top of her right shoulder.

"Oh-ho."

She took a very small sip of coffee and turned a bloodshot eye towards me. "What?"

"You've been busy, you harlot, you. There's a huge hickey, a veritable love bite, on your neck."

She craned her neck at it and grunted. "I wish. Actually, we went dancing. There was this big kid, a wannabe cowboy, who put the moves on me and gave me a massage every time I slowed down. He had thick wrists."

I was rubbing her shoulders and stayed away from the bruise as she continued. "It was a lousy massage."

"A likely story. Changing the subject, he asks, did you have a good time?"

"Wonderful. There were Elena and I and the owner of the hotel lounge and her bartender. They came later. Everything was fine until we switched to vodka paralyzers."

She shuddered again.

"Vodka and Kahlua and Coke and milk. Never again. God did not intend for those things to ever be mixed together."

When she was finished eating, I shooed her off for a needed shower and sat watching the rain. It was very soothing. Finally Fred fell asleep and I tucked him into his crib. Claire came down, wearing jeans and a sweater. She asked, "So, what are your plans for today?"

"Well, most of today is gone, but I was thinking of getting more resumes and then checking out the archery shop and seeing if the owner needs any help. He's weird."

It was said matter of factly and I took the dishes into the kitchen and put them in the sink before assembling a sandwich from a tomato and some lettuce. Claire followed me and pulled a sack of frozen peas out of the fridge's freezer and put them on her forehead.

"There's an implied *but*. As in he's weird, but . . ."

"There's no but here. The little guy's just simply weird. After that, I was thinking of heading down to the library and checking out our friends."

She stood with her eyes closed and pressed the peas to her head. They tasted like shit and we never ate them but we kept a bag around in case of injury. She sensed I was looking and opened one eye. "What do you want?"

"I'm thinking lustful thoughts."

"Good. That would be a good thing. Can we wait 'til I sober up?"

I brushed the crumbs into the sink and kissed the tip of her nose. "If we must. Um, Claire?"

"I said later."

She waited but I didn't add anything more, so she kissed me and then I left.

At the archery shop there were a half-dozen boxes to unload and I had it done in just under half an hour. The driver had blanched when he'd seen me waiting for him and he'd even gone so far as to help pull the boxes off the truck. Up close, he'd smelled of stale sweat and old urine.

I said, "Thanks."

He ignored me and squealed the truck down the alley and out of sight. When the boxes were inside, I went back to the owner. He was busy with a bow on a big workbench beside the cash register.

Sitting on a bench nearby was a young couple, both pretty as puppies, drinking bottled water and discussing being young and in love. Frank interrupted my thoughts. "Finished?"

"All done."

He snorted. "Hell, I shouldn't pay you the full amount."

I waited with my hands clasped behind my back and he went on.

"But a deal's a deal. Here, try this."

He handed me the bow he was working on and I held it awkwardly.

"Bear Two compound bow. About ten years old and absolutely nothing wrong with it. The owner just traded it to me for a new one. Archers are like camera freaks, they got to have the latest and the greatest, they're always trading up to a new model."

I raised the bow and pulled the string back to my ear.

"Yep. You're a natural. You want the bow?"

He said it casually and I looked at him suspiciously.

"How much?"

"Eighty bucks and I'll throw in three arrows. No tax."

I put the bow down and shook my head. "Sorry, I haven't got the money right now."

"Sixty? Shit, try it out first."

He made me hold the bow again and measured my arm before pulling a pair of battered fiberglass arrows from a quiver nailed to the wall. I walked down to the line painted on the floor and faced the target at the end of the room. It was twenty yards away and appeared to be the size of a quarter. The old man startled me as he padded up silently behind me.

"Nock the arrow just above the brass bead. Draw the string back below your ear. Sight through the little ring woven into the string, and line it up with the target and this."

He touched the topmost peg on an aluminum rack just above the grip.

"And let the string roll off your fingers."

I did and missed and tried again. Then I trudged back and did it again. And again. By the time I stopped, my whole upper body ached and I glanced at the clock. "Jesus."

Two and a half hours had passed. I lowered the bow and headed back to the front of the store and laid the bow down on the counter. The old man was back at his seat and he didn't even look up as he carefully glued a new nock into a camouflage-patterned arrow.

"So, eighty, right?"

I massaged my left hand where the string had rubbed away the skin.

"I thought it was sixty."

His hands didn't stop working as he studiously ignored me.

"How about this? I'll come back each week for the next two months, no charge, to help with your deliveries."

"Four months."

"Two and a half."

"Three?"

"Three."

The old man agreed and then looked up and smiled. Before he could answer, I went on. "And, I get six arrows."

"Fine. But I keep the bow for the next month as collateral."

We shook on it and I tried to figure out how to tell Claire about my new toy as I walked down Main Street. I had the address of the library from the archery shop's phone book, so I stopped at a bus stop and checked the routes. No problem, one bus would get me there.

On the way I had my eyes open for a tail, either cops or cons. Cops I probably wouldn't see, they could run a boxcar tail on me with a dozen undercover cops ahead and behind me, switching every few minutes and connected by radios. They could change jackets, hats, whatever, move ahead of me, use cars to leapfrog, all things that were tough to counteract.

No one really said it better than Dashiell Hammett back in the 1920s in California. He said there were four rules for shadowing. Keep behind your subject as much as possible. Never try to hide from him. Act in a natural matter, no matter what happens. And, last, never meet his eye. Cops knew all the rules and broke some of them on occasion, but the basics, the essentials, remained untouched.

As for the cops themselves, there were two things they couldn't change, shoes and attitude, and for both of those, being on foot gave me the best chance to spot a tail. Shoes because nobody wants to change their footwear over and over again. Attitude because a cop is a cop is a cop is a cop is a cop. Also, they hate to walk, most of them have good teeth, and they all carry guns, which pull their pants and coats out of true.

When the bus came, I paid my $1.85 and sat near the rear door and saw two young, androgynous people climb up after me. Either of them could be a tail. I memorized their faces and their shoes and then ignored them.

Now, if it was cons following me, friends of the dead kids, then they'd probably do an amateur job because tailing someone was hard work, requiring patience and skill and talent. And lots of practice, something most bad guys would lack. Them, I'd probably spot right away.

At the next stop two more people came through the doors, a man and a woman, and I checked out shoes and faces again. Over the next twenty minutes and eight stops, twelve more people entered and the young people got off and so did the woman, and finally everyone's faces and shoes started to merge and blend. The bus passed between the library and a church. Then a big hole in the ground with a small shopping mall on the other side, then a powerhouse and a parking lot. Small shops and businesses and coffee places, and, at the end of the street, there was a huge wedding cake of a building with gray lime-stone walls and windows framed in brass. It stretched up over five storeys and filled a whole block, the side off to the left becoming a parking garage half open to the elements.

It was perfect so that was where I got off.

21

The moment I hit the door of the store, I started to count in my head. One, one thousand.

Tails are fun. Doing them is fun. Breaking them off is fun. But the funky thing is that you can never be sure that you ever rid yourself of the whole thing. Shit, you can never really be sure you were ever followed in the first place. But even paranoiacs have enemies, so I acted like I was being tailed, which is not a bad idea, although it does make you look like an idiot.

I was in the main Hudson's Bay department store, a big, open area full of mirrors and cameras and expensive merchandise. Too many clerks, lots of brand names, wide alleys between counters and shelves.

Two, two one thousand.

If there was a tail and they were cops or really organized criminals, they'd have run cars parallel to the bus and maintained contact by radio or cell phones. So they'd be circling the store and dumping off watchers on the entrances to pick me up when I came out. If I came out. And four sides to the store meant four watchers.

Three, three one thousand.

I paused by an elevator and checked where I was on a big plastic map of the store. According to the map, there were exits to three different streets on the main floor and one entrance to the Portage Place Mall on the second floor, plus exits to the parkade on five floors and a big basement full of discount shops.

Four, four one thousand.

So I moved. Straight into the elevator and then up to the fifth floor. Watchers would be just getting out of the cars and hitting the pavement. Whoever was behind me, if there was anyone behind me, might already be in the store. And they might have seen me go up to the fifth floor. Fine.

Out and down to the escalator, run down the escalator to four, to three, to two.

By now, some of the outside watchers would be headed into the store, while the inside watcher would be trying to track me.

Twelve, twelve one thousand.

You can run on escalators, stores don't mind. You cannot run among the displays—store cops automatically think you're a thief or insane. Someone to stop in any case, so to avoid this, I walked briskly, pulling off my jacket and folding it into its hood—it was rip-stop nylon and folded small, then I threaded the pull ties through a loop-in belt and I had an ugly bag and a plain, white, long-sleeved shirt.

Thirteen, thirteen one thousand.

Past men's clothes, some nice jackets, past a furrier, which struck me as odd until I remembered that the store was the Bay. They'd be the last place in the world to stop selling furs. Out the doors and one broad hall led to the mall but a narrow stairway to the right went into another building and down. Bingo.

Fourteen, fourteen one thousand.

Down the stairs and out, almost right across the street from where I got off the bus in the first place. There was an alley to the side and I used it.

Fifteen, fifteen one thousand and end.

I was heading in the right direction and I made it to the library without ever leaving the alley except to cross roads going north or south or both.

"Good afternoon." The library clerk on the third floor had dark hair, bright red lips, a small mouth, and a ready smile.

"I've never done this before. I'm interested in some old issues of the *Free Press*. What do I have to do?"

"Do you know the issues? Some of them are on microfilm and the others are in hard copy."

I consulted the paper in my pocket and gave her the first three dates I was interested in and a few extra dates to confuse the issue. In case anyone wanted to check what I had searched in the records.

"Hmmm. Those are all still in hard copy, but I can only give you three at a time. Write the first three down here with your name and address."

She pushed a scrap of paper over to me and I jotted down three issues and the name of Archie Tiers of Corydon Avenue, along with his address. It was a real name and a real address and a real phone number, I'd pulled them out of the phone booth downstairs. A few moments later she brought the first three papers out and I went over to a round table in the corner of the irregularly shaped room where I could keep an eye on the elevator.

I had a pen and paper and there was also a photocopier in the center of the room for long articles, so I started in no particular order.

The first article was from five years ago and involved Walsh in a case where he was accused of assaulting a suspect. I jotted down names and dates and read on. Half of it was spin on how good a cop Walsh was and the other half was how bad the bad guy was. Walsh was a Winnipeg boy, grew up in Transcona, summers at Winnipeg Beach, high school, police academy, good grades, youngest member of the homicide squad at age twenty-one, ERT (Emergency Response Team) member at age twenty-three, detective at this other age, and so on.

Degree in computer science taken outside work at Red River College. No family. No kids.

He was anti-gang ("Punks and cowards"), anti-drug ("Just say no, for losers."), anti-cop bashing ("Gotta give 'em space to do their hard, hard job."), anti-lenient sentencing ("Do the crime and you do the time, and it should be hard time.").

About the guy who claimed the assault. He was a drug dealer, a thief, a pimp, a knocker-over of gas stations. He claimed Walsh had driven him out of the city in an unmarked car after picking him up at gunpoint. Walsh had then stripped his shoes and socks and pants and forced him to walk ten miles back to the city center. It had been January and twenty-five degrees below zero with a wind chill. Walsh claimed the whole case was ridiculous.

Fact: the man had lost two toes due to frostbite, he had spent a week in hospital, and, when he finally came out, he dropped the case and left town. Fact: police maintenance records showed an error of over twenty miles in Walsh's vehicle log. Fact: Saskatchewan police had been doing the same thing to Natives since the mid-seventies, at least, with at least six deaths attributed to death from exposure.

The photocopies cost fifty cents and I went on to the next three papers.

A retiring cop telling tales about Walsh. When he was a young homicide dick, Walsh had tackled a man who had stabbed his wife. During the fight Walsh had burned out one of the man's eyes with a lit cigar he had been carrying. The incident had been labeled accidental.

More papers, more stories. Walsh graduating from the computer course. Walsh testifying at the trial of a gang of purported drug dealers. Walsh testifying after the shooting of a bank robber. Walsh before City Council, convincing them to buy a robot to deal with "Fortified drug houses, bombs, gangs, and other areas too dangerous for police officers." Walsh testifying in the defense of a cop accused of shooting a Native leader, who had apparently asked why he was being interrogated by a cop on a side street at three in the morning. Walsh using his new robot to detonate a pipe bomb during a strike at an aerospace plant. Walsh setting up a computer program for the child-abuse department of the police. Walsh in a dozen pictures with the robot dealing with barricades and hostages. Walsh working with the Royal Canadian Mounted Police on an anti-gang task force. Walsh involved in the arrests of thirty members of the Manitoba Warriors street gang.

Other stories, more information.

The man with the burned-out eye hadn't stabbed his wife and was acquitted. The dead bank robber had been fifteen and carrying paper and a pen, not a gun. The RCMP had asked that Walsh be reassigned, off the task force. In the end, the big gang trial had cost three million dollars and the average conviction involved the crime of being in possession of less than an ounce of grass. Some wise-ass reporter from the *Free Press* described Walsh as being a "cop who solved crimes in his spare time."

No one had found that funny.

I noted down the reporters who were pro-Walsh and the ones who weren't, and continued to read.

Fitzpatrick and Cairns were less reported. Old cops from old cop families, described as "true-blue" by an especially obsequious reporter. Staunch members of the Police Union and sufferers of the Blue Flu when a hundred cops called in sick after someone complained when a cop had his picture taken beating a handcuffed suspect. They were nice, solid guys, if you were a cop or a rabid law-and-order kind of citizen.

Another article about cop families told me that their uncles were cops, their fathers were cops, their grandfathers were cops, and, in one case, a mother had been a meter maid. As a matter of fact, their lineage as cops went back to 1919, when the city cops had gone over to the strikers during the great Winnipeg strike and the city had hired a whole new police force of scabs to bust heads.

For the three boys, there was nothing. About Robillard, there was a lot. Arrested for dealing grass, charges dropped. Picked up in a sweep of fences, no charges laid. Arrested for assault and battery with weapon (a brush hook), charges dropped by the victim. Arrested for possession of unregistered shotguns, fell apart when another guy copped to it. Arrested for disorderly conduct times four in assorted downtown bar fights, paid fines in all the cases. Finally, a few brief lines that there had been a marriage ceremony three years ago linking his cart to that of one Sandra, née Simcoe.

At about ten to nine, the clerk came over and tapped my shoulder. "Time to go."

I stretched and smiled. "Thanks."

The rolls of microfilm went back to the desk and the librarian started to put them away. "It's like they say: you don't have to go home but you can't stay here."

I left laughing and went home.

22

It was the next day, I'd talked with Claire and we had pretty much agreed that the cops, especially Walsh, looked good for at least some of our current difficulties. I was wandering around the front living room, thinking, when I heard someone coming up the path.

"Knock-Knock Ginger."

I opened the door before the woman outside could touch the bell. She was unfamiliar to me and she stared bug-eyed with something between fear and abject stupidity. "Excuse me?"

She almost dropped the envelope she was holding.

"It was a game we played when I was a child."

She just stared and pushed the envelope into my hands. "Here."

She turned to walk away and her shoulders hunched as though to absorb a blow. At the sidewalk, she turned to see me standing with the unopened letter in my hands. I watched her with my head tilted to the side as she slipped behind the wheel of a new-model car and drove away fast.

Claire came up behind me while I was reading and I handed over the letter without a word. She read it quickly and snorted. "Evicted?"

Fred was wrestling with another pillow under the coffee table and the dog was chewing on a piece of rawhide shaped like a bone. I brushed my hair back with the side of my hand and headed into the kitchen for some water. Claire followed, looking at the envelope.

"There's no postage. Who sent it?"

While the water ran to cold, I answered. "A short woman with green eyes and brown hair. She was wearing a light green pantsuit and driving a silver Lexus sedan."

Claire made a motion with her hands.

"Did she have a lot up here?"

I grinned at the implied chest. "No. Not at all."

"That was Ms. Gantz, our landlord. That means it's official."

I drank the glass of water and filled it again while I read the letter again. "So what are we going to do?"

"I'm going to work in the backyard. You wanna come?"

Baby and dog came with us, one going into a playpen and the other ending up tied to a stake by a long length of strong rope. Claire made me rearrange them and then looked around and pulled on canvas gardening gloves before tossing me a bright pink pair of rubber ones.

"Lots of work to do yet."

I slapped the gloves against my thigh and nodded in agreement. The yard was a mess. Earlier tenants had reshingled the roof and left the trash in big piles all over the yard, where it killed off the grass and the flowers. Someone had tried to grow wildflowers in a big bed along one fence and now that corner was full of weeds and thistles. The lawn that did remain was mostly crabgrass mixed with dandelions and scarred with the treads of cars and trucks, many of them quite deep.

"Where do you want to start?"

"Nowhere. We've been evicted, remember?"

Claire nodded politely and went to work in the flowerbed, ripping the weeds out and stuffing them in a garbage bag at her feet.

"Suit yourself."

In places she'd stop and kneel down close to the earth. Sometimes she'd leave the plant alone; at other times she'd rip it up as well and add it to her sack. When I wandered over, I couldn't see much difference between what she considered weeds and what she considered valuable plants. The smells of the fresh earth and the greenery mixed and I picked up my own bag.

Our neighbors on both sides had headed indoors the moment we had come out, so we had the space to ourselves, which was fine. The yard was about fifteen yards long and ten wide and was covered with grass up to the last five yards before the back alley, where gravel and scabs of concrete started. Someone had driven over a small stand of bushes so I started with them.

"Can I toss these bushes?"

"Let me see."

Claire came over and looked at the ruins carefully. Finally she bent down and broke off one branch and sniffed the end. "Yeah. They're dead."

Removing the hedge was harder than it looked but eventually I managed to dig up the roots of the bushes and manhandle them into garbage bags. While I was working, a police car cruised up the alley and paused next to me. In it were two young white men with handlebar mustaches. They turned in unison to look at me through eyes concealed behind expensive mirrored shades.

"Good afternoon."

They were silent.

"Or is it evening?"

The cop who was driving carefully peeled the Saran Wrap off a toothpick and put it between his front teeth. He said something unintelligible to his partner and then they drove away.

"Nice guys, you know."

Claire had ignored them and worked. She had cleared half the flowerbed and was working on the verge along the outside. She looked at me and then at the departing car. "Morons."

She planted the root back in the garden itself and I went to work on the shingles near the house. They had been there long enough to begin to molder, and white slugs as big as baby carrots were busy among the dead leaves and pale plants next to the ground. When I was finished, I brushed the dirt off my hands and dumped the bag with the others near the alley.

"You still haven't told me why we're doing this."

She shrugged and went to wrap Fred up in a blanket. He had fallen asleep and was happily drooling.

"It has to be done."

Renfield had found something in the grass and was rolling around in it with much glee. She patted him as she went past and then started working again. When she spoke again, she was very precise. "Do you want to leave?"

I thought about it and snarled, "No."

She went back to tearing up the foilage and I filled two more bags and was raking up the remaining litter before she spoke again. "What would you have done before?"

The rake wasn't working so I was reduced to picking up armloads of mold and filth and dropping them into the bags. "Before, before? You mean, in the before time? When I was single and life was great?"

"Yes, smart-ass."

She lowered her head and looked at me from under her bangs. The street lights had come on and we were both bathed in their harsh light. The difference between her and me was that she was beautiful.

"I would have left. It would've been a fight to stay, that wouldn't have mattered to me. I mean, what's a home for someone like me? No roots, no nothing."

She nodded and tied another bag shut. I was pretty much finished so I went into the back porch and came out with a six-foot length of copper pipe a quarter-inch in diameter. I'd found it in a corner of the basement when I'd been cleaning, and I'd soaked it in soapy water in the bathtub to remove some of the grit and verdigris. I rolled it back and forth between my hands and thought some more as Claire went on. "And if the fight was worth fighting for?"

I'd put a piece of string aside and now I tied a nut to the end and dropped it down until it emerged from the other end of the pipe. When I had both ends of string I tied a bit of fine cotton cloth to one end and slowly pulled it through. The cloth came out filthy and I put on a new one and tried again. After a couple more pulls, the cloth started to come out unstained and I dropped them into the garbage bag at my feet.

"Do you mind if I leave the crawl space under the porch 'til tomorrow?"

"Go ahead. Don't change the subject, though."

I put the pipe back into the house and came back out.

"All right. If the fight was worthwhile, then I'd do whatever was necessary in order to win. Lie, cheat, steal."

"So. Do you want to keep living here?"

"Yes."

"Then you have to fight. But. You can't slide back to your past behavior, that would be self-defeating."

"Right. Returning to the past behavior would nullify the present course."

Claire stood up and dusted her hands. I knelt down and checked angles, and when I was satisfied, I picked up a shard of broken mirror I'd found and put it near the fence. From under the back porch I'd be able to see the mirror clearly and the door reflected within it.

"You are snotty and overly precise, but an essentially correct prissy bitch. So that means no violence."

She was grinning when she said that and so was I and she added, "Well, how about this for a rule? Don't kill anyone."

We hugged and traded dirt.

I slept until 3:45 in the a.m. and slid out of bed. Over the years I'd trained myself to wake up when necessary and the skill remained.

When I was up, I took a few minutes to stretch before heading downstairs into the basement. I'd chained the dog up in the front this time and left the back undefended. I hoped the note passers would notice that.

The piece of pipe was where I'd left it, along with a shorter piece of heavy hardwood the size of a police flashlight, good-sized for cracking heads and breaking bones. I found both items in the dark and moved slowly and carefully. I'd tied a string around the pipe, and attached to that was a cork into which were stuffed nine darning needles, four inches long, with a tuft of cotton glued to the end and a second tuft glued midway down for stability.

Moving through the dark basement was difficult but I'd strung a length of clothesline from the end of the stairs to the rear window, and by holding the rope in one hand, I could move almost soundlessly. At the window I listened but couldn't hear anything, so I opened the dirty pane of glass on freshly oiled hinges and listened again to nothing.

Wiggling through the window was easy and then I found myself in a little nest of dirt and broken wood, leaves, and shards of plastic wrap. The floor of the rear porch was six inches above me when I was folded in half, so I carefully cleared away some of the rubbish in front of my face and hunkered down to wait. There were spiderwebs everywhere but I focused my eyes on a narrow line of light coming in between the tops of the piles of trash and the bottom of the back porch.

Nothing moved so I carefully pushed the pipe into place and inserted the dart into the end with the tip of my thumb. When it was properly seated, I kissed the end and tasted the metal, which reminded me of fresh blood and electricity. I made a seal with my lips and inhaled through my nose until my lungs were full and then I held it. The pressure was uncomfortable so I only held it for a few moments and when I released it, I found myself panting.

Outside, nothing was happening. The dogs of the neighbors on both sides snuffled loudly and lay down with sighs audible over the sounds of distant traffic. The dogs were a familiar thing to me, every poor neighborhood has dogs, they're burglar alarms and companions all rolled into one. It's when you find a neighborhood with no dogs that you find real poverty, that's where you get the true ghetto. Since the neighbors on both sides had dogs and Renfield was in front, the note passers could only come from the alley and across the yard in front of me.

About five yards away I could see the mirror I'd placed. It dimly reflected the rear of the house but I could not see myself in it at all. While I waited, I emptied my mind and relaxed all the muscles in my back and legs. Every few minutes I tightened everything, starting at my toes and moving up to my face and then I consciously loosened them again but I did not move.

A bird made a sleepy noise across the alley and I waited but it was not repeated. It was tempting to daydream or to think about food or sex or any positive thing but in that way lay inattention, so I just waited in the dark and the dirt and listened. A long time later, just when the sky was starting to turn light with false dawn, a car pulled up. It was a low-slung, four-door sedan with bright whitewalls and it was driving without lights, including interior ones. I watched it wait with the engine running and I gathered my breath, but a few minutes later it drove off.

To distract myself I laid the possibilities out. If there were two of them, I'd deal with whoever had a weapon first and if neither had a weapon I'd deal with whoever was biggest. I'd put three darts into each of them to get their attention. A four-inch needle wouldn't kill, unless I aimed for the face and had unusual luck. Having said that, there were dozens of good targets on a human that would disable. Belly, groin, throat, those would all incapacitate a human quickly, and a dart to the back of the knee would drop anyone, if I could find the right angle.

From where I was, I would probably end up with a good shot, probably a series of good, silent, unexpected shots. I twisted my neck a little and stared some more into the darkness, stared until I started to see things that weren't there, so I throttled back and went on to more idle thoughts.

I like blow guns, they're instinctive, you don't aim them, you point, and, with very little practice, you can put ten absolutely silent darts into a target the size of a human face at ten yards, and I had been much better than that not all that long ago. There were other targets on a human as well as the face. Just below the elbow is a large concentration of useful muscles like the supinator longus and the extensor carpi radialis and especially the extensor caommunis digitorum, which moves the fingers. Any of those would do in a pinch. And if I had a shot at a leg, well, there was the foot. Halfway through it was a big muscle called the flexor accesorius. Injure that and walking becomes problematic.

Before I could hit anything, I needed a target.

Ten minutes later one presented itself. The sky was slowly turning pale and opalescent when I heard a door slowly creak open in the neighbor's house to the right of ours and a voice request that doggie sit and that doggie be good. Then there was silence interspaced with grunting, and a large head suddenly appeared over the whitewashed fence. The head swiveled left and right and vanished, to be replaced by a large rump wearing dark blue polyester.

"Shit."

There was a pause and a short rip and then another longer one.

"Shit."

One of my neighbors, a big, wide-bodied woman with blue hair, crouched there in our yard and looked left and right. In her hand she clutched a piece of brown paper.

I put the pipe to my lips and started to inhale. She rushed forward at a cumbersome trot towards the house and I could hear her panting and snorting. As she passed by, I could see that she was barefoot and her toenails were painted with some kind of glitter paint and I had to exhale to avoid swallowing the dart with suppressed laughter.

The stairs creaked as she went up and she grunted some more while attaching the note to the door. A few seconds later, she trotted back across to the fence and hoisted herself up. For one beautiful and shining moment I had an incredible shot at the right hemisphere of her ass but I was shaking too hard to take it.

When I'd recovered somewhat, I went back through the window and up to the kitchen to make coffee. I'd left the blowgun and the piece of wood downstairs and I had to turn on the radio to cover the sounds of my gasping laughter. That was how Claire found me.

"Sam? What are you doing?" Claire's voice was full of sleep. I was still laughing and I tried to give her a hug but she pulled away sharply.

"You're covered in dirt and cobwebs."

"I'll take a shower."

She followed me upstairs. "Um, what the hell just happened?"

There was a big cocoon of some type in my hair and I combed it out with my fingers and looked at it curiously. "I found out our neighbor is one of the people leaving the notes."

She shook her head in disbelief and then she nodded and said calmly, "I'll kill them."

"No."

Dust and more cobwebs fell.

"We'll have them over for a barbecue."

"Huh? You're not making sense."

"Sure I am."

"Oh. When they come over, then I kill them, is that the plan?"

"No, that's not the plan."

"So I can't kill them?"

"No, but we'll make them wish they were dead."

23

I had to wait until 10:00 the next day for the hardware store on Main Street to open. While I was waiting, Claire made me do the exercises the doctor had recommended, and after that I had to take an extra shower just to get rid of the sweat. When I was done, I made myself a second breakfast under Claire's disapproving eye.

"You're going to get fat."

Fred was busy trying to build something with oversized wooden blocks in the living room, while Renfield was trying to knock them down. They both thought this was great fun so we let it go on, despite the increased decibel level of calls and howls.

"A second breakfast was common in the British Navy of the early eighteen hundreds."

"It's not the early eighteen hundreds."

"It could be. Maybe we're in some kind of time warp."

She ignored me. My eggs were done so I slid them onto the toast and ate standing up by the sink.

"What did you mean last night when you said we were going to invite our neighbors over for a barbecue?"

"Exactly what I said."

I finished the food and dumped the crumbs into the sink and washed them away.

"Can we afford a party?"

"Yes, if we keep the whole thing cheap."

She poured herself a cup of coffee. I was trying to obey the doctor and avoid caffeine so I just looked longingly at the black, hot happiness. She ignored me, made sure I knew she was ignoring me, and then agreed with herself. "Yes, we can afford it. Especially if the guests bring something."

I forgot the next question I was going to ask and asked a new one. "Why would they bring something?"

"Oh, it's just common courtesy."

I filed that away. Thieves don't do that. If someone invites you out, then they pay, it's only right. "Can I also get about twenty dollars from you, right now?"

She gave it to me and I explained. "It's for our neighbors. The next time they want to come over uninvited, I want to give 'em a treat."

The sun was only starting to cut through the clouds when I reached the hardware store. It was an oddity, a small store still owned by a person and not a corporation. When the door swung open, a small bell made a cheerful noise and the owner, a slim, white-haired man with prominent teeth, came out of the back room. When he saw me, he blanched and started to recoil, but when he recovered he came forward much more aggressively and stopped only a few feet from my face. "I don't have a job here for you."

I stared at the old man and put my hands behind my back. "I don't think I asked for one."

The shop was full of racks and shelves of tools and fasteners, strange devices and spools of wire and chain. When I looked back at the old man, he was biting his lower lip.

"You mean you're just here to buy something?"

I walked past him and he put the countertop between us. As I wandered the aisles I could feel his eyes on me, peering myopically from the big mirrors in each corner of the store. It was kind of funny as I watched him watch me keeping a careful watch on him. As we did that, I filled a shopping basket with odds and ends: some heavy-gauge wire, a pair of cheap wire cutters, two pounds of two-inch-long roofing nails, some flexible lengths of plastic designed to be used for trim, and a big ball of twine. At the register, the old man spoke harshly, like his throat had been burned. "Will that be all?"

He kept jars of glue behind the counter and I pointed at the rack. "A jar of an epoxy resin."

When it was in front of me I read the instructions and the old man tallied up my bill on a very new cash register. He mumbled something I couldn't quite hear so I smiled and asked, "What was that?"

"Nothing."

"Oh. It sounded like *sniffer*."

The old man glared some more and I paid him.

"Have a nice day."

That was too much for the old man. "You too, Mr. Haaviko, you too."

Outside, I thought about heading home but turned the other way. Where had he learned my name? To check out a theory, I went to the bakery, where the young waiter I'd met before was making change for an ugly lady with a big box of Danishes. When he saw me, his face shut down and he muttered in a dull voice, "Oh."

I nodded to him and sat down at one of the tables while he vanished into the building. After five minutes I went back to the counter and yelled. "Coffee. Please."

It took five minutes before he slopped the cup down in front of me and turned and trotted away.

"Curious."

I ran a finger around the edge of the cup and felt the cracks and chips and finally dipped my finger into the liquid itself to find it cold.

When I tasted it, I discovered it was bitter as well. I glanced up to see the waiter's head pull back into the doorway.

I left exact change and walked back home. Claire greeted me with another letter.

"We got a notice to evict immediately. What do you want to do?"

I brushed past her and laid the stuff I'd bought out on the kitchen counter. "Call her up. Tell her I have to go to Brandon but I'll be back soon."

"And if she presses . . ."

"Be evasive. Tell her I had a relapse."

When she asked a relapse of what, I blew her a kiss. "Make something up."

The bus for Brandon left at 1:15, I'd checked the schedule. It cost me twenty-three dollars and a few cents for a round-trip ticket. Just outside of town I went up to the driver and crossed the yellow line beyond which passengers are not supposed to go.

"Can you let me off here?"

The highway was empty and he pulled over.

"This isn't Brandon, you know."

"Are you sure?"

The driver let me go. Five minutes later the bus to Winnipeg showed up and I waved it down with my ticket and wallet in hand.

"I'm glad you stopped."

The driver, a short Native woman who was slowly turning from muscular to obese, didn't say a word while she took my sixteen-dollar fare.

I sat down in the seat behind her, where I could hear if she used the radio, and said brightly, "I almost ended up in Brandon. Can you believe that?"

She didn't say a word and a few minutes later I was back in Winnipeg.

24

The building that housed the Residential Tenancies Branch was downtown on Edmonton Street, about ten minutes at a real slow walk from the Greyhound bus terminal and about twenty minutes from the library. I was thinking about the persistence of old habits, which was brought about by the fact that I was wearing clothes more suited for stealing than any honest endeavor. I had on a black denim jacket with extra pockets sewn into the reinforced inner lining, the left arm heavy with handmade chain mail around the forearm in case I ran into a dog, and a hidden inner pocket in the back that used to hold handcuff keys and a Gem razor blade in case the cops used plastic cuffs. Even the jeans were gimmicked, they had extra long pockets, good for loot or a gun, and they also had big leather patches sewn into the knees and ass for protection against skids and scrapes. To top it off I was wearing a black baseball hat with a broad bill to deal with security cameras. All this and I had absolutely no intention to do anything against the law, although there was a brisk snap in the air, enough to make a young man's fancy turn to theft, murder for profit, and casual arson.

"Spare any change?"

It was only a short distance to walk and three people panhandled me. The first was a man in his late fifties with scars from bad acne all across his cheeks. He smelled minty fresh but I shook my head and kept walking. "Sorry, tapped out."

I considered the term 'tapped out.' I seemed to remember that the term came from bartenders who drew from the big kegs of beer. When they were opened, someone would have to drive in a spigot, thus tapping them. When they were empty they would be 'tapped out.' Of course, the same ideas and terminologies also applied to maple trees but that didn't strike me as being very romantic.

Halfway to Edmonton Street I veered into Portage Place, a big shopping mall, and then down into the parkade underneath. I'd left the house without a weapon except for my Swiss Army knife, on the off chance someone searched me, but being unheeled made me a little nervous. The knife had been a wedding gift from Claire's parents, they'd given it with the file extended and they'd had the handle engraved with the motto 'cake to follow' and it vaguely annoyed me each time I used it. In the parkade that file served to cut off a telescoping radio antenna from an older model Chevrolet sedan. When it was free, I pushed the antenna shut and then tucked it into my right-hand jacket pocket.

I headed up the stairs out of the parkade, put my knife in the left-hand pocket, and whistled cheerfully. No one suspects someone who's whistling because nervous people don't whistle, their mouths are dry. Therefore, my theory is that when you whistle, people will not suspect you of anything. Although it's probably a lie, it does make me feel better.

The stairway emptied onto the main floor, and I went to the information kiosk and asked the guard for directions.

"It's just across Portage behind me and then you head to your right for about a block."

Behind the guard I watched a bank of TV monitors and saw two guys wearing black pants and white shirts with Sam Browne belts walk up to a car that looked familiar. I realized that the car they were approaching was the one that had donated the antenna, so I thanked the guard and left.

"Uh, right."

There was some kind of huge sale going on, which packed the whole area in the center of the mall with people scrambling for footwear, and I felt much better outside. Before I'd gone six feet, though, another person panhandled me, this one a pale woman with dark blue hair and blond roots. I stared at the snake tattoos on her face and shook my head.

"Well, fuck you."

She said it politely enough so I kept on going and thought about other stuff. I didn't think I'd actually get into a fight but if I did, then the antenna would give me a long reach to bring an opponent in close for the knife. Although the blade was only three inches long, it would serve. It was as sharp as a razor, perhaps sharper, and three inches in the right place would kill anyone. The antenna was longer but it was just for dramatic effect, somewhat annoying but mostly distracting. It was the knife that would kill.

It was uncommonly warm downtown and the buildings blocked out some of the wind. The clouds were very high up and scattered. I passed by a bookstore named Book Fair and made a mental note to stop back after I'd done my business. Claire could use something new to read. As I walked past the store, the idea of using the pocket knife as a weapon triggered a memory and finally it came to me that Lawrence Sanders had written a book about a pathetic female serial killer who'd killed using a Swiss Army knife. There was something else, though . . .

A panhandler, a new one, interrupted me.

"Could I have a dollar for coffee?"

The request chased the idea from my mind and I stopped in mid-stride. The panhandler was in his twenties with dark skin and brown eyes. His hair had been cut short and he was fingering a stocking cap as he talked to me.

"No."

I started to walk on and then I turned back. "Why don't you just work?"

"Don't want to."

"Then why don't you steal?"

"Okay. Stick 'em up."

He said it listlessly and I walked on, trying not to smile. It was when I was about three doors down from the short and squat office building that housed the residency office that the other element of Sanders's story came to me. The killer had worn a bracelet that read 'why not?' With my memory satisfied, I went up the stairs happily and into the reception area, where a secretary took an interest.

"May I help you?"

The woman was polite and faked attention fairly well. She was also quite photogenic, with red hair and brown eyes and a nice torso, from what I could see. When she smiled, I noticed a little bit of green stuck to one tooth.

"Why not?"

She stared at me blankly and I went on. "I mean to say, yes. I need to ask someone a few questions about the rights and obligations of landlords and tenants."

"Certainly. Do you have an appointment?"

There was no one else in the waiting room and I shook my head.

"Well, if you want to take a seat, I'll speak with Mrs. Claren."

Before I even reached my Naugahyde chair in the far corner, she was on the phone. I had picked up a fishing magazine and was leafing through it when the receptionist spoke again.

"It'll be only a few minutes."

She made it sound like it was some kind of honor so I nodded in appreciation and she beamed at me. A few minutes later, a middle-aged woman with shockingly white hair came out of the back offices and motioned for me to follow.

"Mr. . . . ?"

I offered to shake her hand and passed her a business card. "Leung, Dr. Leung actually."

The doctor had been rather casual with his cards in the hospital so I'd pocketed a few dozen, just in case. She looked at my clothes somewhat askance and I chuckled loud and long.

"I know. I don't look like a doctor."

"Well, actually I was thinking that you didn't look Chinese."

I smiled. "Oh. Well. You see, in 1905 the Germans invaded Shang-hai . . ."

I let it trail off and she led me into a plain little office where she sat behind a cheap desk with her back to the window, which overlooked a long, narrow alley full of clean garbage cans. In a few corners there was still dirty snow, black almost with soot and full of leaves and twigs and empty bottles of hair spray. Down the block, three kids were huddled in a brightly painted doorway and passing a cigarette back and forth, and when the cigarette was down to practically nothing, one of the kids started to strip down a handful of thrown-away butts for the remaining shards of tobacco. When he had enough, he anted up for a piece of rolling paper and made a new cigarette, which they lit and began passing around. I couldn't see exactly what they were doing but I'd done the same thing enough times to know the motions by heart.

"Dr. Leung?"

"Oh, right. Distracted myself for a moment there. Just looking at the kids."

She turned her head and shook it as though she was trying to dis-lodge something.

"Tsk, tsk. Animals. Filthy animals."

When she turned back to me she was focused on me and the kids were right out of her mind.

"And how can I help you?"

"Right to business, I like that. Actually I'm doing a favor for a patient of mine who's having some troubles with his landlord. My patient is schizophrenic, which he treats with medication. The landlord is, frankly and bluntly, bigoted and wants him to leave."

Mrs. Claren made a little moue with her mouth and stuck out her teeth but I ignored her and kept talking.

"In my professional opinion, it would be criminally wrong to force my patient out onto the street. I'd like to intercede with the landlord and, to do that effectively, I need some information. How, for example, does a landlord go about forcing a tenant out if the tenant does not want to leave?"

She opened a drawer below my level of vision, took out some papers, shuffled them, and then put them right back, apparently into the same drawer. "I didn't know doctors did that kind of thing."

She managed to make it sound insulting and vaguely degrading at the same time.

"They do if they're any good at their job. The oath I signed reads 'First do no harm.'"

She looked at me blankly. "Hmmm. Well, basically a landlord can evict a tenant only under certain circumstances. I have a pamphlet around here somewhere but this is a synopsis. A tenant can be asked to move out immediately if they don't pay the rent, although they must be given four days' notice. Not paying the security deposit is also grounds, so is a failure to keep the residence clean, damaging the premises, disturbing the neighbors, changing the locks, endangering the safety of the neighbors, or too many people are living in the residence."

She paused and took a drink of water from a big, plastic, penis-shaped bottle about a quart in size. "Of course, in most of those cases the landlord has to give the tenant a written warning to correct the problem. In my experience, the tenants just ignore the warning."

"I see."

She went on. "The landlords can also ask the tenant to move out if they need the space back for certain reasons, like demolition, renovations, etc. In those cases the tenant gets three months' written warning to leave."

I listened politely and then asked, "Out of curiosity, just what are the legal obligations of a landlord? What do they have to do?"

"How do you mean?"

"Can a landlord cut off the heating to the property, paint the place with no warning to the tenants, stuff like that?"

"Well, no. A landlord has duties such as maintaining the appearance of the residence, doing repairs, and ensuring the supply of heat, water, and other essential services. They also have to investigate reasonable complaints in a reasonable period of time, and so on. Basic stuff really."

She fumbled around in her desk and came up with a pamphlet that she passed over.

"There are some other pamphlets around here. A landlord has to provide a fire alarm on each floor of the property. They have to make sure there are working locks on the exterior doors and they have to provide a written receipt when the rent is paid in cash. They have to guarantee the privacy of the tenant, they can't just barge in whenever they feel like it."

I listened and wondered whether there was anything the woman knew that was not neatly encapsulated in some pamphlet.

"And if there are problems between landlord and tenant?"

She drank some more water. Again, she didn't offer me any. "In that case the Residential Tenancies Branch will investigate and try to mediate. In other cases the police might be called or the Human Rights Commission, but that happens only in the rarest of circumstances."

I stood up and reached over to shake her limp, uncallused hand

and barely repressed a shudder. "Well, thank you very, very much. I'll get back to you if I have any problems."

Then I left, wiping my hands on my pants as I went. In the foyer I went over to where I had been sitting and picked up the magazine I'd been looking at. I held it up until the receptionist noticed.

"Yes?"

"Can I take this with me?"

She looked startled. "No one has ever asked that before."

She thought about it while I stood there.

"I suppose you could, I mean, it's just one magazine. Why do you want it, though?"

When I held it open she could see the article I'd been reading. It was titled "Absolutely the World's Toughest Ten Fish" and was filled with pictures of improbably large fish being caught by very tired-looking men wearing very stupid clothes.

"Actually, I'm kind of embarrassed but I can't put it down."

She read the title silently and then favored me with a bright smile. "Wow."

"Yeah. Anyhow, if you let me take the magazine, I'll tell you something you may not realize."

"What?"

"Is it a deal?"

She raised and lowered her head just a little and I leaned in close.

"There's spinach between your teeth."

Laughing in the back of her throat, she reached up and touched the exact spot. "This? It's not spinach. I had an emerald inserted into the enamel of the tooth."

I looked closely. "Oh."

Finally, I was out of there. A half hour later I was on a random bus to shake any tail anyone had pinned on me. In my hand was a plastic grocery bag full of previously loved books and a vegetarian submarine sandwich for supper.

25

By six o'clock that night I was receiving a kiss from my wife and dog while the mouse glared balefully at me from a dry aquarium tank placed carefully in the room's center.

No one offered so finally I had to ask. "Why is the mouse there?"

Claire kissed me again and smiled gently at the rodent. "He escaped from the cage in our room and tried to make a nest in the futon."

I walked over and looked at him through the plastic wall. His fur was matted and he was industriously licking it back into order.

"Why is the mouse wet?"

Claire linked her arm through mine.

"Well . . ."

Renfield came over and sat down beside the aquarium and gave me a dimly lit dog-type smile.

". . . I used the dog to catch the mouse."

"And, how did that go?"

The mouse glanced at the dog and then crawled into an empty toilet paper tube to sulk.

"Well. The dog was very good but he held the mouse in his mouth for quite some time. We had a Sylvester and Tweety moment of back-slapping to free the little bugger."

She went on brightly. "So. Are you hungry?"

"Not after that story. I have some work in the backyard if you want to help."

"Sure. Oh. I dropped off invitations to our neighbors on both sides and across the street, asking them to RSVP. We received another note at the front door, though."

Claire followed me as I retrieved the blowpipe from the basement and headed up to the bathroom on the second floor. There was a nar-row, little, dormer window there that overlooked the backyard and the panes of glass were tinted to provide privacy, but when the hinges were oiled they would open without too much difficulty. I opened one and rested the blowgun on the sill, which was covered in flaking white paint.

"What are you doing?"

The dart went into the end of the pipe and I put my lips in place. "I need some dark so I'm gonna shoot out that light on the telephone pole out there."

She looked over my shoulder. "No way. I'll give you two to one."

"Two to one what? Sex or money?"

She thought about it for a minute. "That really puts some meaning into the saying."

"Which saying?"

"Put your money where your whatever is. No, I need the money. I'll bet five bucks."

"You're on. Watch me. This is going to be the second easiest ten bucks I ever made . . ."

I pointed and exhaled fast.

Chuff.

Nothing happened. I tried again twice more.

Chuff.

Chuff.

The light remained brightly shining.

"Let me try."

I loaded it for her and she looked down the length the pipe.

"What are the darts made from?"

"This and that."

She looked at me suspiciously so I went on. "Okay. I used some of your darning needles. I'll replace them with the ten dollars I'm gonna win from you. Now you don't aim, you just point and . . . You're doing it all wrong. Hold on a second."

Chuff.

I heard the tinkle of the dart hit the metal post the light was on and then I shut up. Claire reloaded and grinned at me.

"And for my next trick . . ."

Chuff.

The light went out in a tinkle of glass and I went down to go to work, somewhat subdued. Halfway down the stairs, I figured out that I could take the money from Claire's purse and pay her that way.

In the backyard it was as dark as pitch and I stood listening as I thought about what I wanted. I certainly didn't want anyone to die. That would be bad. I also didn't want anyone to end up in the hospital, which would be bad as well. There was a bit of military doggerel I said under my breath as I prepared. "Mines and booby traps can kill so be alert and stay alive . . ."

I put the lengths of thin plastic down on the grass along with a carpet-cutting razor to cut them into strips.

"If possible, don't be in too much of a hurry . . ."

Well, my neighbors would definitely be in a hurry and they wouldn't be looking for traps. I ran a length of thirty-pound-test monofilament line from one side of the yard to the other. It was maybe eight inches off the ground. I measured from that and scratched my head.

"Never take anything for granted: it might look harmless, but it might be a killer . . ."

Figure the visitors were five feet plus tall. They'd come in over the fence and then head to the house fast and on their way they'd hit the line and trip. They'd go down and their arms would go forward to try to catch themselves so their hands would probably end up about . . . here. I ran a single strand of barbed wire from one side of the yard to the other and thought about the wounds that would cause. If my visitors were lucky, they'd have tetanus shots kept up to date.

"Evidence of old camouflage may indicate mines and booby traps . . ."

If they missed the wire and line, then they'd reach the stairs and head up. All the notes had been left on the door or on the mat just before the door. I cut one length of plastic to fit exactly on one step and then hammered in the carpet tacks in an irregular pattern pointed up. When I was done, I spray-painted it black and let it dry.

"Suspect all objects that appear loose or out of place . . ."

Almost forgot about that one. I took a five-dollar bill from my pocket and put it beside a paving stone leading up to the back porch. It looked good there so I dug a little hole underneath it and put in the big rat trap with a thread running from the bill to the trigger.

"Always look for trip wires . . ."

A second and third monofilament line went on both sides of the house in case the neighbor went that way. I'd collected some of Renfield's bowel movements so I scattered those on both sides of the line and then went back to the yard.

"Never bunch up and become a good target for command detonated mines . . ."

I took some shards of broken glass from some water glasses broken during the move and crushed them fine with a rock. Then I cut one of the plastic strips into a half-inch-wide length and emptied a tube of glue on it. Before it hardened, I dribbled the glass onto the surface and then put that aside to set. When it was done, I'd spray paint it white and put it on my side of the fence where I'd seen my neighbor climb over.

"Destroy mines and booby traps in place or mark, report, and leave them alone . . ."

Small plastic tiles cut from the strips served to hold more nails pointed upwards and I scattered forty or so of them across the yard, after giving each a quick shot of black paint. They'd be invisible at night and easily picked up during the day.

"Before cutting trip wires, check both ends for booby traps . . ."

I coated some lengths of the fishing line in more glue and draped them in the bushes near the end of the yard. The glue would dry on the surface and make a film that would remain sticky, and anyone disturbing it should pick up a memento. It would be annoying and embarrassing but hardly lethal.

"Objects should not be disturbed without checking for booby traps . . ."

I tied both ends of the glued line to some empty cans and dropped a few pebbles into each can. With luck, the noise would scare the neighbors and they'd run, which would make more noise so they'd run faster, which would make more noise and so on.

"Only the enemy's imagination limits his use of mines and booby traps . . ."

With the plastic end of the can of black spray paint removed, it would spray in all directions, so I took it off and then placed it in a hole under one of the paving stones. Small clumps of earth held the stone in place at each corner but stepping on it would still give a healthy dose of paint out each side. It would also make a hell of a loud hiss, and strange noises and sights in the night are discouraging to the untrained.

"Be especially careful in areas where you are expected to slow down, bunch up, or become a good target . . ."

I made running nooses in four lengths of the line and hung them under the windows around back, just in case anyone decided to come look in. I tied them off with two yards of line to nails driven into the windowsill. If they looked in, then they'd probably get their hands caught and the reflex would be to yank them, which would close the noose, which would scare the snot out of anybody.

"You can learn a lot from the local people: seek their help locating mines and booby traps."

More nooses went out in the yard, these about a yard around to catch feet and tied to pieces of sharpened dowel I pushed into the ground to act as anchors.

"Trails and roads should be suspected: check refilled holes, areas covered with straw, littered with dung, pavement repairs, and other suspicious spots . . ."

With that done I tied a piece of plastic stripping into a circle about six inches in diameter. In each strip I pushed nails through and angled down so that anyone reaching through would be fine until they withdrew their hand; then they'd get nails in the wrist. These went around the stakes the foot nooses were attached to.

"Report mines and booby traps immediately . . ."

Of course, there was a way out—they'd have to release the stake, though, and then they'd still be stuck by a noose attaching their leg to the ground and they'd also have a bunch of small holes in their wrists.

"Always check your area for evidence of mines and booby traps when you set up your defenses . . ."

I went around and scattered dirt and leaves over my works.

"Probe gingerly when mines are suspected; don't depend solely on mine detectors . . ."

Claire was standing in the doorway and staring at me and I suddenly realized I had no idea how long she'd been there.

"Do you always talk to yourself?"

"Beats singing. You take the first letter of each sentence and it spells 'MINES AND BOOBY TRAPS.'"

She thought about it and I added, "But I forgot the S at the end. That stands for, 'since there was nothing in the area yesterday, don't assume there is nothing there today.'"

I put the final pieces into place and then went back inside and Claire followed.

"How do you remember where you put all that stuff?"

"Practice."

She gave me a hug and I kissed her.

"In addition I'm very talented, skilled, lucky, smart, wise . . ."

"That explains all the jail time."

I ignored her and cleaned up before we went to bed.

26

At quarter past four I heard the screams start, but they were quickly silenced as though someone put their thumb on the mute button during a scary movie. At the first peal of noise I'd rolled out of bed and was crouched at the door with the bayonet in hand. By the time I started to think, the screams were just echoes. Listening carefully, I could barely hear *sotto voce* cursing, so I relaxed and put the bayonet back under the pillow. Claire rolled over and threw an arm onto my empty side of the bed.

"Whazamatta?"

I kissed her and she rolled back. When she was breathing deeply again, I went to the bathroom and stood off to the side of the window where I'd cut a slit in the drapes. Through it I could see most of the yard but anyone down there wouldn't be able to see me. The dog came in and I scratched him behind one ear as I let my eyes adjust to the dim light. In the middle of the lawn, there was a large, pale shape lying prone. As I watched, the figure crawled a body's length forward towards the fence and then paused.

"Good boy."

I scratched the dog some more and knuckled his ear until his rear legs started to spasmodically kick. The figure in the yard was moving like a half-squashed bug and I began to admire its perseverance as it finally reached the right-hand fence. That would mean that the visitor was one of the Kilpatricks, either the big, fat husband or the equally big, fat wife. I wondered if it might be one of the big, fat children but I decided against it, the two girls and a boy were all in their early teens and they weren't as big as the figure seemed to be in the dim light.

The figure had reached the fence and levered itself upright when suddenly it began to spasm wildly before dropping to the ground and shaking its arms wildly.

"Hmmm. I'd forgotten that one."

Renfield looked up at me uncomprehendingly and I scratched him some more.

In the first light of morning I went out and gathered up the traps. I found the note the intruder had left in the middle of the yard. It was butcher's paper again and it had "LEAVE, YOU FUCKING KILLER!" written in yellow crayon. As I was reading it, Mr. Kilpatrick, senior, came over to the fence and put his arms gingerly on the top. He was moving very slowly and carefully, like an old man dealing with new pain.

When I noticed him, I waved cheerfully. "Good morning."

"You know . . ." His arms and face were covered in small, flesh-colored Band-Aids, and he had a pronounced limp. He swallowed audibly and started again. "You know . . ."

He stopped and his wife edged out of their back door and peered at me. They were both big people and looked quite alike, both over two hundred pounds and squatly built. They had pale skin, frequently washed, that was rarely exposed to the weather, and lank brown hair that was rapidly graying, although they seemed to be in their early forties. I walked over to the fence and gestured with the folded note.

"Know what, sir?"

I looked into his eyes from an extremely close distance. Mr. Kilpatrick found it uncomfortable so he started to back away until his wife made a *harrumphing* noise and he froze in his tracks and continued.

"You know, it might be a good idea for you to leave."

It almost came out as a question and I shifted my weight onto the other foot and ignored his statement entirely. Their house was beautifully kept with aluminum siding and bright red paint on the lintels and around the edges of their windows.

"Isn't it a beautiful day?"

He swallowed convulsively. "Me, and the other neighbors . . ."

I interrupted him again. "Yep, a beautiful day and my wife and me, we were thinking about how lucky we are to have such beautiful neighbors and to live in such a beautiful neighborhood."

His wife, I think Claire had said her name was Emily, took a step out onto the porch and I could see she was holding a frying pan in her meaty palm. He glanced over at her and went on. "Well, we think that maybe . . ."

"Yep, beautiful neighbors and a beautiful neighborhood and a beautiful city but we don't know them very well, at all. It's really quite a shame."

He stopped trying to talk and stared so I added brightly, "So, of course, you'll be coming to our barbecue. Right?"

He turned full face to his wife, who began to shake her head violently from side to side. I looked at her for a moment and then nodded, and she stopped as though someone had cold-cocked her. Mr. Kilpatrick shivered then and turned back to me with his mouth a little bit open so I repeated myself and made it into a question.

"Right?"

He nodded dumbly and I handed over the note he'd left behind. "You dropped this."

He clutched at the paper until it crumpled and then bolted inside, so I finished cleaning up the booby traps. I'd barely picked up the last item when Renfield squealed and darted between my legs and through the open door of the house. I was still rubbing the muscle he'd bruised during his passage when a triple fork of lightning split the sky and a hard spring rain started.

After breakfast I'd handed Claire a highlighter marker and half the stack of the pamphlets I'd brought back from the Residential Tenancies office. We sat down at our kitchen table and twined our feet together underneath and went to work. Every few minutes the thunder would come and finally Claire looked up.

"Huh. I didn't know that."

I criticized her idly. "Don't grunt, it's not ladylike. What didn't you know?"

"I didn't know about the fire alarms. We're supposed to have fire alarms, three of them, one on each floor. Where's your dog, by the by?"

"In the basement. The thunder scares him. Where's Fred?"

"Trying to escape from his crib. And, dear?"

I looked up and she kicked me in the shin with the side of her foot. "I'll grunt if I want to."

"Isn't that a song? 'It's My Party and I'll Grunt if I Want To'?"

She sighed and brushed hair back from her forehead. "You're not funny, you know."

"I know."

It took us until past noon to go through the piles of paper. After that, we wrote out our lists separately and then traded pamphlets and went over them again. It was while we were checking for duplication that the doorbell rang.

"I'll get it."

The crowbar went behind my back, just in case, and I opened the door a crack to see Frank from the archery shop, standing in the rain and looking like a drowned Chihuahua. He sneezed and wiped his nose on a sleeve. "Can I come in?"

"Sure."

He was wearing a pale blue poncho made out of some kind of

rubberized material and he stood and dripped water all over the foyer of the house as Claire came forward with her best smile.

"Hello, I'm Claire Parker, and you are?"

"Frank. Frank Wyzik. Your husband sort of works for me on Wednesdays."

"I know. It's a lovely bow you sold him, or so I've heard."

I put the crowbar back with the umbrellas. "Would you like a cup of coffee? Or some lunch we're about to have?"

He shook his head, ran his hand through his hair, and turned to look at me carefully. "Wanted to tell you, I got a call yesterday saying you were a killer and thief, that you were living in the neighborhood and that it might be a good idea if you left town."

He left a space after his words and I waited politely so he went on. "Anyhow, I figured I'd tell you. The man said to call Detective Walsh for information."

Frank scratched the side of his leg through the poncho. "Anyhow, I asked some of the other businesses around and they all heard the same thing. Some of them confirmed it with Walsh too. They say he seemed real enthusiastic and nasty. Showed up to visit a couple of them with your picture in hand and talked about raping and killing and stealing."

Claire put her arm in mine and I waited.

"Just wanted to tell you."

He pulled up his poncho hood and opened the door behind him.

"So, I'll see you at noon tomorrow, right?"

His words hung there and I could barely understand them until Claire squeezed my arm.

"Yes."

My voice broke suspiciously and he stomped off into the storm without another word. Claire closed the door and relocked it and then I spoke. "I think I have a friend."

* * *

That night after supper, Claire went out jogging. On the previous nights, she'd gone out alone and I'd wondered about her safety until she'd showed me the sixteen-inch bayonet taped under her left forearm with the hilt towards her hand.

"I pity the fool who tries to mug me."

I eyed the set-up. "You can't draw that fast enough."

She pulled on her warm-up jacket and pulled the sleeve over the blade with difficulty. Then she tried to reach the hilt. "Hmmm. You may be right, oh wise one."

"Professional opinion."

The blade and her hand and her arm were all parts of the problem and I touched her right palm gently.

"Here."

I tore the sleeve along the seam from her wrist to her elbow and then sealed it with a couple of pieces of electrical tape. "There you go."

"You gonna sew it back?"

"Sure. Cloth sews easier than skin."

"Guess it does."

She reached with her right hand and easily pulled the knife free. I taped it back together and gave her a kiss.

"Remember. Stab, don't slash. Short, controlled arm motions. Yell 'fire' throughout."

And off she went. I tidied up and did my exercises, and while listening to the radio and thinking long thoughts, I was looking forward to love and sleep. At the hour the CBC announcer came on with the local news full of good cheer, minor mayhem, and unhappy businesspeople. My hand turned the radio off and I went upstairs to bed and waited for Claire. It would be a busy day tomorrow and meanwhile, out there in the dark, people were working against me and mine.

27

When Rebecca Gantz finally answered her door, I was standing on the porch holding the gold-lettered NST folder in both hands. From the house she used as an office came the smells of coffee and the sounds of distant typing.

"Good afternoon."

The rain was still falling and it beaded off my plastic jacket and pooled on the garishly tiled concrete patio at my feet. My hair was plastered back, which made me feel oddly refreshed and clean but probably explained why she didn't recognize me. She stared for a moment and then spoke. "Good afternoon. Can I help you?"

"You can help me by reading this."

I handed the folder to her and stepped forward confidently until she had a choice of moving to the side or letting me walk through her. She moved to the side and limply accepted the folder in manicured hands. I knew the moment she recognized me because she went rigid and squeaked at a pitch so high I could barely recognize it. The sounds of typing stopped and a young woman came bounding up through an open doorway from the basement.

"Ms. Gantz? Are you okay?"

The new woman must have ears like a bat. I stared at her for a few moments until she blushed. Then I said, "She's fine. My name's Sam Parker."

She recoiled from my hand and I let it drop. Gantz managed to find her voice. "I don't want to talk with you."

"Landlords and Tenants Act. Landlords, in other words, you, must talk to tenants, in other words, me, when there are problems. There are problems. We'll talk."

She was panting now like she'd just had a good orgasm, but finally she nodded and retreated into the house, all the while keeping me within her line of sight. I followed cautiously and the other woman followed close behind me. We ended up in the kitchen. The landlord went to a phone mounted on the wall and picked it up. "I'm calling Wal . . . the police."

There was a nice table and chair set in chrome and brass with a heavy glass top tinted gray, and I sat down and rested my arms on the top. I'd heard her start to say *Walsh* but I didn't react.

"Call whoever you want. But why?"

"You broke in here."

I shook my head.

"No. You let me in. I came to talk with you as a tenant talking to a landlord. If this is a bad time, I can come back. However, the Landlords and Tenants Act does allow us to set an appointment within a reasonable space of time. How's tomorrow for you?"

The braless young woman came over, staying out of my reach, and the two looked at me for a few seconds in silence.

"What are you talking about?"

"Read the letter, it's short."

She went to where she had dropped it and came back, scanning as she went. I waited and let the water drip off my coat onto her kitchen floor. In the corner, a small ceramic coffee urn steamed and perked away merrily but none was offered to me. When she'd finished reading, she looked at me. "This is ridiculous."

I stood up, ready to go.

"I'm glad you think so too. Just make the repairs in the next two or three days and we'll forget that pesky little complaint. It's nice that you're being so reasonable."

She looked confused and handed over the two sheets of laboriously typed paper to the woman beside her, who began reading them. As she read, she developed a slight smile.

"No. You have to leave my house you rented."

"Not really. Again, referring to the Landlords and Tenants Act, you haven't given me enough notice, so we don't have to leave. But that's just part of the problem. Do you want me to forward this to the authorities or do you want to deal with it here and now?"

I lowered my voice. "Mano to mano, so to speak."

She started to pace, three steps forward and three back, and she began to waggle her finger and lecture me. "You're a dangerous criminal. You lied to me. You haven't kept the place in good repair. You've irreparably damaged both my property and my reputation."

I sat down again and put my hands on the table. "Are you done?"

She stood there triumphantly and accepted the papers back from her assistant.

"Okay. First, the police cleared me of any charges, so I'm not a criminal, and even if I was, you can't refuse to rent to me on the grounds of past behavior. Secondly, I never lied to you, my wife made all the arrangements and you'll find that I am listed everywhere with both my birth name and my legal name, and my employment status is also listed. Third, we've only been in the place a brief period of time and we've kept it in fine condition. Fourthly, your professional reputation is fine, unless you want to try to press charges against me under a slander/libel suit, which, I tell you three times, you'll lose."

Unconsciously I raised my voice. "Regarding the property we've rented. The locks are bad and the roof leaks. The damage done during a robbery attempt has not been repaired. The heating vents are badly maintained and heat doesn't reach to the second floor. There are insects in the basement. There are no fire alarms."

I controlled myself and managed to lower my voice. "You refused to meet with me when I asked. And, lastly, you attempted to evict me and my family for no reason at all."

I started to walk to the front door. "A copy of that letter will go to the authorities tomorrow morning. You have until 9:45 a.m. to respond to the letter in specific. The mail pickup near our place is at ten."

Both women followed me to the foyer and Gantz blurted out, "You're bluffing."

"No, I'm not."

"Then you're delusional."

"Probably, but your response should be in writing. As a matter of fact, I insist."

It was still raining, harder now, if anything. I went on. "Find a lawyer. Talk to them. I assure you that I'm within my rights."

"You can't be serious." She had grabbed my arm and was looking at me from about eight inches away, and I felt a surge of anger.

"Of course I'm fucking serious. You've tried to kick my family out. What did you think I would do?"

The assistant was about two yards away and probably couldn't hear me over the rain outside, but I really didn't give a shit, so I leaned in and whispered. "You're lucky I'm not as bad as you seem to think, or I'd cut your throat from ear to ear."

Her face went white and I smiled and left. Before I'd made it to the end of the sidewalk, the assistant came running out. She had stopped to pull on a clear plastic overcoat. "Mr. Parker? Please wait."

I waited and she stood between me and the street. "I'd like to talk to you about this."

"So talk."

She bit her lower lip and looked over her shoulder at the house and her boss.

"Not now, I've got to get She-Who-Must-Be-Ignored calmed down. She's ready to send in the marines and I'm sure we can come to some kind of reasonable agreement."

"She-Who-Must-Be-Ignored? Cute. Come to my place in an hour. I'll be a little less pissed off."

"Okay."

She waited but I didn't ask, so she offered.

"She-Who-Must-Be-Ignored is a name from the *Rumpole of the Bailey* book series. It's what he calls his wife. Actually he calls her She-Who-Must-Be-Obeyed, but I like my version better." She smiled engagingly. I walked home. All in all, I was relatively cheerful. I'd found out it was Walsh behind some of the crap that seemed to be coming down and that made me feel a little bit more in control.

28

It took her slightly longer than an hour to show up, which was fine by me. I arranged the dining room table so it was clear and then I stacked the pamphlets from the Tenancies office in the middle. When I was done, I put a chair for her in the middle of the biggest stain on the carpet.

"What the hell are you doing?" Claire had been working at finding me a job, using the newspapers and telephone, and when she came out of the kitchen, she had a pad of scrap paper.

"Our landlord's assistant is coming over right away to talk. I'm just setting the stage."

Claire looked at the table and the chairs and sat down on the stairs. "Trying to take the moral high ground?"

I went into the kitchen and came out with the good china service, which we kept in a large wooden wine crate, and I carefully removed each piece and dealt them around the table like cards.

"Nope. Just trying to make her queasy. Think it'll work?"

"Maybe. She's smart, I think. I dealt with her personally when renting this place." Claire stared at the set-up and tapped the phone book with her fingers. Then she added, "Should work. I'm going to sit in, if that's okay with you?"

It was so I got out another setting and then brought the missing chair from the back room where I'd stashed it. A few minutes after everything was ready, Fred started to nod off towards his afternoon nap and I took him to his room and tucked him in. Ten minutes later the assistant rang the bell and Claire let her in just as I reached the door.

"Hello, Mr. Parker, Mrs. Parker."

She stood in the foyer until I felt constrained to offer her a hand removing her coat and motioning for her to remove her boots.

"Come in, Ms. . . . ? You know—I don't know your name."

She was right behind me and she laughed. "I guess we haven't been formally introduced. My name is Vanessa Rose. Should I call you Mr. Parker or Mr. Haaviko or what?"

"Just Sam."

We went through the living room into the dining room and I watched carefully but she didn't have any reaction I could see to the stained carpet. Claire was already sitting down and pouring coffee by the time I reached my seat. "Do you take milk or sugar or fake sugar or none of the above?"

Vanessa sat down and put an oversized canvas purse primly in her lap. "The first two, please."

She accepted the cup and drank from it with her little finger partially extended. Claire refilled my cup and then turned a little in her seat. "Dear? The dog's outside, do you think that's all right?"

"He'll be just fine. He hates the weather, you see."

I addressed the comment to Vanessa but it bounced right off her meaningless smile. From where I was sitting, I could see that she had her feet raised so they weren't touching the carpet but were hooked on the rungs of her chair. I had to bury a grin in the cup and then I continued. "So. You wanted to talk."

Claire watched patiently as Vanessa put down her cup and set her purse on the table. She glanced at the pamphlets and focused on me. "I've read your letter and there is some merit to the points you've raised. However, at the same time, we do feel that you misrepresented yourself to us and, therefore, we have grounds to evict you."

She raised a hand to fend off any anger that I might be feeling, but I wasn't feeling any so the gesture was wasted. Claire had to drown her own grin in her coffee and Vanessa just rattled on when she figured out that neither of us was going to react. "We do feel that perhaps we were, shall we say, overly enthusiastic about the eviction notice. If we were to extend the time involved by, say, three weeks, would that be acceptable?"

Neither Claire nor I said anything and she went on. "And, of course, we'd add in some money to help in your moving expenses, perhaps five hundred dollars. We would also return your damage deposit, all four hundred and fifty, for a total of nine hundred and fifty dollars."

She looked expectant and Claire spoke up. "So we'd have three weeks before we'd have to leave?"

"Yes."

Vanessa drank some coffee.

"And you'd give us five hundred dollars on top of everything?"

"Yes. We think that would be fair."

Claire smiled. "But why should we move? I mean, we're in the right, right?"

Vanessa didn't react and Claire went on. "And we, my husband and I both, really like this town and this house. So you see our problem."

"Well, we could go as high as a thousand dollars to help with your relocation."

Claire looked at me and I gazed blankly back and she nodded and answered. "No."

Vanessa was startled. "What?"

"No. We don't want to leave. We'll go right away if you find us another equivalent residence here in town but, other than that, no."

Vanessa leaned back in her seat and let her feet touch the ground. "Under the law we can ask you to vacate if we give you three months' warning."

"Sure. So, are you going to give us our warning now?"

She gritted her teeth, both figuratively and in reality. "I don't want to, but I will."

"Fine. Do it in writing."

Vanessa reached into her purse and came out with a sealed envelope but, before she could put it on the table, I spoke up. "Wait a second. What about the repairs to bring this place up to standard?"

"They'll be done."

"When?"

She put the envelope down and Claire opened it and read it. When she was finished, she nodded and then held up a hand to me before asking another question. "You know that this letter says that the property is going to be, and I quote, 'extensively renovated'?"

Claire gave her a chance to answer but Vanessa didn't say a word. "You didn't have to say that. Now you're actually going to have to do it."

Vanessa shrugged again and Claire went on. "We'll want a replacement carpet in right away. Is there a place in town or do you use a contractor?"

Vanessa growled a little and poured herself a refill without asking. "What does it matter?"

Claire looked at her with the sweetest possible expression on her face. "I'm going to call them tomorrow. I just want to make sure I get the right place."

"Don't do that. I'll do that. That's my job."

Claire tapped the letter in front of her. "Just like you kept the place up to standards? You're not stupid, you knew what your boss was doing, why'd you go along with it?"

"She's my boss."

Vanessa looked a little confused and Claire tapped the letter again.

"Even though all the repairs can be written off? Even though the repairs build up the equity of the property? Doing it this way is not very smart at all."

Vanessa thought about it for a moment and when she spoke again her voice was compounded equally of mild anger and distaste. Oddly enough, it didn't seem to be directed at either of us but more towards the world in general and her boss in specific.

"I agree. I'm quite money-oriented. However, my boss doesn't see things in quite that way and she's the boss. In the end, it's her decision."

Claire put her pad of paper on the table and picked up a pen. "So the name of your carpet place is . . . ?"

"Hansen's. It's in the North End nearby."

"Good."

I looked back and forth at the two women and then spoke up. "So we'll be gone in three months. That's plenty of time."

Vanessa had refilled her cup from the pale pink and gold pot and was idly stirring her coffee.

"Plenty of time to do what?"

"Oh, mostly to convince you and your boss to let us keep the place. We really are very fond of it. It's just right for us."

She snorted, which was a very unladylike noise indeed. "Fat chance. My boss does not change her mind."

"Wanna bet?"

She looked at me and then at Claire and then back at me again. "No. I don't bet."

Claire reached over and patted her arm. "That's very wise of you." She turned to me and said solemnly, "See, I told you she was bright."

I laughed and Vanessa closed her purse and looked around the room for a few minutes. I could see the muscles tense in her throat a couple of times and then relax, so I waited until she said what she needed to say. "Well, now that that's all settled, can I ask you a question?"

"Shoot."

"You don't seem like a, I don't know, bad guy, I suppose."

Before answering, I drank some more coffee. "Well, not now. I used to be one, though. I used to be really bad but I stopped."

There were more words in my mouth and more ideas but I held them back with difficulty and continued on a different track. "I just stopped."

It sounded lame and it hung there for a long time while Claire held her hand out where I could take it, but I didn't reach out and she pulled hers back.

"But . . . killing those three boys. How did it make you feel?"

I stared at her and fought down a surprising surge of rage. Claire noticed and moved around to kiss me on my cheek. When she spoke, I could feel her breath tickling the hair around my ear. "She didn't mean anything."

Vanessa was starting to look a little worried and I exhaled loudly through my nose.

"It made me angry and sad."

She stared at me and shook her head. "Really?"

Claire was holding onto my shoulder quite tightly and I looked up and addressed what I said to her alone. "Yes, really."

For a second I thought there was a tear in Claire's eye and then she squeezed my shoulder again.

Vanessa deadpanned, "Strange. I wouldn't have felt a thing."

I started clearing the table. I wanted to say something nasty, but instead I spoke very carefully. As though it was something important to recount. "I didn't feel a thing the first time. Or the second. Or even the third. After that, well, sometimes I felt happy and really good and that scared the piss out of me. Eventually I started to feel a little pleasure every time. It was right after that that I decided to stop being bad."

Vanessa stared at me and a slow flush came across her face. And then, abruptly, she left.

29

Thompson phoned a little after 5:00 p.m. I'd just finished taking the last load of garbage out of the basement and packing it neatly in the same cardboard boxes we'd used for moving. While I was coming in from the back door, the phone jangled and I caught it on the second ring. " 'Lo?"

Thompson sounded sober. "I just received a phone call from the Crown attorney. The RCMP are serving a warrant tomorrow morning at your residence and they're giving us notice."

"That's great. Why?"

He answered, confused, "Why what?"

"Why give us notice, that's not standard procedure, is it?"

"Well, no. They probably wanted to make sure everything went by the book. That makes sense, right?"

"Sure. Oh, are you and your wife coming over on Saturday for the barbecue? We sent out a note but haven't received a response yet."

Thompson was quiet for a few moments. "Sure, I think so. I guess my wife has the letter, I haven't seen it yet. But sure. Now, about tomorrow, the cops are coming at 9:00 sharp."

"Can you make it yourself?"

"Sure. Wouldn't want to miss this. I'll see you then."

Claire came down from the second floor, holding a half-filled garbage bag. "Who was that?"

"Thompson. The cops are going to search the house tomorrow morning."

"Ah, shit. No point in cleaning, then."

She dropped the bag and sat on the stairs.

"Well, we can finish cleaning up after they leave."

I nodded agreement. "Right. So I declare a holiday for the rest of tonight."

"Before we do that, let's check the house for anything that shouldn't be there."

"Like anything planted?"

"Right."

So we did. Claire found it in the garbage pile in the back by the alley: a slightly torn, ziplock bag of white oblong tablets and cracked crystalline pebbles. We both stared at it for a moment and then I put the garbage bag back on top.

"Leave it?" Claire was biting her knuckle.

"Yeah."

We found a piece of particleboard and put it on top of the stuff before going back into the house to look some more. The last thing we did was both sign our names in marker on the board, along with the time and date.

Then we sat and listened to the rain for a few hours until we fell asleep.

The first person arrived at exactly two minutes before 9:00. When I opened the door, there was a big man in an expensive suit standing along with the Crown prosecutor, McMillan-Fowler, and Thompson. Behind them, and looking sodden in the rain, were three Mounties in their patrol uniforms.

McMillan-Fowler spoke first. "Mr. Parker? Good morning, I am here with Inspector Atismak of the RCMP and these other officers to serve a search warrant. Your lawyer, Mr. Thompson, is here as well." She tried to walk past me but I didn't let her.

"One moment. May I see the warrant?"

She had it under her coat and handed it over as Thompson crowded up to read it as well.

". . . search the premises . . . address is right . . . firearms, narcotics and biker paraphernalia. . . . What the hell is *biker paraphernalia*?"

McMillan-Fowler gestured expansively with one hand. "Patches, literature, signs, stuff like that."

"Oh."

I turned to Thompson, who was holding his own copy of the paper.

"Looks okay?"

"Looks fine."

I stepped away and made a grand gesture. "Come in, come in, *mi casa es su casa*. Coffee and donuts are on the kitchen table. And there's what looks to be some crack cocaine and some kind of tablets planted in our garbage pile by the alley."

Everyone froze at that but then the big cop and McMillan-Fowler went out the back while the others stood staring at the table and at me. Claire had gone out at 6:00 that morning before I had woken up and the pastries were arranged on little napkins along with a big urn of coffee in the dining room. The big RCMP officer stepped back in and slung his jacket over his left arm. He didn't mention the stuff outside and gestured at the table.

"Looks familiar."

McMillan-Fowler came in and the cops scattered through the house while Thompson scurried after them to keep them honest. Claire and Fred were sitting together on the sofa by the window and playing with a bit of string. I'd chained the dog up outside and he barked every few minutes, more curious than angry.

I turned to the Mountie who'd commented on the coffee and donuts. "It should. I got the idea from *Twin Peaks*."

He looked blankly at me and I continued defensively. "Obscure social referent."

"Yes, I was just remembering. The table in the rear of the town's cop shop, the flaky secretary set up a spread like this every day for the local police."

I was impressed. "You've got a good memory."

He nodded politely and faced me silently before walking back into my home. The front door was still open and I could see a big, black panel truck parked just down the street. Leaning against it were five men wearing black uniforms and carrying heavy-assault weapons. With difficulty I ignored them and Claire came up beside me, still holding Fred. "Whatcha thinking, love?"

I motioned at the cops with a twist of my neck. "Two Heckler and Koch MP5 submachine guns, blow back action, very accurate, reliable, prime; five thousand dollars each. One Colt M-16A2 or assorted variants assault rifle, full or semi-auto; two thousand dollars. One Remington 870 pump shotgun with extended magazine; about five hundred dollars. One Remington M-700 accurized rifle with variable scope, probably in 7.62 mm or 7 mm magnum, maybe point 300 Winchester; about twelve hundred."

"Hmmm. So, in other words, college for Fred?"

"Yep. Or you."

She kissed my lips and we turned back into the house before answering.

"Not me. Been to college."

"You dated frat boys, there's a difference."

She held my hand and responded, "You're probably right."

* * *

"Sir? Sir?"

One of the cops from upstairs came racing down the stairs, holding a big plastic bag. In it was the Mauser bayonet that I had left beside the bed, but before I could say a word, Atismak spoke.

"What is that?"

"A sword. I found it upstairs."

The Mountie was young and had barely grown into his black walrus mustache and he looked very happy indeed. Atismak, however, did not look happy, he looked very tired all of a sudden.

"May I see it?"

He took the bag and held it up. "Not a sword. Not a knife, either. A bayonet?"

Claire was tense but I was watching Atismak's face when I answered. "Right. From a Mauser rifle, model 1871. I bought it in an Edmonton pawn shop. They used great steel back then, keeps a good edge."

Atismak handed it to me. "Right. Now, Officer . . ."

He turned to face the cop, who kept his eyes on the bayonet. "Did you read the search warrant I gave you yesterday?"

"Yes."

Atismak didn't wait. "That's, yes, sir."

"Right, sir. Yes, sir."

"Good. The warrant read '*Narcotics. Guns. Biker paraphernalia.*' Is that bayonet you grabbed narcotics, guns, or biker paraphernalia?"

The cop was silent and Atismak went on. "So, it's cutlery. Why don't you wait outside and we'll talk later."

The young Mountie went and I brought Atismak one of the mismatched pairs of coffee cups.

"Coffee? Cream and sugar are over there."

"Thank you."

He limped over in considerable pain to doctor his own cup and I squeezed Claire's shoulder gently through her blouse. "That is a smart cop."

She blew into Fred's belly, which made him squeal, and answered in a monotone. "Contradiction."

"Well, that's that."

McMillan-Fowler had come back down with Thompson as the other cops trooped out. Atismak had never left my side and now he put down his fourth cup of coffee, shrugged into his coat, and gave me a barely perceptible nod, like he was thanking me.

Before they could go, I asked, "Now that it's all over, can I ask why you searched my house?"

Atismak looked at McMillan-Fowler, who made a polite face, before answering. "I don't see why not. I can't see that investigation going anywhere."

I looked at both of them. "Right. Okay, ignoring the stuff out back . . ."

I had seen Thompson and McMillan-Fowler debating beforehand. They both nodded and Atismak took over speaking.

". . . which we will be investigating, although not in relation to you folks."

He smiled briefly and went on. "The provincial tip line received a call indicating that firearms and narcotics were stored here. The call was very specific and believable and we had to check it out."

Claire looked at me, it made sense to her. Me too. "Can my wife and I listen to the recording?"

Atismak shook his head and shrugged. "Sorry. But it wouldn't matter even if you could, whoever it was disguised their voice. They mentioned a Glock pistol along with considerable quantities of crack cocaine and crank speed, along with PCP and Viagra. Frankly, Mr. Haaviko, considering your past history, the call sounded credible."

Thompson was trying to say something but we all ignored him and finally he just blurted it out. "Viagra?"

Atismak looked amused so I answered. "Yeah. It goes for twenty-five dollars US per pill in Russia. It's smuggled to Churchill, put on ships, and offloaded in the Black Seas ports."

I turned back to the Mountie. "Let me guess, it's the details in the call that raised flags for you. That's why you gave me warning of the search and let me have my lawyer present?"

Atismak smiled. "We also put some watchers on you with long lenses last night in the hope you'd move something, which you didn't. You didn't even touch the drugs back there."

His smile was cold and smart. "We're not all bad, Mr. Haaviko."

Then they left, except for Thompson, who walked to the door and looked down the driveway at the cops by the van. His face flushed bright red and he fumbled in his jacket pocket for a silver flask about a pint in size. With trembling fingers he unscrewed the top and took several swallows before putting it away. When all the cars outside had left, so did he.

Claire came over and threaded her arm through mine. "You look concerned."

"I am."

"Why?"

"Someone tried to set me up and didn't care if you and Fred got in the way."

"Who?"

"Walsh, maybe. Robillard. Whoever it was called the cops and claimed we were armed and running drugs for bikers. All in exquisite detail."

"Oh." She held on to my arm and kept a smile on her face but I could feel her whole body go rigid.

"Fuckers."

"Yeah. If we'd had a slightly dumber cop than that Atismak, we would have had the whole riot squad down here. Local cops and not the Mounties."

She turned to face me. "And they would have found something, right?"

"Sure. They would have come down like the wrath of God, and those weapons outside would have been in here with us. Someone would have started shooting and no one would have been able to prove afterwards it wasn't me or you. Clean, simple, elegant, and some cop becomes a hero, the city gets to avoid embarrassing questions, the world goes on."

We were quiet and she turned and went back for Fred. When she came back, her voice was artificially calm. "So. What are we going to do?"

I shrugged and now I was trembling too. My hands vibrated and my vision tunneled as the adrenalin pumped through me. "I don't know. We tried. I tried, I mean. I really did but I don't want to try anymore."

I was pleading and she kissed Fred on the forehead and he turned to look at me. "Cry havoc," she said.

"Huh?"

She put Fred between us and we made a sandwich hug.

"It's a line from a bad movie with Christopher Walken, 'cry havoc and let loose the dogs of war.' "

"Right."

Neither of us was smiling and she went on. "Or a song by Pink Floyd after Roger Waters left."

"Right, or even a comic book hero."

She squeezed closer and I put my head down to her ear.

"Woof."

Claire answered just as softly.

"Woof."

When the cops were long gone, I took a quick walk around the neighborhood and found a pay phone in the back of a bowling alley. The Red River Community College administration office answered on the third ring.

I said, "Hello, this is the alumni association. We're checking the mailing address of one of the graduates for a pamphlet we're producing."

"Ummm. Yes, hold on."

There was a pause and I crossed my fingers, I was playing percentages but that often works just fine.

"Name?"

"Enzio Walsh. Computer course graduate."

She gave me an address in the suburb of Transcona and I thanked her and then held my head against the glass frame of the booth to feel the coolness.

"Woof."

No one was around and I walked off with my head full of vague thoughts, strung-together memories, and ideas. It was free thought, the same way it had been when I'd been stealing. Elements of ideas, concepts, free floating, diffuse, they would spin together and form something in time, as long as I let them alone. Robillard and Walsh, Walsh and Robillard, but Walsh first.

About a block away, I had the parameters down pat. He was an enemy I couldn't and shouldn't kill but could and should ruin. An enemy full of pride like a frog full of fart and armed with arrogance in his reputation. An enemy backed by his organization.

Some dead French cop said that it is not enough to destroy a man unless you destroy his reputation. But all I wanted was to be free. And have a family. And make a living. Which was actually quite a lot, if you thought about it.

30

It took me two days to find Robillard's address, using the library records, the phone company, the gas company, and City Hall. Getting to the library was half the fun, taking different routes each time, avoiding any tails, dumping surveillance, if it was there, making an idiot of myself, if it wasn't. Practicing old techniques, moving fast and well.

At the end of the second day, I took a bus out to the St. Norbert end of town and then took a walk around Robillard's neighborhood. His place was on a nice street called Athlone, and it was a ranch house with an attached two-car garage sitting on about four acres of wooded land. I walked by once and then hopped back on the bus and used the same transfer to pay my way downtown.

While the bus jerked and spasmed through very little traffic, my hand itched for a gun and my veins itched for the heroin rush and my nose itched for the coke and my throat itched for the whisky, and my eyes itched for seeing the bad things. Taking what I wanted and not taking any shit and wanting things and not giving a rat's ass . . .

We passed by a pawn shop. Source of all good things, knives, money, guns, so my hand was right near the stop cord. Pull it and walk in, nail whoever the fuck was behind the counter with a fist between the eyes and then a knee to the jaw. Flip the sign in the window to CLOSED. Lock the door. Do unpleasant things to the shopkeeper until he handed over the money, the guns, the videotape of me coming in.

It was all eighteen inches away. And that would be the start. Acid to take you away and grass to smooth the ride. Cash on the barrelhead and sleek, slick, steel instruments of destruction. Headlines and blurred camera images. Fast cars and that crazed, myopic, adrenalin rush.

The voice inside my head said, Hey. Just one more time. Help me out, help yourself out, do some good.

Against all that old shit was a baby who, when born, measured exactly as long as the distance from the tip of my fingers to the crook of my arm. Waking up with the same beloved breath on the back of my neck. Yard work and house work. Something to own that wasn't stolen, borrowed, or bought with blood.

My hand relaxed. I was going to bend, not break.

And then the pawn shop was gone.

That night Claire and I made love until I couldn't even remember my name.

The next morning I left much before dawn and played all my little avoid-the-tail games and moved on foot until I could steal a bike and then by bike to Transcona. About a mile past Walsh's house, there was a big junkyard surrounded by a wooden fence topped with razor wire, so I paused there and threw the bike over the fence to land behind a pile of gutted cars. Towering high into the sky over the fence was a bright yellow crane hoisting a massive electromagnet and I paused to admire it before walking back. It was almost 8:00 when I reached Walsh's bungalow and it was still ice-cold out with a bitter wind.

Cops are hyper-stressed most of the time; there really are people trying to get them. For that reason I stayed far away, walking once past the front of the place using a brisk race-walker's stride, no one looks twice at those guys. Walsh had a small bungalow with attached garage, thick hedges between him and his neighbors, and a smallish backyard, carefully fenced in. Changing my pace and my jacket, I walked along the back alley and saw that the property ended in a field with an old railway line cutting neatly across it.

Through his fence I could see a neatly manicured lawn, a field-stone patio area, and a small shed. But no toys that indicated children, and no patches of dog crap or urine that indicated pets.

Back front and about a block away, I waited until Walsh had left in a small Corolla and then walked up his driveway to where a dark gray van sat in front of the attached double garage. I took my hand out of my jacket pocket and looked at the para compass resting in my gloved palm. I'd picked it up at a marine supply house in Prince Edward Island, prepping for a score that hadn't worked out, and I'd kept it since. Sailors used it on small boats but it was strong enough to detect magnetic fields, like those around alarm systems, at close range, and it was small enough to be easily concealed. I was using it to check for an alarm on the van. In my pocket was a flexible metal shim and a Robertson screwdriver to strip the steering column and start the engine once I was in.

Some jays sang nearby as I held the compass near the body of the van and slowly walked around it, watching for the needle to deflect. Nothing happened but the needle took a little dip near the front driver's side wheel.

"Nah. Nothing's that easy."

I circled the van and came back to the same place and felt around until I found a small, magnetized box where Walsh had put a spare set of house and car keys. I opened the box and slid into the van. In the back there was a nice set-up with a chair on a heavy-duty rotating bracket, some shelves, a locker built into the back of the driver's chair, and a little cooler resting between the seats. I left everything in place and arranged myself behind the steering wheel.

My palms were sweaty under the gloves and I turned on the ignition, holding my breath. It would be just like a cop to install some kind of extra gimmick in his own car, parked in his own yard, but nothing happened.

The van started on the first try and I turned it off and fingered the house key.

Oh well, nothing ventured.

31

Walsh had a nice place but very masculine. The front door opened right onto a living room with dark wood paneling on the walls, black leather and chrome steel couches and chairs. The furniture all faced a pale birchwood entertainment unit from Ikea that covered one side of the room. A stereo, good TV, DVD player, and so on were all prominently displayed along with racks of movies and music. In the corner near the closet, there was a stand-up bar that showed signs of use, big glasses and supplies of Johnny Walker Blue and Gold scotch, Hennesey cognac, Drambuie, Jack Daniel's bourbon. Hard liquor for hard men.

No books but magazines on tabletops: guns, computers, cars, fitness, self-defense.

Under the coffee table was a Bushnell Spacemaster Spotting scope, about six hundred dollars' worth of quality optics, and one of those ashtrays with a built-in fan to suck up smoke.

The kitchen was small and functional and full of appliances. The bathroom was equally small and had a well-thumbed selection of *Playboy*, *Penthouse*, and *Maxim* magazines in a rack beside the tub.

His medicine cabinet was full of vitamin supplements, herbal compounds (what the hell was St. John's Wort or even ginseng for that matter?), condoms (ribbed and regular), and a big bottle of industrial-strength pain medication with codeine.

As I moved through the rooms, I listened but didn't hear a thing.

The dining room had been turned into a study with narrow tables along all the walls holding too many computers. I shook my head and counted: eighteen towers, three laptops, sixteen screens of various sizes, along with three printers. And stuff I'd never seen before.

Along one wall was a bookshelf full of manuals and a three-drawer file cabinet full of warranties. The one window in the room had been sealed with a great deal of care and laid over it was a patch of corkboard that reached from throat height to the ceiling.

Pinned to that were about fifty pictures of me and Claire and Fred; at home, in the yard, shopping, in the hospital, on the street, working at the convenience store. The pictures were printed on computer paper, not standard photographic stock.

Off to the side were six pictures grouped together, pictures of Robillard talking to someone I couldn't identify in the front seat of a Taurus station wagon down the street from my place. Pictures of Robillard walking. Pictures of Robillard driving out of my neighborhood in a big SUV.

I wanted to check the computers but didn't know anything about how they worked, so I stuck with what I knew. Under one desk I found a barrel safe bolted into the floor. The lock was a good one, twenty million possible combinations, but the steel was shit and I could have opened it with a claw hammer in about two seconds. I left it alone.

There were two bedrooms. Walsh had turned one into a storeroom by filling it with boxes upon boxes of stuff. At the same time, he had left an open space down the center, where he'd strung a length of braided steel wire upon which to hang his clothes, all his clothes, right down to underwear and socks, which hung on their own little hangers.

The second bedroom was his own with a big, expensive mattress on an antique cherrywood frame, two matching end tables, and a small vanity table set into the wall with a huge mirror that did double duty for sexual stimulus and grooming. In the drawers of the vanity, I found more condoms, breath spray, nail grooming equipment, a selection of cigars sealed in aluminum cases, and a pair of Zippo lighters.

I resisted the temptation to put pinholes in the condoms and kept looking.

Where the closet had been, Walsh had installed a Sentry 14 gun safe. Steel frame and full construction with a combination lock. Capable of holding fourteen long guns. Locked, of course.

I stared at the closed door for a moment and then retraced my way back to the filing cabinet in the study, where I found a sheaf of warranties. A Taurus Raging Bull magnum revolver in .44, Ruger Model 77 bolt-action rifle in .30-06, a Browning Buck pistol in .22, a Mossberg Model 500 pump shotgun in 12 gauge. There were also bills of sale for more weapons bought at gun shows and second hand. A Ruger ranch rifle in 7.62 Russian, a Derringer in .45 ACP, a Colt Commander pistol in .45 bought at a place called Gunsite down in New Mexico. The bill for that was over twenty-five hundred, US. About four times more than a Colt should have cost.

I backtracked some more. In the living room there were three framed diplomas, all for Walsh. One for graduating from Red River. One for graduating from the Cooper Gunsite pistol course down in the States, where he had apparently gone to learn combat shooting. The last was for graduating cop school.

If Walsh had a Colt worth two and a half grand from Gunsite, then it would have been accurized and modified. Which meant he knew how to shoot.

Back to the warranties. Grown-up toys, a Nikon SLR digital camera bought at a police auction, a Meridian GPS Gold system from a local sporting goods store, black combat fatigues from a mail order company called US Cavalry, body armor from Second Chance, good knives from Gerber and Buck, a laser range finder from Leica, night vision binoculars from Bushnell, the warranty for the spotting scope in the living room, and surveillance equipment like bug finders and sonic amplifiers from a variety of companies, most of them in England. I put the papers back.

Downstairs the basement was unfinished but Walsh had a weight bench set up with free weights, a Bowflex gym, as well as a stationary bike and a treadmill. Beside the racked weights was a big punching bag about a yard long, a heavy-duty Everlast, which I checked out for wear marks and found quite a few low and on the left-hand side and some centered.

I reached his garage through the kitchen. It had been turned into a workshop with woodworking tools, billets of lumber, and many racks of tools. There was nothing that jumped out so I closed the door softly and stood there. I could have done a lot of things. I could have broken into his gun safe, loaded a shotgun, pointed it at groin level down the front hall, and set up twine to trigger it when he opened the door.

I could have cut the bolts through on his weights. Or wired his gas stove. Or sawn halfway through the stairs leading to the basement. Or drilled a hole into his tub with a live wire from his basement and painted the end white. Or spilled black powder around his hot water heater. Or dissolved codeine invisibly into his whisky.

But I didn't.

I stopped in the living room and collected the Bushnell telescope and stole his van.

32

The van drove like a dream and I wasted some time driving around the industrial lots along the perimeter highway before finding what I wanted in a back lot outside a trucking firm. Parked near the back was a Dodge Caravan of the same year, model, and color, so I stole the front and back licence plates and replaced them with the ones off Walsh's van. Then I came back and went around to the driver's side and opened the gas cap. No one was around so I poured a bottle of Coke from Walsh's cooler into the tank and headed back onto the highway. I felt sorry for the poor van owner, who comes back and finds his van won't start and calls a tow truck, who probably won't look at the plates. Tow truck comes and drags the van back to some garage somewhere where it is off the street. Which means the licence plates are not available to the cops. Which means confusion.

I headed down the highway until I found a small hotel for breakfast in the coffee shop. I chose a table near the front and had to wait until the waitress finally came over and stifled a jaw-cracking yawn. I put her at maybe seventeen and pretty enough in a flyblown way, blond and heavy-set with thick calves and a weak chin. She stood and slowly scratched her neck with the end of her pencil. "Whadday-awant?"

I opted for simple and scorched. That way the germs would be dead or at least stunned and easy to eat. "Scrambled eggs, bacon, rye toast, and a can of diet Coke."

She went off to place the order and came back with the pop and a fresh table setting. I drank the Coke and waited for the caffeine to hit.

"Hereyago."

The toast came and I ate it without thinking about what was going into my system. I needed money, but not a lot of it, maybe a grand. I thought about that for a second and then doubled it on general principles. I also needed it fast and without heat.

"Hereyago."

She delivered my eggs, which were watery, and my bacon, which was limp and tasted mildly of dish soap. I ate and thought about money, not food. Fast meant I needed cash, not something to sell. At the same time, avoiding heat meant I couldn't steal by force, which was the fastest. Fast also meant I didn't have time to run any complicated cons. I finished my food with about three good ideas and one I didn't like at all.

"Will that be all, sir?" The waitress had saved her best effort for last, good pronunciation, a pleasant smile, and a little bit of leg. I tipped her three bucks I couldn't afford and left.

I spent the next hour driving around the city until I found a fair-sized mall leeching off a residential area in the southern part of the city. I parked in front of a two-storey house with a big FOR SALE sign on the yard and high grass, and then I walked to the back end of the mall, where the parking lot was blocked off by a chain-link fence. I was wearing an old black raincoat over my suit and I took off the coat and slung it around my neck before climbing over. Three kids, the oldest about ten years old, watched me in astonishment and I winked at them and then put on dark sunglasses.

"Don't try this at home."

They laughed and took off, playing hooky, I guess, and kind of nervous. Once over, I walked around into the mall and checked out the property board in the front entrance, where it listed a big bookstore, a grocery store, one of those amateur handyman places, and a bunch of smaller boutiques selling clothing and perfumes and such. There was also one of those ubiquitous mall wart stores so I decided to start there.

Just inside the mall entrance an elderly man greeted me. "Welcome to Walmart."

I thanked him and asked where the sporting goods section was.

There were a few people wandering the aisles but I ignored them and headed to the racks of hockey equipment near the wall. The sticks were racked along about five yards of space and I snagged a Bauer Jetstream with a one-hundred-and-fifteen-dollar price tag and leaned it casually on my shoulder. The store had two customer service kiosks, one at the front and the other near the entrance to the mall lot. I chose the one near the lot entrance and only had to wait in line for a few minutes before a bright-eyed young woman greeted me.

"Good morning, sir. How can I help you?"

I suspect that these stores hire pretty young women to take complaints because they figure most people won't yell at them for the following reasons: A) they're pretty, B) they're women, and C) they're young. In my experience, though, most people complaining are women who are neither young nor pretty and I think they like to yell. The who is probably unimportant. It's just a suspicion, though.

"Good morning. I bought this hockey stick yesterday and it's not what my son wants. I'd like to return it, if that's all right."

Her smile grew although it appeared somewhat brittle. "Certainly. Do you have the receipt?"

"I'm sorry, no. I seem to have lost it. I paid cash, though, if that helps."

The look she gave me said plainly that, no, it didn't. "I'm sorry. The store policy is that we can't accept returns without receipts."

She waited while I digested that and then I perked up.

"Well, can you do a trade, then? I can bring my son back later to choose for himself but I do have one or two other things to pick up today."

She agreed that that would be okay and I turned over the stick and got a voucher for one hundred and thirty-one dollars, which I pocketed. As I left, she piped up, "And have a great day!"

I did. In the jewelry section of the store I found a woman's Timex with a price tag a little more than the voucher, so I bought the watch using the voucher and most of my remaining cash and then headed towards the other customer service kiosk.

"Good morning, sir. How can I help you?"

It was another bright-eyed young woman, although this one had red hair.

"Good morning. I bought this watch and it's not what my wife wants. I'd like to return it, if that's all right."

"Certainly. Do you have the receipt?"

"Yes."

I handed it over and she glanced at it and put it in her till. "You understand that it's our policy that we can't accept a return without a receipt."

"Of course."

She paid me slightly more than a hundred and fifty dollars and I walked out into the mall.

Of course, that kind of hustle wouldn't work in small places, I needed a big, busy store with set policies and indifferent management; still, it gave me some working capital and that was what I needed. My next stop was at a shop specializing in work clothes, where I bought a generic baseball cap, a pair of cruddy steel-toed boots, and a set of coveralls, all for slightly more than a hundred dollars. The bookstore provided me with a clipboard, blue and red ballpoint pens, and a pad of legal paper for ten bucks. On my way out, I stopped at a big hardware store on the other end of the mall and picked up one of their complimentary catalogs. Then I went back to the van and drove around to park beside a name-brand, chain-operated steakhouse near the mall. There I changed into the new clothes and waited.

Most restaurants do the basic cleaning at night and more during the morning just before they open and the steakhouse was no exception. Many managers wait until morning to do the bookkeeping and then dump the records, and that was what I wanted, the credit card receipts.

Sometime after 11:00 the back doors opened and two Filipino kids came out, carrying big plastic bags, and dumped them into a steel bin near the kitchen vents. When the door was closed, I walked over and found that the first was leaking fluid but the second crinkled when I touched it and so did the third. I tossed those in the van and drove back to my original parking spot.

I opened each bag separately and went through them. Anything I didn't want went into the bags that had held my new work clothes. The first bag was full of old menus, order slips, and paperwork but the second one had what I wanted near the bottom.

"Gotcha."

The strips of paper were yellow and crumpled and I smoothed them out and looked them over carefully to be sure. These days no one uses the old-style carbon slips for credit cards, the numbers get run through computers rented from the bank and those computers eventually spit out these long, narrow, double strips of white and yellow paper with all the information neatly printed on them. The accountants take the white copies, and the yellow copies get tossed, which was fine by me. I found two readable sheets and put them in my pocket and cleaned up the van, then I went over the sheets until I ended up with two complete credit card numbers and the expiry dates attached to good-sized sales. My stomach growled and I checked the dashboard clock.

"Time for lunch."

Out of kindness and a sense of fair play, I went back to the steak-house for lunch, it was the least I could do. They had a pretty wait-ress who brought me a rare roast beef sandwich and a spinach salad with hot bacon dressing and I said goodbye to my diet. The girl had a small tattoo of a crucifix above one eyebrow and something metal in her nose and we flirted gently back and forth while I ate my lunch and drank my iced tea. Eventually I asked her the name of the man-ager and she looked a little concerned.

"Gee, I hope everything's all right."

"No, it's all fine. I'm a general contractor and your place here needs some landscaping right away if it's going to look good for the sum-mer. Mebbe I'll bid on it. So, who's the boss?"

She scratched her head with the nub of a pencil. "Well, the main manager's Peter Dalrymple, but he's off today. Would the assistant be able to help?"

"No, I want the head honcho. It always works better that way, I'll call tomorrow."

After I ate, I went over the hardware catalog and wrote down the items I needed along with their cataloged numbers and costs. On the way out I stopped at the bar in the lounge and bought three dollars' worth of quarters. No one noticed when I pulled around back and slung the repacked pillaged bags back into their bins.

At the outside phone booth, I looked up the corporate number of the steakhouse in the Yellow Pages and asked to talk with someone in the accounts department. When a woman named Arlene-something came on, I cupped my hand around my throat to change my voice slightly and spoke louder than normal.

"Hi, this is Pete Dalrymple out of the Winnipeg Corydon store. My contact number at the bank for the customer service is coming back as out of date. Do you have a new number?"

The woman sounded worried.

"All right. Read me back the number and I'll double check that I've got it right. I just retyped the list and maybe I screwed it up."

She read me back a local number and I repeated it carefully and wrote it on my clipboard.

"...0...2...2. Got it. I've got 202 written down. Thanks."

Arlene-something accepted it as a compliment and hung up.

The next call was to the bank, where I was eventually patched through to a young man with a thick East Indian accent. "Commercial Accounts."

"This is Mr. Dalrymple, manager of the Corydon Steak Academy. Account number 5-4-3-8-9."

I'd pulled that number off one of the sheets from the garbage. He tapped the number into his computer and grunted.

"Go on, Mr. Dalrymple, how can I help you?"

The most promising credit card numbers from the garbage were written on the clipboard in front of me and I picked the one that had the highest charge.

"I've got a party that wants to book twenty seats this Friday. They gave me their Visa number and I want to check the name and make sure they can pay before I reserve tables on my busiest night. Can you tell me if the card can handle a charge of fifteen hundred to two grand? Something around there." I read off the number and the expiry date and listened to some more tapping.

"That's an account for Rachel Divischuk, Incorporated. There's no problem with that amount. Is that all you needed?"

"Yes."

We both hung up at the same time and I looked up the name in the phone book.

Apparently Rachel Divischuk, Incorporated was a modeling agency specializing in "The Fresh Faces of Tomorrow!!!" Go figure.

No one was waiting for the phone so I dialed the mall's hardware store and used a non-accent. "*Bon jour.* I'm sending down our handyman to pick up some items right away but I'd like to use my credit card to pay for them over the phone, is that possible? He will sign for the order, of course."

The young man transferred me to another department. "Hello, order desk?"

"Good afternoon. We need some items to build a stage for our models. Can you package them up for me and I'll send our handyman Allan down to pick them up?"

"Ummm, certainly."

"Wonderful. Do you have a pencil handy?"

He did and took the order in silence.

"We need a Dremel rotary tool package, the battery-powered one with the extra bits numbered . . ."

When I was done the man totaled the bill. "That'll be four hundred and thirty-two dollars, including the tax."

I gasped and he apologized.

"The most expensive piece is the Dremel, that's more than two hundred dollars just by itself. I have included our corporate discount."

"Oh dear, thanks. Well, that's why they invented credit cards. Here's the number . . ."

He made sure he had it right and put me on hold. A few minutes later he came back to tell me that the bill had gone through just fine.

"Wonderful. Now, I'll send Allan over right away. Where should he go, by the way?"

"The customer service entrance."

"That's fine, should he ask for someone in particular?"

"I'm Scott, I'll pull the stuff together at the loading dock. Your driver can ask for me."

"Alrighty then. Now, Scott, can I ask you a question?"

"Sure, I guess."

I lowered my voice to a whisper. "Do you think all this stuff will be tax deductible?"

He laughed out loud and told me he thought it would be, as long as I kept the receipt.

33

Scott was a well-tanned man in his late forties and he was waiting at the loading dock when I arrived. I backed in and hopped up onto the platform to greet him. "You Scott?"

He nodded and held his hand out in greeting and I took it.

"I'm Allan. My boss ordered some shit."

He gestured with his head at a pile of boxes on a steel shelf. I went over what was there and shook my head. Scott was holding a clipboard and he nodded politely and handed it over. As I checked the totals I kept repeating to myself, "Shit."

"Anything else you need?"

I scratched my chin and lifted my hat a bit while I ran my finger down the invoice.

"Nope. Guess Rachel's gonna make me earn my pay. Let's see, Dremel, assorted hand tools, five pounds of assorted nails, five pounds of assorted screws, three tarps, three sets of overalls, five hundred yards of heavy-gauge copper wire, twenty yards stainless steel chain, and a dolly. Looks good."

I signed the bill illegibly and was given a copy in return.

"Thanks. I haven't used one of the Dremels before, does the battery come powered up?"

"No. You've got to plug it into a standard power outlet for about two hours to get a full charge."

I loaded the dolly into the van and lowered it onto its side where it wouldn't move. Then I put the boxes on the passenger seat and on the floor beside the dolly.

"Thanks."

Scott nodded. "Good luck."

I grunted and drove away.

Walsh had a copy of the *Sherlock Homes Guide to Winnipeg* map in the compartment under the passenger's seat and I opened it beside me as I drove. I was still short of cash and I was running out of time and energy. On the north side of the city was another big shopping mall. I aimed towards that and parked nearby beside a small hotel with a big beer vendor built into one corner.

The vendor was covered in glass and neon signs and right past it were a half-dozen stalls for cars, each with a separate electrical plug and a freshly painted sign that read "not for block heaters." I ran an electrical cord from one of the plugs through the passenger's side window of the van and plugged in the Dremel. When I finished that, I changed back into my suit and overcoat, both of which were starting to look wrinkled.

While I was closing the van door, I realized a young guy in an Adidas track suit was leaning against the wall and watching me. He was slightly built with thin, ropy muscles and in his late teens or early twenties with pale blue eyes, the deep tan you get from skiing, and short brown hair that stuck out from under a baseball cap that advertised Moosehead beer.

"Howdy."

He nodded at my parking space. "Those are for staff only."

"Sorry."

He shrugged. "Not that I care but you should know that those plugs only run for half an hour and then shut down for an hour. That's when they're on and I don't think they're on this month."

"That's cheap."

He shrugged again and lifted a coffee mug that advertised a strip bar and some event called "Legs! Legs! Legs!" "That's the owners. Lithuanian-Poles. Cheap through and through. Stingy."

I looked at the cord and the van and thought. He went on.

"You need power for what?"

"Hmmm? To recharge the batteries on some power tools."

He drank some more coffee. "I could help. Run the line into the vendor and plug it in the back outlet."

"How much would it cost?"

"How long do you need?"

"Two hours. Two and a half."

"That'll work fine. Twenty bucks?"

"Ten?"

" 'Kay."

I nodded and the kid took the plug through the door behind him before holding his hand out to me. The bill vanished and I shook his hand to seal the deal.

"You are . . . ?"

"Seth Varaniuk. My grandparents own the place."

He spat carefully onto the concrete from between his two front teeth.

"Okay, Seth. I'll see you in a few hours."

All that done and I still needed cash, that hadn't changed. The new mall was maybe three times as big as the first one and I wandered it with my hands in my pockets and my eyes moving over everything. There were electronic stores and music stores, watch repair places and banks, stores selling jewelry and more selling overpriced women's clothes. Stuff you wouldn't believe or need or want or wish on your worst enemy. Halfway through, I had to stop to rest and sat down on a bench across from a giant sporting goods store.

When I'd recovered, I went into the place and used some of the last of my cash to buy an assortment of hats, some better quality hand tools, and a cordless electric glue gun. There were racks of lockers near the information kiosk so I put my purchases there and kept looking. All through the mall I found things I could use but nothing to help my central problem, which remained money.

A song from the creepy movie *Cabaret* went through my mind. "A mark, a yen, a buck, or a pound . . ."

Or Pink Floyd. 'Cause it's all about the Floyd and the *Dark Side of the Moon*.

"Money . . ."

I bought ten yards of rocket ignition fuse from a hobby store. The clerk was looking down the blouse of the lady behind me in line so I also pocketed a set of Exacto knives and some electrical tape. At a Radio Shack I picked up AA batteries, copper wire, and a cheap-model Polaroid camera and film. At a big drugstore I found an electric toothbrush, a box of cotton pads, some double-sided carpet tape, a tube of generic super glue, and a package of latex gloves. Which took care of the rest of the money.

When I went back to the locker, I noticed a woman feeding a five-dollar bill into a bright red machine beside the information kiosk. The machine licked the bill in, chirped, and then dumped five loonies out for change through a slot in the bottom.

I said, "Praise the Lord."

The woman, a tight-faced bottle-blonde with big pores spaced far apart, turned to me and frowned. She looked as though she was in her late fifties and hadn't enjoyed a single day of her adult life. "You should not blaspheme. It's not proper."

I grinned broadly. "I agree and I'm not."

She stared coldly at me and her lips pursed tightly, so I asked her gently. "Have you accepted Jesus as your own personal savior?"

She nodded once abruptly and walked away briskly but I kept smiling because I'd found the missing cash I needed. To make sure, I reached into my pocket and pulled out a quarter, which I let roll onto the floor and under the drink machine beside the change machine.

"Oops."

No one seemed to be watching and there were no cameras that I noticed, so I leaned down between the machines to retrieve my change. Amid the dust bunnies the cash machine was attached to the wall by a quarter-inch steel chain that ran through a narrow pipe welded to the bottom of the unit. The power cord was a normal, rubberized one that ran straight from a hole in the wall to the machine itself and no plug was visible. I was very careful to touch nothing with my fingers or palms.

Standing up, I found that the machine was owned by Apex Machine Works, which had been servicing the public's needs since both 1975 and 1981. That confused me a little but I just smiled and patted the machine gently with the edge of my left hand before emptying my locker and leaving.

Seth, the beer jockey, was gone by the time I reached the hotel but the guy who had replaced him handed over the other end of the cord with no questions and I drove back to the mall. In a far corner of the lot I checked to make sure the Dremel was powered up and then I changed into the overalls. Before I did anything else, I opened the tube of glue and used it to varnish my fingertips until there were no more fingerprints. The glue dried in a couple of seconds and that was that. Then I wiped down the tools and my clipboard.

I opened the attachment pack that came with the Dremel and installed a ceramic saw blade onto the tool and pocketed two replacements. Stealing a set of licences from a random van took only a second and I used four lengths of the carpet tape to stick them over the ones the van was already wearing.

34

There were some parking spots reserved for emergency vehicles next to the mall's entrance nearest the change machine. I used one and walked in wearing a gray baseball hat and wheeling the dolly in front of me with the Dremel and a roll of electrician's tape sticking out my back pocket.

"Howdy."

The girl behind the information desk was wearing a dark blue jacket and skirt with the name "Candy" in gold lace just over her heart. She looked at me disinterestedly and then went back to reading a glossy brochure. I stood there patiently until she bothered to look up again. "Can I help you?"

"Sure can. You can write Out of Order on a piece of paper and hand it to me so I can put it up. I'm from Apex and they need to re-calibrate the cash machine back at the shop. There have been some problems."

She looked me over and shook her head. "So why don't you have a, you know, company-insignia-type-thingie on?"

She was writing on a piece of paper and doing it quite elegantly.

I answered. "I'm a private contractor doing salvage and hauling. Apex just contracts me to do the heavy lifting and grunt work."

She handed me the note.

"Wanna feel my muscles?"

She sneered. I went and posted the sign over the change machine, using her tape, and then knelt down with my back to the desk. There was a small chance the cops might be able to pull fingerprints off the tape or the sign but the odds weren't good, what with the glue on the tips of my fingers.

There were a few shoppers around but no one paid me any interest as I went to work. In about twenty seconds, the Dremel had cut through the chain. Then I took a deep breath and started on the power cord. I figured I was insulated, using a ceramic saw blade plus the heavy-duty gloves, but if I was wrong, I'd get zapped into a crispy critter right away. In two seconds, though, the machine was free and I was unscathed, so I sealed the cord with electrician's tape and then taped it to the wall with a big X of tape.

"That's loud."

I looked at the girl and shrugged. "Almost done."

The machine was heavy, around three hundred pounds, and awkward, but I finally walked it out and levered it until the dolly could slide underneath. Then I tied it down with the canvas straps and tested the buckles.

"You'll get it back in a day or two."

She went back to reading her brochure, moving her lips slowly.

I wheeled the machine awkwardly out to the van and levered it ungently into the back before tucking the dolly beside it. With that done, I drove away at a sedate pace, stopping behind a convenience store to rip the stolen plates free and dump them down a storm drain.

It was almost 5:00 and getting dark so I kept my eyes open for some place to park and crack the machine. I was starting to feel nervous, when I found a brewery that was being demolished. It was surrounded by a high cyclone fence topped with barbed wire and right beside was another fenced lot where a produce company kept their trucks. It was just off a minor highway, so, to find me, someone would have to be looking right into the setting sun, heading south, and turning right immediately down a bad gravel road.

"The love of money is the root of all evil."

A preacher in Drumheller had said that, over and over again. I repeated it as I switched heads on the Dremel and used an expensive tungsten drill bit to make an eighth of an inch hole in each corner of the access hatch in the front of the machine. Then I used one of Walsh's screwdrivers from his tool kit in the back of the van as a lever and ripped off the whole heavy-gauge plate, pushing it at each hole and moving the unit just a little each time.

"Charity begins at home."

The preacher had said that too. The machine opened and inside was twelve hundred and fifty dollars, nine hundred in fives and tens, three hundred in loonies and fifty in quarters. I pocketed the cash and dumped the coins into a plastic bag. That was awkward because of the gloves. Then I switched heads on the Dremel and hopped out, kept talking to myself.

"And of course the Petshop Boys, who said, 'Let's make lots of money.'"

The next bit was the riskiest part of the whole thing so I worked fast to cut a two-yard gash through the fence and into the brewery. And when it was done, I cut a second gash along the bottom and levered the wires inward until they stayed put.

"Allez . . ."

The gutted cash machine slid painfully out of the van.

". . . Oops."

There was no need to be gentle so I muscled it upright and walked it through the fence and toppled it into the weeds. If I was lucky, no one would even notice it there. The two Dremel heads and the screwdriver also ended up in the yard. They'd match the cuts and abuse on the cash machine so they had to go. Resealing the fence took a couple of minutes and four yards of baling wire to lace the cut closed and then I was done.

My stomach grumbled as I started the van so I drove fast to a garish casino nearby. I pulled my suit on in the rear of the van and went in to a poor dinner in an overpriced, well-staffed restaurant under a fake waterfall. No one seemed to mind that I paid for the meal with one-dollar coins and a couple of quarters.

The waitress admitted she had a copy of the *Free Press* in the back and she generously allowed me to read it over coffee while I free-associated through the next set of problems. I was really no closer to where I wanted to be: I had rough ideas.

My coffee grew cold as I stared into space.

"A refill?"

I looked at the waitress and nodded so she poured and left. I folded the paper and put it off to the side. Then I went driving around.

35

I stopped on three separate occasions to get rid of stuff. The dolly I left beside a moving company's rent-all store and I shredded the overalls and dropped them into Omand's Creek. Lastly, the Dremel and its heads went into the brush at the foot of a stubby hill that looked seriously out of place in the middle of the city.

Because you can never be completely sure about the capacities of forensics.

I had stolen a copy of the Yellow Pages from the casino and I marked down the places I wanted to visit on a piece of paper: a sporting goods store, a home hardware place, and a party supply store. All of them within a mile of each other in the St. James industrial park. I parked in roughly the middle of a triangle formed by the stores and walked from there.

First was the sporting goods store, a big place called S.I.R. They took my money with no questions asked and sold me a cheapish pair of Tasco binoculars with low light capacity, range finder, and a built-in compass. I could have bought real infrared or starlight light amplification, but they were generally unreliable, extremely heavy, and ridiculously expensive, and the battery always wore out at the worst possible time. So I stuck with the Tascos, which had a pretty effective passive light-gathering system. Which would never run out of power.

It's a sore point. I went to jail once because some batteries failed.

Some long underwear. Spring or no spring, it was still cold. A suit of ridiculous-looking leafy camouflage two sizes too big so I could wear a tuxedo under (if I wanted, which I didn't). Wearing the suit, which was brown and green and had tufts of cloth sticking out in all directions, would make me look like a walking bush but I'd be invisible to anyone beyond ten yards in the right terrain. It might be useful, or I could save it and use it during deer season with my new bow.

I lingered over the hand and long guns in the far-left corner but resolutely turned away. No firearms acquisition certificate in the first place and some stupid judge had banned me from ever (legally) owning firearms forever in the second place. But guns were not what I wanted, not what I needed, nor did I need black powder or gun cotton or primers or any of the stuff so useful to turn into bombs.

I lingered some more over the knives. They had some Spydercos, made popular by Hannibal the Cannibal in the movies and books, but they were folders and not my favorite because folders sometimes folded their blades at the wrong time.

I have scars to prove that.

Further down the line under the glass, they had some Cold Steel knives and I picked up a small and very cheap Bushman's knife. It had good steel, the blade would never fold at the wrong time, it would keep an edge. And it was cheap enough so I wouldn't weep if and when I had to dump it.

Finally I found a heavy-duty backpack and added that to the cart.

The girl at the front counter was very pretty. "Would you like to sign for our giveaway?"

"No, I'm married."

"What?"

"No, I'm not from around here."

"Oh."

"What did you think I said?"

All my purchases went back to the van and then I went to the party supply store.

"Greetings."

The place was a two-storey brick building with a bright neon sign reading PARTY HEARTY.

The clerk was a fairly unattractive, black-haired man wearing a French maid's outfit. I didn't answer his first greeting so he tried again.

"May I help you?"

"Umm. No. I'll just look around."

He nodded serenely and went back to data entry. I found a plastic pail with handle to hold my selections. The store was big, maybe twenty aisles, and I wandered back and forth until I had found what I needed.

"Did you find everything you needed?"

"Yep."

He rang it through and came up with a big chunk of money. Press-on instant tattoos good enough to look like homemade ones, cheap sunglasses in a variety of styles, cheap glasses with plain glass in the lenses, a fake scar and two fake warts that looked surprisingly good, a plain black eye patch, cotton pads for changing the shape of a face, some good-quality buck teeth to fit over real ones. Even a decent wig of short, graying hair and a novelty voice changer, an idiot toy to make you sound like an alien.

On my way back to the car I detoured to the hardware store, where I picked up a new Dremel and a selection of cutting, drilling, and other heads. At a donut shop inside the store, I got the morning edition of the newspaper, and at the key-cutting place by customer service, I had two extra copies made of Walsh's car keys and one of his house keys. On my way out I saw a small kiosk selling cellular phones and I stopped and stared.

An idea was coming to me. Now, you have to understand that professional crooks don't like cell phones. There's no security, anyone with the right equipment can listen in.

Like Scott MacKenzie, a bank robber I'd worked with once or twice, used to say, "Just lie down and spread your legs. You will be getting fucked."

He'd believed in tailored dark suits, good guns, magnum shells, eight-cylinder engines in big cars, hollow point rounds, buckshot, and stocking masks. The cops had caught him in a crossfire outside a Regina credit union and put more than eighty rounds through his suit.

But cell phones did have their uses. I walked up to the guy there getting ready to shut down.

"Hi. Just a few questions, how do the payments work?"

He was about eighteen and tired of standing in a hardware store selling technology many of his customers only had contempt for.

"Hi. 'Kay. You pay for the phone here. You pick the plan you want off the list. You sign up for three, six, or twelve months. That's it."

"What kind of ID do I need?"

"Nothing really."

Five minutes later I walked out two hundred poorer with the cheapest model cell phone possible in my pocket and the cheapest possible plan in place. I had registered as Ken Graham with a fictitious address, job, and other pertinent data.

The only thing that had been real had been the money I'd paid.

Back at the van, I closed the door firmly before looking over my purchases. Most of the bulk was made up of cardboard boxes, plastic wrap, and so on. When all that was removed, I was left with a very full backpack and a slightly less full canvas shoulder bag. First I took the garbage out and stuffed it into a big bin behind a bakery, then I drove the van to a parking lot serving a restaurant across the street from another shopping mall.

With the bags in hand, I cleaned the van down with a rag soaked in gasoline siphoned from the tank. It made my head hurt but was guaranteed to ruin any fingerprints. Then I propped a copy of the current *Winnipeg Sun* on the steering wheel and put my new copies of Walsh's keys in the ignition. The original ones went back into the case under the van. I unfastened the stolen licence plates and dropped them into a bag for later disposal.

Then I came back and took a Polaroid of the paper with the keys prominently visible.

On the back I printed with the pen held straight up: "The son of a bitch Walsh is lying, he lent me the van, how could I have stolen it if he gave me the keys?" That went into an oversized envelope, which I addressed to the Manitoba Public Insurance Agency and dropped into a mailbox on my way to the bus stop. I had ten minutes to spare so I went into the mall and bought a bouquet of roses. Only then did I get on a bus towards home and sleep.

Moving through town towards home, I went from hedge to hedge and down alleys and across small parks and it took more time than I'd thought and twice I had unpleasant almost-encounters with dogs. I started to wonder about my sanity and desire to avoid surveillance. By the time I got home, it was past eleven and Claire was asleep on the futon upstairs with Renfield on my side of the bed. Her arm was thrown possessively over the dog and I had to nudge him hard before he left.

"You have an unnatural relationship with that dog."

She sounded sleepy. "Means nothing to me. Nothing. There's only you."

"Likely story."

She cuddled up to my naked back and kissed my neck. "Have a good day?"

"Well, I met a nice man in a French maid's outfit. You'd like him."

She laughed. "I let you out too much."

"I also bought you flowers."

She practically purred. "Good boy."

36

I woke up before four and crept out before Claire and Fred woke up. Renfield noticed but accepted a large piece of cheese as a bribe for silence. The night before, Claire had made up a half-dozen sandwiches for lunch with a gallon plastic jug of weak tea with lemon. That went into the backpack and then I headed out the rear door and cut through yards and down alleys.

It took me ten minutes to reach the park near the river, where I found an overgrown thicket of brush. There I settled down and watched my back trail for the next hour. While I waited I ate a sandwich and watched to see if anyone was following and when I was sure I wasn't being tailed, I cut out across alleys and backyards. I moved that way as long as I could until the river started to have houses and then I cut back towards Main. Once, to my surprise, I startled a deer along the riverbank that bolted abruptly into the false dawn, its tawny hide speckled with dew and its fat, little, white tail flashing a warning I couldn't understand.

At a grubby motel I phoned for a cab. A half-hour later I was crouched in the empty and sere field behind Walsh's house, getting ready to start generating some pressure.

A smart German general named Model once told his subordinates to "Attack, regain the initiative, impose your will on the enemy." He had used the line during a war he lost but it struck me as good advice.

Later on, he and his army ended up surrounded so he surrendered his troops and shot himself in the head. But it was still good advice.

I was about two hundred yards out and had the Bushnell scope from Walsh's house focused on his property. Nothing was happening, though, so when I got bored I would flip the scope over to the house two doors down, where an anorexic-looking woman in her early twenties was doing aerobics naked in front of her wide-screen TV showing CNN. When she was done, I guess she was over-stimulated because she climbed onto her bed and masturbated with a big yellow vibrator she kept in the top drawer of her bedside table.

At that range and with that magnification I could see she shaved everything—and the phone number on the cell phone propped up on her purse. I noted the number down.

It was about eight when she finished and I was trying to decide if I should buy Claire a vibrator when Walsh came out of his house and climbed into the Corolla I'd seen before, his second car, probably. The scope was so good I could even read the little sticker by the rear licence plate, "Don't Mess With Texas." When he drove away I flipped the scope back onto the bedroom of the self-help girl and left the scope there before retracing my path about half a mile to where the Schmengis brothers had their auto-wrecking and salvage yard.

There were crows in the sky cawing for love, and seagulls too, but those were looking for food and much quieter about it. I had decided that Claire didn't need a vibrator, and if she did I'd get her a smaller one, the other one intimidated me. Around the front of the Schmengis yard was a narrow access road but a chain stretched across the entry-way to the yard itself. Hanging from the chain was a large sign that read "Closed. Back in fifteen minutes," but it was old and tattered, as though it had been there for a long time.

Which was fine with me. I used the cell phone to call a cab and made it back downtown in forty minutes. Right beside the police station was a half-open concrete parking area, full of ramps, elevators, space for anything up to and including an SUV. I figured Walsh would either be parking there or in the parking lot under the station house itself.

Inside the building, security was pretty good with wide-angle-lensed cameras in the corners and more outside the elevators and fire doors. Across the street, though, was an open area with a phone kiosk so I went there and dialed Crime Stoppers.

The novelty voice shifter filled my hand and to the end of it I had taped a cleaned-out soup can to add resonance. To top it off, I spoke in a nasal, atonal voice, turning me into a nasal, atonal Darth Vader talking out of the bottom of an empty well.

"There's a guy called Sam Parker who lives in the North End of Winnipeg, I don't know where. He just scored a Taurus 44-magnum pistol off me along with a half box of Teflon-coated rounds. I think he's gonna use it to pop a cop."

The old woman on the other end became real excited and I waited 'til she shut up.

"How do I know? 'Cause Teflon rounds are for busting up Kevlar vests, you . . ."

I let it trail off.

"Right. So what's the number I need to get my reward?"

She gave it to me and I hung up and went home.

37

I spent the rest of the day cleaning house with Claire and making plans for the barbecue. My new purchases stayed in the bags and I figured there was no chance the cops would be doing a surprise raid on the house. Not after last time.

In fact, I imagined Atismak getting the report and putting a little tick against Walsh's name and going about his business.

At ten I asked if Claire minded making a phone call from any downtown club she chose to name.

"Any particular phone call?"

"Yep. A very specific one to a very specific lady. Don't leave a message, though, either talk to her directly or hang up."

"Right . . ."

"And it would help if you sound drunk . . ."

"Sure."

I spent ten minutes explaining while she dressed in blue jeans and a black turtleneck sweater.

"So I'm a neighbor to this woman, I saw someone in the field behind her place with a big camera pointed right at her place. I don't want to be involved but feel that girls have to stick up for each other. Right?"

"Bingo."

"Don't say that. I'll call from a gay bar, then."

"A gay bar?"

She smiled sweetly. "Yep. It's a great reason not to give a name. Repressed lesbian longing . . ."

After she left I realized she was enjoying this far too much.

The next morning I was up before dawn and put together a bag before catching the bus downtown. I changed into a new jacket, hat, sunglasses, and pants in a restroom under a big mall and then slipped into the service area through a locked but poorly sealed door in the corner. Twenty minutes later I called for limo service out to the Winnipeg International Airport and then from there to the downtown Delta hotel. From the hotel I made it to St. Norbert by bus and foot. No way anyone followed me.

The rest of the day I spent wandering around Robillard's neighborhood but the house was tight. No one came in or out, the garage door was down, the yard was serviced by an agency, they had a satellite dish for TV, along with a short-wave antenna for either ham radio or a CB receiver. A working-class neighborhood.

Every hour or so I changed clothes. This hat with this jacket. This jacket with those glasses. Those glasses with this hat.

For half an hour I borrowed a poodle from a house down the block where it had been chained up under a dying tree. We walked around, she peed on everything, sniffed everything, and licked me a lot. When I left to go home, I put her back in her yard and she whined.

After supper Claire and I checked the house for bugs or surveillance, didn't find anything, and finally bundled Fred up in the *uber*-stroller for a walk. The dog came too.

"Stay. Sit. Wait."

Claire laughed.

"You better not be laughing."

"Right."

I untangled the dog from a tree and we continued. When Claire had caught her breath, she leaned into my arm. "So what happens next?"

"Walsh's life is becoming strange. His van is stolen but someone had the keys so it can't be stolen and they send a message to the insurance company saying exactly that. That's a problem. Walsh is receiving grief from the cops because he didn't get in trouble for beating me but two other guys did. That's a problem. Atismak is probably asking some questions about the first call to Crime Stoppers and he's definitely asking questions about the second call. And that's a problem."

I untangled the dog from a woman in a wheelchair and apologized, then we went on.

"Then some neighbor calls the cops and says there's some pervert peeping her. The cops find his scope with his fingerprints in a field behind his house. That's a problem."

Claire listened well. "But it's going to get worse?"

"Yep. Now, Robillard's not so easy. I can't see him giving up and walking away."

"That's another problem."

"Yeah."

"So deal with this one first."

The next morning I took a bus to a new mall and used one of the bank of phones outside a restaurant. In quick succession I made calls to the major crimes unit at the police station, victim's services at the court, and then Walsh's home. The results were that the cops told me that Walsh was at the courthouse, the courts told me he was scheduled to testify and, to top it all off, no one answered when I called his home. Which all made up my mind for me.

A new bus took me to within ten blocks of the Schmengis junk yard. From there I walked until I was outside the front gate, where I didn't pause at all.

Without thinking about it, I pulled a balaclava down over my eyes and crossed the invisible line into someone else's property. With an eighteen-inch length of heavy-gauge iron pipe, I was ready for anything. I had padded the striking surface with duct and electrician's tape in case I had to cosh someone. In the backpack was the fully charged Dremel, a selection of heads for it, a length of bike chain, and another padlock still in its plastic case with the price sticker neatly affixed.

Seagulls and crows and ravens picked over the piles of neatly organized piles of garbage as I walked towards the rear of the yard. I could see most of the crane I was interested in. It hung motionless in the sky with its round, hockey-puck-shaped cargo swaying not at all in the wind. Finally I saw the cab of the crane itself. I had seen it before and it had been moving scrap machinery around but now it was simply sitting there on big caterpillar treads with the control booth stuck on like an afterthought. Beside it was a tiny lean-to built right onto the back fence of the lot and there was no one around that I could see. The pipe slipped into my gloved hand and I listened but could hear nothing, no voices, no radio, no movement, nothing. Was there really no one around?

It couldn't be so easy.

In the lean-to I found a bright yellow hard hat, some earmuffs, and a set of keys attached to a billet of wood on which was carved "Crane." When I walked over to the crane I found that the batteries were ninety percent charged and that the diesel tanks were more than half full, so I got into the cab and stared at the sixteen separate levers and nineteen separate buttons.

The engine started with a half twist of the key and I lowered the crane until it was parallel to the ground with the deactivated electromagnet maybe two yards above. It was kind of funny, really; you can learn lots of stuff in prison. I know how to build a bomb out of what

I can find in most janitor's closets. I know four ways to kill a man with a piece of newspaper. No, five.

I know how to torture and kill, maim and wound, steal and con. I can hot-wire most cars, build a gun out of pipes and some duct tape, and sew a knife wound shut with fishing line and wax. I learned how to drive a Caterpillar tractor while working in Drumheller Prison, moving a prefabricated greenhouse to the right place a piece at a time.

Avoiding the access road was simple. I backed out through the three-yard-high plywood fence and turned right. The ground, though, was soft and slippery, so I angled up onto an unused railway bed and drove on the pebbles and gravel with the rails themselves far under the treads.

It took ten minutes to reach Walsh's house and then I reversed again and plowed through his backyard towards the house. When I was close enough, I maneuvered the crane with the parallel switches and finally lowered it until it was almost, but not quite, touching the roof of his house.

Then I turned the electromagnet up to full power and snapped the key off in the starter.

I hopped out and wrapped the chain around to seal the cab and then I put the padlock on the chain and locked it. That key I pitched over my shoulder, then walked into the field and started a roundabout route home.

I wasn't sure what an industrial electromagnet would do to Walsh's computers or files or toys, but I suspected it wouldn't be good. As I walked away, I wondered how long it would be before someone called someone.

According to Mildred Penny-something's news report later that night, it took four hours until a neighbor realized maybe the giant crane in Walsh's yard shouldn't be there. During that time the magnet completely erased the hard drive of six computers and more than six thousand floppy and CD-Rom discs. It also irretrievably damaged three TVs, a microwave, a short-wave ham radio receiver/transceiver, and sundry other devices.

On the bus ride downtown the next day, I thought about bombs and stared blankly into space. Wiring, detonator, timer, shrapnel . . .

"What the fuck are you smiling at?"

There was a man standing beside me in the corridor of the bus. He looked to be in his early twenties with black hair cut short, a nose frequently broken, and eyes hidden behind dark sunglasses. He wore blue jeans and a denim jacket covered in copper studs. His right hand was behind his back and his left hand was on the rail in front of me. His fingers were covered in thinly drawn, organically shaped tattoos, designs whose name I had forgotten.

"Was I smiling?"

He leaned down and I could smell cigarettes and stale sweat and just a hint of grass. "Yeah, you fuck."

I looked mildly at him. Could this be a set-up? If so, cops or Robillard? Did it matter? No, so I said it quietly. "Well, then I will."

He stared at me through the sunglasses and I stared back until he flinched and I knew he was going to back down. And he mumbled out loud, "Alright then."

He fled the bus and I went back to thinking about bombs. There were other things to worry about, like the casing or body of the device, anti-tampering devices, back-up fuses. . . . All in all, easy as pie. I had a few good ideas so I stopped at a convenience store and bought a huge mug of thoroughly toxic coffee along with a pad of generic graph paper and some pens. With that in hand, I went back and found a bench in a small park about two blocks from the house and started to sketch.

38

Near as I can tell, it was an accident, it certainly wasn't due to my own observation or alertness, I was just in the right place. Blind luck.

I was sketching on a bench at the rear of the park where there were deep shadows cast by big elms and small pines. After a while a very old-model, dark blue station wagon pulled up and parked. There were four adult figures in it, one driving, one riding in the passenger seat, and two in the back, and, as I watched, one of the ones in the back seat climbed into the cargo space in the rear.

A sedan full of adults was warning enough, but a couple of seconds later the windows on one side rolled down and I heard the ratchet-click of a pump-action shotgun being loaded. Before I knew it, I was off the bench and moving around to the side, keeping close to the trees and next to the redbrick front of a Baptist church that bordered the park. The last elm was about three yards from the van and I moved up beside it and waited in the shadow.

"... so where the fuck is he?"

The man was young with a tinny, nasal voice.

Another voice answered, older, still male. "No idea. No idea at all."

I could vaguely see that all the men in the car were white, mostly young, and wearing dark blue Nike track jackets with the white piping on the sleeves and black toques sitting high on their heads. Gang bangers? Cops?

"I feel like an idiot."

A third voice. Was this a hit? A drive-by? A home invasion? I chanced another look. The car was idling. The guy in the passenger seat was fiddling with something between his legs.

The guy in the back bench was leaning against the door nearest to me with his legs stretched out on the bench itself and a towel stretched across his lap. The last guy was crouched in the trunk area, holding two, big, gallon glass pickle jars full of fluid with rags stuffed in the tops. Molotov cocktails? Simple to make, gasoline and dish soap, and I wondered if the fuckers had scored the jars with a glass cutter to let 'em fragment when they landed.

"So where the fuck is he? His bitch is there, so's the brat. Should we just go ahead? I mean, the wheels is hot, right? I mean, we gotta do this, right?"

I realized the whole neighborhood was quiet, no kids on the street, no one working in their yards. Nothing. Some kind of ESP, maybe. Some kind of group consciousness.

"Shut up."

Not cops and not a home invasion, which meant a hit. I looked down the street and saw that my house was on the same side the guy in the bench seat was facing, along with the guy in the shotgun seat. Funny that name, not enough to laugh but funny anyway, aptly named. In my head I could imagine them driving up with the windows down and parking across from my house. Guy in the back seat opens up (he probably had the shotgun), guy in the passenger's seat opens up (a pistol, maybe), driver just drives when he has to, parks when necessary, so boom-boom-boom, then, after a second, the guy in the rear opens the door, hops out, lights the cocktails, tosses them through the blown-open window.

My house. Shot up and burned with my wife and my son inside.

I moved in a rush. There was half a red brick on the ground, fallen and half-rotten from the church wall, and I scooped it up in my right hand and took two steps forward as I wound up and let fly. It hit the half-open driver's side window like a bomb and blew it into a cloud of safety glass that still managed to razor away about half the driver's face.

"Shit!"

I was still moving and I opened the rear door with brutal force. The guy in the back fell halfway out of the car. There was a shotgun on his lap and I plucked it from his nerveless fingers as the station wagon surged forward three feet into a cargo van parked in front of the church. Someone else in the car swore.

"Shit—shit—shit . . ."

Pump shotguns are all the same. Slide the fore-end back to put a round into the chamber, pull the trigger, and fire. Then spray and pray. I aimed at one guy in the rear of the car and caught a glimpse of his terrified face as I changed the point of aim.

The gun was loaded, which was nice.

"Boom!"

It was smaller than a twelve-gauge, maybe a twenty or a sixteen, and the tongue of fire from the muzzle flash went into the Molotov cocktail in his right hand. With a whoosh it went up and filled the back of the wagon with flames and screams.

The passenger in the front had retained his cool and now he was leaning around the screaming driver and shooting at me with a short-barrelled semi-automatic pistol, one of those useless nine-millimeters cops are always bitching about. "Crack."

The bullet hit the tree beside me and peeled off a big square of bark. "Crack—crack."

The bullets went past me on the other side as the wagon was bucking and grinding against the van, but by that time I had the shotgun re-aimed.

"Boom! Ratchet-click."

The barrel was almost touching his hand as it went off and took off about half his forearm. For a brief moment I could see the twisted chunk of plastic and alloy that had been his pistol buried in his arm up around his elbow. He started to scream and lost interest.

"Fuck. Fuck. Fuck."

The guy with his head on the ground was fumbling at his belt for something, a gun, a knife, who knew?

"Boom."

The barrel was actually touching his right knee and suddenly the guy had more and better things to worry about than me.

The heat was unbearable so I stepped back to the tree and looked at my handiwork. Guy in the back, still screaming, cooking and howling, guy on the ground, holding a knee that wasn't there, guy in the passenger seat minus an arm, driver silent now, either bled out (maybe), or hit by stray pellets/bone fragments/bits of the pistol and out of it. I flipped the shotgun into the rear of the wagon just as the fuel tank cooked off.

Time to go. I went through the park, fast as I could sprint. The park ended in a chain-link fence and I went up over it and down the alley.

As I walked downtown, cop cars and ambulances passed me, and I walked and thought and in about an hour, I reached a thrift store that sold me new-used blue jeans, a black turtleneck, black runners, and a generic black baseball cap. Once my original clothes were in a garbage bin, I sat back and counted money before taking a cab back to the archery shop, where three teenagers were using recurve bows to make small holes in paper targets. I watched them for a moment while Frank did something under the level of the counter by the cash register.

"Yee-ha!"

He held up a scratch-and-win lottery ticket and waved it in my face.

"Won ten bucks."

His eyes were alight with glee and he barely registered as I counted bills out onto the counter.

"I'm gonna do something nice for myself."

He looked at me suspiciously. "Yeah?"

"Uh-huh. Gonna take the bow home today."

His face split in a grin and he took it down from the rack behind him. "That's great. She misses you."

I looked carefully into his face but he seemed serious so I didn't say a word until he'd put the money away. "I'd also like to get some broad-head arrows."

"No problem. Got just what ya want."

He pulled out some sealed foil packets and I examined them gingerly and poked them with the tip of my finger.

"All right, I don't understand."

He tapped the foil packets. "These are the edges. Surgical steel so sharp they're only good for one shot before they're dull. They're called Thunderhead Broad heads and I can let you have six of them for sixteen dollars each, which is my cost."

I winced and made the exchange.

"Good hunting and remember that deer season hasn't started yet. So don't be caught."

He had provided me with a garbage bag to hide the bow. Outside the shop, a police car whipped past with the sirens wailing and I turned back to Frank.

"Oh, I'm not hunting deer. You still coming to the barbecue?"

"Yessirbob. Wouldn't miss it."

Outside, I used a pay phone. "Hi, Claire."

"Hiya, babe. Still working?"

"Yeah. Still working."

"No problems here. Bit of excitement down the road, though. Car caught fire."

I gave her a chance but she had nothing to add.

"Anyone hurt?"

She sounded concerned. "Four of them. Two dead and two really badly burned."

Hey, I was getting better at this not-killing schtick. "Well, that's good. Talk to you soon."

"Love."

"Love."

39

With Frank's permission I took over one of the lanes and started to shoot. An hour later my arm was exhausted so I took off and went around to the rear and stashed the carefully bagged bow behind a dumpster.

It was still light outside so I took a bus downtown and started to walk around, thinking about Walsh until it was dark enough to deal with Robillard. Inside, the anger roared for release.

But I didn't let it go.

A block away from Buttes, I stole a Honda Civic and drove off to pick up my bow, then headed to Robillard's. I parked nearby and walked into the woods beside the road, where I pulled a balaclava down over my head to blur my outline and eliminate the shine of exposed skin. The dark clothes helped and over top I pulled a dark green, hooded, fleece jacket about four sizes too big that the owner of the Civic had left in his trunk. That blurred my outline even more.

But the main thing to being invisible is how you move. It's the hardest thing there is to teach anyone, how to move invisibly. If you want to be unnoticed and invisible, move slowly. Go as slow as you can and as quiet and precise as you can. Are you there yet? Good, now move slower.

Lift your foot an inch, pause, scan slowly by moving your eyes first and then your head, rely mostly on the corners of your eyes, they're more sensitive to movement. Move your foot forward a couple of inches. Put your foot down, toe first, brush any twigs or sticks aside now with the edge only. Scan again. Put the weight on that foot, raise the other an inch. Scan again. If someone is ten feet away from you in the dark, they won't recognize you as being human if you move that slowly. Half the time they'll edit you right out of what they see.

And you can kill them.

It took an hour and a half to cover the hundred yards to the house and another ten minutes to find a window that led into the basement. Crooks don't like alarms in general so I took a chance and popped the latch with my pocket knife and then went in headfirst. It was luck and skill that I caught myself before falling into a sink some ass had put directly under the window. My muscles ached as I held myself there for a good five minutes while I listened for any sign that anyone had heard me. After, I lowered myself the rest of the way through and reached back for the bow on the grass outside.

Only when it was ready with the arrow in place did I look around the room. It was a small utility area with a washer and drier and a rack for fine clothes that needed to air-dry. The surfaces were so clean that I could see in the pale light reflected through the open window. Off to the side, bright light was shining under a door. I took two steps and listened.

After the noises of the crickets and the frogs, the two human voices seemed strangely pedestrian. One was male and agitated and the other was female and calm. Underlying the voices was a strange sound that took a minute before it finally registered, the tinkle of glass on glass, as though something was being drunk. Carefully, I turned the knob of the door until it opened a little and pulled it towards me until I could hold it in place with my foot.

No one reacted so I took a deep breath, pulled the string back to full draw, and stepped out into the main part of the basement.

"Just the man I want to talk with."

Robillard's wife was on the padded cocktail stool nearest the wall and she froze in the act of pouring a drink while the man himself stood closer to me with nothing in his hand. The woman was three yards away and beside her was a short-barrelled, lever-action carbine with its barrel resting in an ornamental (I hoped) spittoon.

"Don't move."

He froze and I looked hard at him. The tracksuit he wore was a deep purple and it had the tiny design of a devil with raised pitchfork above where his right nipple would be. Sandra put her glass down and placed both hands flat on the bar, but I focused loosely on the circular sight installed in the bowstring itself. It lined up neatly with the tiny plastic marker just above the bow's grip, which in turn lined up with Robillard's stomach.

"Great. Now let's keep this civilized. If I let the string go, then the arrow goes whoosh and plants itself right into fat-boy's belly. The arrow is made of fiberglass and is tipped with a broad head tipped with three blades. The blades are sharper than a scalpel and come in foil pouches as an added guarantee of both cleanliness and sharpness. The arrow will burrow a two-inch-wide hole through your stomach and come out your ass at the same speed."

He made some kind of gobbling noise.

"Now, the arrow won't kill you right away, not where I'm aiming. You will be, in hunter's parlance, 'gut-shot.' Sorry about that in advance in case you get stupid and this gets out of control."

Sandra cleared her throat but I rode over whatever she was going to say. "So let's talk. Oh, yes, one more thing: you should know that I am holding the string back against fifty pounds of pressure, so I can't keep this up for too long. That should encourage conversation. If someone shoots me, then I let go of the arrow anyway and the same gut-shot situation comes about."

Robillard spoke in a cold voice full of imitation arrogance. "You can't be serious, to threaten me with a toy?"

"I am. You tried to hurt my family, of course I'm serious."

The woman looked at me intently but I paid no attention to her.

"So, fat-boy. Do I have your attention?"

His voice came out in a kind of enraged croak. "Yes."

"Good. Now why shouldn't I shoot you?"

"Fuck you! You ain't got the balls."

He gobbled some more and it sounded like a question and a statement so I shook my head.

"I thought we had an agreement."

He snarled and tremors ran across his body. "You killed my cousin and fucked up four of my boys and threatened me and then Walsh comes around and . . ."

The woman didn't move but her eyes were shifting to the rifle even as I answered Robillard.

"Slow down. We had an agreement, right? You were to stay away from my family and me. Right?"

"FUCK YOU!"

His roar made Sandra twitch violently.

"I said: RIGHT?! Or don't you fucking UNDERSTAND?!"

Robillard flinched, Sandra edged her fine-boned hand a little bit along the edge of the bar and Robillard gathered himself, so I changed aim and let the string roll off my fingers. I forced myself not to move while the arrow purred off the rest and slashed through the air across the rec room. While it was in the air, I reached out with my right hand for the second arrow in its holder mounted beside the bow's grip. My fingers closed on the nock of the arrow as Sandra reached for the carbine. Robillard twisted to the side and started forward towards the pool table.

The next arrow came free and I put the still quivering string into the nock of the arrow and put the shaft of the arrow on the rest just above the grip. The woman's hand touched the slender part of the stock of the carbine, just below the receiver. Robillard stared blankly with his left hand on the top of the table and his right snaking underneath, feeling for something.

I drew the string back until the nock was right under my right eye and the first arrow struck the carbine right between the barrel and the tubular magazine below it.

With a sound like fingers on a chalkboard, the metal parted and tore, and the split carbine hung there, pinned to the bar itself. With that noise, Robillard stopped moving and the woman withdrew her hand from the wrecked weapon. The next arrow pointed right between Robillard's panicked eyes and he blinked frantically.

"Fat-boy. Why don't you show me what you've got under the table? Remember, if you shoot me, I'll just let the arrow go and you try to digest it."

Slowly he raised his hand and showed off a brightly chromed revolver the size of a small cannon. He put it on the table and took a step back.

"Another magnum? Fuck, you're civilized. Very civilized. Now, what do we do? Should I just walk out of here and . . ."

He didn't say a word and neither did his wife and I went on, "No, doesn't sound all that . . ."

The woman spoke up. "Bottom line it."

"The smart thing for me is to kill you both and burn your house down around your dead asses. See if the crime scene geeks can or want to pull my DNA out of the ashes."

Robillard spoke up. "Now, WAIT a minute."

I answered him conversationally. "And my arm is getting tired."

"No, wait. What if I promised to back off and leave you alone?"

The woman pursed her lips and listened.

"You already did that and you didn't," I said. "I've got no reason to believe you'll be honest this time."

Sandra spoke. "Okay, what if I promised? Not him, me?"

I switched aim at her and she didn't flinch.

"You?"

Her voice was soft. "Yeah. Me."

"Come here."

She got up and walked over very slowly with her hands held out to either side. Robillard's eyes flickered to the pistol on the table and back again and I addressed myself to him.

"Go ahead."

He stopped looking and stared off somewhere above me. The woman stopped about three feet away with the arrow pointed squarely at her chest.

"You'll promise?"

"Yes."

She took a deep breath. "We'll leave you and your wife and your son alone. We'll stop helping Walsh. We'll back off and let whatever happen naturally."

It was almost funny.

"Why should I believe you?"

She shrugged and there was no humor in her eyes. "Because I promise. I didn't know about whatever my husband sent at you. I would have stopped him. And I'll promise."

Robillard was getting angry. "Well, what about me? I already fucking promised."

She glanced at him. I shook my head and answered. "Your promise is worth nothing. Hers might be."

I looked her over again and saw a young, thin woman in mended blue jeans and a soft wool lumberjack shirt with a black and red checkered pattern. By no means would I have called her pretty but she did have character and her dark eyes were steady and unflinching.

"Can you control him?"

She glanced at him again and his face was turning purple with rage.

"Yes."

"Or?"

"If he breaks my promise, then it's my problem. May I?"

I nodded and she reached over and picked up the big pistol and held it loosely in her right hand while I lowered the bow and relaxed my arm. She turned to face Robillard and spoke slowly and carefully.

"Hon? You understand I gave my promise?"

"SHOOT HIM! Shoot him now, you dumb bitch!"

She went on as though he hadn't said a word.

"I gave my promise and I won't break it. Neither will you."

He roared something inarticulate and started around the table towards me.

"Kill him, you dumb bitch, just kill him. Here, let me do it . . ."

He kept coming and his right hand came up and dipped into his back pocket. A glittering straight razor with a pearl handle appeared in his fist and he moved easily towards me on the balls of his feet. Like a man intent on his enjoyment, he was riveted on me and breathing heavily. He passed Sandra and she slipped aside to let him go with an apologetic glance at me.

"You're . . ."

I never did find out what I was because she waited until his back was to her before she touched the barrel of the pistol to the back of his head.

"Put it down, hon."

She waited and he did nothing, and she whispered, her mouth about six inches from his ear, "Or I will shoot you."

I waited and he finally dropped the razor when she cocked the hammer.

" 'Kay. Mr. Parker, you can leave."

I walked over and pulled the arrow from the carbine and then put both away in the holder attached to the bow. For a moment I was at a loss for words and then she spoke. "I'll deal with this."

She touched the side of her husband's face with her free hand but the gun stayed steady.

"My promise still stands."

Robillard's eyes were focused inward and his mouth opened and closed in confusion.

Behind him, Sandra kept her eyes veiled while the corners of her mouth turned down slightly as though at an unpleasant memory. When I spoke, his eyes caught mine and then the gaze slipped slickly away.

"Never doubted it for a minute."

Oddly enough, I never had. Less oddly, I never heard of Robillard again.

40

The Civic ended up parked behind a strip club and I washed up in a ditch before taking a cab back home, where the cops and the firemen and all their superhuman crew were still working down the road. Claire took the bow and put it aside and then kissed me gently on the forehead before putting me to bed.

I dreamt of nothing and awoke to a large mug of tea sweetened with syrup. And another kiss.

"Long day?"

"Yeah. Longer. Longest."

She brought Fred in and he slept beside me on the futon while I held my wife and let the tea work.

"So what time is it?"

"One."

"'Kay. Gotta go to work."

"I figured. Is it almost over?"

"Yeah."

Claire watched while I dressed and then kissed me again before leaving.

In the rear-most booth of a Salisbury House diner, I lowered my head and exhaled bacon fumes and fried onion toxins. The coffee went down like a bomb and drove me into the bathroom and the cramps made me flee back onto the streets.

Walsh was in the Princess Street cop shop. That's where he was stationed. That's where he felt most secure. Surrounded by a blue wall.

That's where he was weakest because he felt most secure.

Cop shop. Off to the side was the Winnipeg Police Force Credit Union. On another side was City Hall. Down the street was a big parking garage. Past that was the Chinese Cultural Centre.

Walsh was a senior officer and the police station had underground parking, but would he park there? I remembered the figures I'd read in the paper: there were a thousand plus cops in the city, at least three hundred stationed in this one building. How many patrol cars? Fifty, seventy-five?

They'd be underground along with the EMT vans, and the surveillance vehicles, and the motorcycles, and the supervisor SUVs, and the paddy wagons, and the identification wagons, and the mobile Breathalyzer vans, and the. And the. And the.

Not enough space left for a sergeant to park, no matter how senior.

So I climbed the low concrete wall into the parking lot and started to walk up and down the ranks of cars. Everywhere there were cameras, small suckers the size of pop cans with wide-angle lenses to cover every inch of the structure. Undoubtedly tied to monitors downstairs, where the clerk gave out parking tickets and took money. I ignored the cameras, trusted my hat and high collar, and kept walking.

On the third level, parked near a walkway to the police station, was Walsh's car. Backed into a spot prominently labeled with a "Reserved" sign. Without a second glance, I walked until I reached the top of the structure, where I took the elevator down to the ground floor and out into the afternoon.

My head ached and I went in to the Chinese Cultural Centre to hide from the sun. And found myself staring into a glass case holding a terra cotta warrior from the Chin dynasty. A grim man with a sparse beard and mustache. A serious man.

According to the plaque on the wall, the statue was part of an army buried by the first Chin emperor to protect him in the afterlife. One member of an army of thousands of men and horses, all made out of clay. All the men with different expressions. Different faces.

A black-haired woman came up beside me. She was wearing the basic black blouse and skirt of a university student and carrying a backpack over one arm.

"Look on my works, ye mighty, and despair . . ."

She looked at my incurious face and blushed.

"'Ozymandias.' The poem. Magnificent statue, huh?"

"Gorgeous. Glorious."

The figure was dressed in clay armor and his hand was held out in front of him with the grip closed around air.

"Why isn't he carrying a weapon? He was a soldier, right?"

It was rhetorical but the girl answered anyway. "Oh. Originally they all were. The emperor had banned all weapons from the peasants so they wouldn't rise up against him. When his son took over, the peasants revolted. They had no weapons so they dug down to the clay soldiers and took their weapons. And overthrew the son."

She stared at the statue and bit her upper lip. I thought about what she'd said, about the arrogance that doomed the son. And then I left.

Outside, I ducked into an alley and changed hats and jackets before continuing. I had some useful stuff in my backpack, the Dremel with some spare heads, the binoculars, the electric toothbrush I'd modified, the cell phone, some spare hats, jackets, and sunglasses. They'd have to do. Pulling on latex gloves, I put the toothbrush in my pocket and checked building fronts and angles before walking up to the front door of a small, brownstone, office building. The doors were open and I walked in and past the receptionist, who was signing for a package.

She didn't even notice me as I headed up the stairs, taking two at a time. On the third floor there were three businesses, an import/ export business, a chiropractor, and an attorney. All busy. On the fourth floor there was a camp office, a travel agent, and a large bathroom at the front half of the building. Even luckier for me was the fact it had a window facing the parking structure about eighty yards away.

No one was in the bathroom so I took out the binoculars and focused them on Walsh's car. It was like I was in it and I started to hum to myself, repeating the incorrect words to an old Eagles song as I watched.

Scanning down, I looked into the tiny kiosk, where a uniformed security guard sat in front of three monitors. The picture constantly changed and every little while someone drove out and needed change or a ticket stamped and the clerk moved. Other than that, he was pretty much an inert lump.

I focused on one monitor at a time. First the one on the right. I'd watched the picture change five times when someone opened the door and I had to let the binoculars thud onto my chest while I washed my gloved hands, the quickest way I knew to hide the latex. A nervous bit of peeing later and a man in a white smock left and I went back to spying. The cell phone had a clock, which told me that it was almost three.

The monitor switched and I saw Walsh's car. In the bottom right-hand corner of the screen was written "Unit 250" and something else, and then the screen switched. Starting at quarter to three, a torrent of cars filled the parking lot and the passengers filed into the police station, the 3:00 to 11:00 shift coming to work. At five after three, a torrent of white men and women started to come out, the 7:00 to 3:00 shift leaving.

The monitor switched again and I saw Walsh's car with Walsh getting into it and the same words on the screen: "Unit 250—1509."

I put the binoculars away and took a walk through the rest of the building. On the eighth floor, I found an office in the back with no lettering on the door. I knocked briskly to be heard over a class of tap dancers one floor down but no one answered. So I pulled out the toothbrush and pressed the head to the lock and flipped the bugger on, keeping my body close by to absorb the noise.

Bzzz.

It was quieter than that.

bzzz.

I'd modified the Plaque Buster 2000 by removing the plastic bristles and gluing a tiny disc onto the front plate. Into that disc I'd inserted fifteen tiny lengths of copper wire as thin as hair, each of different length and bent at different angles. Insert said copper wires into a lock and turn on the engine, which makes the wires oscillate, vibrate, and turn. These wires in the lock are now caressing the tiny little faces that make up the working surfaces of a lock. Give it a few seconds and by sheer chaos theory, the lock is opened and the wielder of the toothbrush is allowed entry.

Of course, the lock would be very scratched up but it would take someone who knew what he or she was doing with a magnifying glass to discover that.

The room beyond was small and dreary, filled with a dusty, over-sized desk, armchairs, and a wooden filing cabinet. I relocked the door from the inside and walked to a closet in the far corner. It was the work of seconds to slip inside and crouch down on the floor with my knees drawn up to my chest. The door of the closet I left open an inch, both for air and because people are less likely to check a door if it's open.

Then I settled down to wait.

41

At 6:30 a security guard made a very noisy patrol of the building, shouting as she went, "Closing down for the night. Everyone out."

Thirty minutes after that, I stood up and did some quick calisthenics in the middle of the room to start my blood flowing. My eyes had adjusted to the half-light from the dying spring day and when I was feeling limber, I prepared to go to work. For the sake of silence, I pulled off my shoes and put them in the backpack before making my way downstairs to the lawyer's office.

There was one more thing I needed.

With a jacket around the toothbrush, it was even quieter but the lock was better and it took a good six seconds to make my way into the lawyer's office. It was even brighter in the office with light coming in the windows and from a computer screen with its screen saver on. I checked left and right for a security panel that would indicate a separate alarm system but saw nothing. Behind the receptionist's desk there was a closet, a likely location for a panel, so I slipped over and checked but there was nothing and I relaxed.

Again I locked the door and checked the suite out: reception area, two offices, one much bigger than the other. Windows with alarm wires set into the glass. Conference room with a big wooden table and comfortable chairs for six people, and a big, wall-mounted entertainment unit with sliding dark wood panels.

Inside the entertainment unit was a big TV along with a VCR, probably for viewing video wills. It took fifteen minutes to figure out the wires and separate the TV from the VCR and stuff the VCR into my pack. Followed by all the necessary cables, like video and audio.

The security guard made another noisy, clompy, sighing, sweep of the building, this time with a big flashlight throwing a lance of brilliant light ahead of her as she went. I checked the cell phone and found it was 8:05 on the dot. When the guard had headed upstairs, I looked through the rest of the office and finally found a bright orange extension cord in the closet of the bigger office, tucked away in the back.

At 8:15 the guard stomped back down the stairs to her post. I waited but I could hear nothing else so I kept working.

I wrapped a jacket around the cord and tied it around the backpack, and then snooped around and found two blank VCR tapes still wrapped in plastic in the receptionist's desk. I took one and sat down to wait. At 9:06 the guard came down the outside corridor, shining her bright light into every office and then continuing upstairs.

At 9:09 I opened the door, slipped out, locking the door behind me, and moved down the stairs, keeping near the edges where there'd be less creaking. At the top of the second-floor landing I leaned down and checked just in case she had a partner, but there was no one. At 9:10 I was outside and sprinting away from the building.

"Nice night for a walk, huh?"

There were three girls and two boys, about sixteen, standing under a street light, and the first boy was grinning as he went on. "Nothing to wear, huh."

They all laughed at that and one of the girls brushed her short hair back from her eyes. "You forgot your shoes, man."

"Oh." I sat down and put them on and one of the girls gave me a hand up.

"Thanks."

I still had the tools I'd used so I walked a distance before tossing the toothbrush with the gloves wrapped around it into the muddy Assiniboine River, where they vanished like they'd never been. On my way back towards a big government building and a bus route, I detoured to check out a statue blocked from view by a concrete wall and found that it was supposed to be in commemoration of Louis Riel, one of Canada's more endearing madmen-slash-politicians-slash-rebels-slash-saviors. I stared at the twisted nightmare and then patted its flank.

"I know just how you feel, pal."

42

Claire woke me up by sinking her fine teeth into the side of my neck.

"Okay. I'm awake."

She bit harder.

"No, really, I mean it. I'm awake. Honest."

She growled and shook her head and Renfield came over to sit about six inches in front of my face. He tilted his head down and to the side and flared his ears, and I realized that he was probably thinking that Claire's actions meant I was no longer Alpha male. His tail wagged half-heartedly and I figured he was possibly considering eating me. Claire let me go and Renfield slowly stopped wagging.

Claire looked over at me and smiled. "We've got a lot to do."

I cuffed the dog in the head and he rolled onto his back. Claire watched as I went down on all fours and grabbed his throat with my teeth and growled into his ruff.

"What are you doing?"

I spat fur free and got to my feet. "I'm showing the dog who's boss. And then I'm going back to sleep."

She cuffed me with an open hand and growled again, which made Renfield roll over and wag his tail. I laughed and kissed her. "Okay, okay, I've been wrong before."

She let me pull on my bathrobe before I went downstairs and midway down the dog caught up. I scratched him behind one ear. "Man's best friend, my ass."

Claire forced me into the kitchen and started me boiling eggs. Many eggs, lots of eggs, six dozen, to be exact. She had bought them the day before from a woman who sold them out of the back of her pickup, fresh from her farm. No tax and no packaging. To boil them all at the same time I needed every pot we owned.

"This is an unreasonable number of eggs."

She stood beside the kitchen table and peeled potatoes into a garbage bag. "It is."

The last eggs went in and I turned the burners on full.

"Why?"

"Egg salad and deviled eggs. Two dozen for the salad and the rest for hors d'oeuvres. You need to cook them for eight minutes at a full boil."

I sighed and sat down to watch the clock. At least it wasn't a difficult job. Claire came over and put a cutting board on my lap along with a bundle of green onions and a sharp knife.

"Cut them fine."

After the eggs I started to make iced tea. Five gallons of the stuff.

"This is silly."

Claire had two large bricks of butter she was whipping, one with garlic and one plain, that were supposed to go with the six dozen Kaiser buns I was still supposed to go get.

"No. It's a barbecue. Hot out, remember."

It was hard to forget that while I was stirring boiling water and adding cups of refined sugar and chugs of honey. According to Claire, the lemon went in later. She finished the butter and went out to check on the meat she had hung in the back landing.

"Perfect."

She had bought beef ribs and cheap cross-cut roasts and flank steaks and all the worst and cheapest cuts of meat, and now she intended to serve them.

"Some help here."

With my help we brought them down and laid them out on the kitchen table. She made her final scoring cuts and then started piling them on specific plates, depending on the size and the length of cooking time. As she worked, she rubbed handfuls of garlic and rosemary into the meat and then started to shovel about half of it into the oven, at which point I complained.

"That's not a barbecue."

"You poor sap. It's not the cooking method that's important, it's the sauce."

She gestured at the stove top where a pot was slowly roiling. Then she carried the rest of the meat out to our hibachi, a huge charcoal grill that had been our first purchase together. She had apparently started the fire before she'd bit me, and now plumes of smoke and steam emerged as she forked the meat on. I was curious, she had made the sauce when I wasn't there, so I finally asked, "So what's in the sauce?"

She was putting meat on the grill and whistling merrily. "Secret recipe. Are you sure you want to know?"

"Yeah."

"Okay. Rotting pork and beef fat along with really rotted anchovies, although minnows will do. All that gets simmered along with garlic, bay leaves, oregano, salt and pepper. Then white and yellow onions, more garlic and chili peppers. Then you add in tomatoes, dry mustard, and some dry red wine. To get a really good flavor you use hickory wood, which was why I started cooking the sauce two days ago."

"Minnows?"

"Minnows. The shiny ones are best."

"Gag."

She looked beatific. "I told you you didn't want to know."

She shooed me out.

I brought buns back from the bakery. "Much left to do?"

"Not really. There's the cutlery to set up and the Caesar salad to be assembled."

"So can I have a shower?"

She wrinkled her nose. "Wish ya would. Shave too, if you don't mind."

There was nothing to do but wait for the guests. And then they began to arrive and I had my hands full all over again. As I took coats from guests, I wondered if I was wasting my time. And as I wondered I worked, taking coats, smiling, playing the host.

43

All the guests came, at least I think they did. There were our neighbors from all sides, Ramirez and her mousy husband and quiet son. Thompson and his wife showed up a little late, but that was fine, at least they showed. Vanessa Rose showed up with a hulking boyfriend and they brought good will and cheer and an understated optimism that everything would be all right. The first thing Vanessa did was take me aside and tell me her boss had reconsidered and that we could keep the house for the full lease. Claire accepted this as our due and conned Vanessa into helping to baste the meat.

The weather was good so we set up in the backyard. Claire had reminded me not to put out the booby traps the night before, so I didn't have the extra chore of dealing with that. I have no skill with small talk so I handed out iced tea, grinned, shook hands, handed out plates of meat and salad, thanked people, agreed the weather was nice, hid the last of the beer from my lawyer, although he had brought it himself. That made his wife pleased with me.

More greetings, more thank-yous, more schmoozing. More small talk.

Thompson took me aside and asked if I'd heard.

"Heard what?"

He was very loud. "Walsh. Burp. He's in deep shit . . ."

There was one of those strange pauses in the conversation so everyone heard him.

". . . he's apparently been spying on a neighbor, he's accused of trying to steal his own car for insurance, he got insubordinate with some RCMP honcho. He's falling apart."

Thompson's wife walked over and grabbed his arm. "It's time to leave."

"Apart. Hic. 'Scuse me."

He started to say something to his wife and then he took a good look at the corners of her mouth. Then he agreed and they both left. Gradually, the rest of the party left too, fading away like mist and leaving behind litter and good feelings and, if not love, then an absence of fear. And when they were all gone, Claire and I cleaned up and laughed and then we went inside and made love and I fell asleep with my arms around her and hers around me.

I woke up at 5:00 in the morning and lay there. Claire still had her arms around me but I had rolled over onto my back at some point and above me there were dark shadow stains on the ceiling, the predawn blackness by which all others were measured.

In the quiet and the still, with my wife sighing, my dog snoring, my son whimpering, and my mouse walking very slowly on its wheel, I listened to my mind and my instincts.

In Walsh's house he had a framed diploma that showed he had gone to a very good combat shooting school. I had looked it up on a computer hooked to the Internet in the University of Winnipeg's library and found that the school taught "Combat Pistol Craft," along with fast draws and instinctive shooting. Unlike many other schools, though, Walsh's also encouraged students to carry a backup weapon and the instructors recommended something small but of large caliber, like a derringer or something similar. The logic being that most small, concealable guns were in smaller, weaker calibers. But derringers could hold one, two, even four shots and could be found in very large calibers indeed.

In Walsh's house were myriads of toys for grown-ups. He liked toys. He liked gimmicks. Tricks. He liked fancy. He had certificates showing he was good with batons and shotguns, unarmed combat and collapsible clubs, Tasers and first aid. He liked being a cop with a cop's tools and toys.

Claire sighed some more and outside a crow made an unlovely sound.

In Walsh's house his punching bag had slick spots on the left-hand side and low. As though he punched mostly with his right hand and aimed for the torso. Or else he kicked with his right leg.

In Walsh's house in his filing cabinet had been pistol targets marked ten yards with the center X blown away. Also rifle targets marked three hundred yards with groupings of five and four shots you could cover with the palm of your hand. But there were also pistol targets marked five yards with a scattering of five or six tiny holes all across. From what?

In Walsh's career he had killed several times. He liked it. He was good at it and people were happy when he did it. Twice, bad guys had taken his pistol away from him and he'd killed them. What with, the accounts weren't precise. Maybe with a backup gun he carried.

It was possible to lose a gun once in a struggle, but twice? That was carelessness. Cops aren't supposed to do that, they're trained not to lose their guns.

Walsh liked the adulation he received. He liked being tricky. He was vain. And proud. And he liked to do it all himself.

So maybe Walsh had let the bad guys take his main gun. Which made them real bad to anyone who heard the story. And made Walsh into an almost-victim. Until he shot them. And became a hero.

When he'd interrogated me he'd almost waved his Colt in my face. Why?

So I'd take it.

And he'd shoot me. With the backup gun he was trained to use. And he'd be a hero again. Which he liked.

Outside, the crow made another noise, which was answered by another bird farther away.

Suddenly I knew what to do. I'd been willing to set it up so Walsh would beat the shit out of me and someone would film it. Someone like my wife or my lawyer or Atismak. But this was better. What I now had in mind was much better.

I woke Claire up with a long kiss that grew in insistency. When she was fully awake we made love and the whole fucking world waited. And outside the crows sang to their gods and, for all I knew, their gods sang back.

44

At 10:00 the next morning I reached Walsh's car and walked past it, looking for the camera marked with 250. I had on dark sunglasses so I could look up with impunity and I remembered the angles so I found the camera in three minutes.

There I paused and looked around but there were no other cameras nearby. I was in a blind spot at the base of a pillar about ten yards from Walsh's car. Above me was the camera, set onto a steel platform bolted into the concrete; above that were heavy-duty air vents.

It took only seconds to jump onto the hood of a pickup truck and climb on top of one of the vents. The vent creaked but held and I had maybe two feet of space, which was just barely enough for my purposes. After laying out the tools from the backpack, I went to work, stopping to listen every few minutes for anyone coming or going.

I still had the car antenna I'd stolen from the parking garage days before and I'd used a clamp to attach a young girl's compact to the end. With that and some practice, I managed to get a look at the back of the camera a yard under me, using the small mirror. On the back of the unit were two, big, female receptacles, one for video and one for audio, and only the video was plugged in to a thin line leading into a hole drilled into the concrete. I checked through the accessories I'd bought the day before at a Radio Shack and found something that matched and fitted it first to the VCR, which I'd wrapped in a clear plastic bag. The VCR stayed on top of the vent and I started looking for a power source.

Again I was lucky. Less than three yards away there was a plug set into the wall, for what I don't know. Since the garage was indoors, they wouldn't need to run block heaters in the winter. The Dremel had a heavy-duty drill that served to put holes in the vent and into those I screwed two dull silver hooks to hold the extension cord until it reached the concrete pillar.

Then I hopped back onto the pickup truck and drilled more holes down the pillar until I could run the extension cord in a professional fashion to the outlet. I plugged it in and checked the VCR.

"12:00. 12:00. 12:00."

The blank tape went in and I folded the plastic back into place over everything and pressed the Stop button on the VCR. Twice I'd had to stop for cars or drivers walking to work, but I still had time as I checked that the wires from the VCR were dangling in the right spot, just below and to the side of the camera. With everything in place, I got into the blind spot of the camera and waited.

I emptied my pockets into the backpack, change, wallet, knife, but I kept the cell phone, I'd need that. I was wearing a dark blue windbreaker and a pair of loose track pants with tennis shoes laced tightly.

I had a few tricks to match Walsh's. Around my left forearm from just below my wrist to just past my elbow, I had on a plastic and aluminum guard. It had cost fifteen dollars (with tax) at a sporting goods store and its purpose was to keep skateboarders and in-line skaters from fractured wrists and hands. The hand guard came down over my palm and ended in a raised bit of plastic so I still had most of my dexterity.

Under the jacket I was wearing a sleeveless rubber T-shirt a half-inch thick. I had bought it over the counter at a sex shop that catered to fetishists of all sorts. I was hot and sweaty and really couldn't see the sexual appeal of rubber, but so it goes. It had taken twenty-eight minutes to put it on in a pay toilet and I was wearing it in case Walsh was carrying a Taser.

I was also wearing a hockey player's cup. Which made me feel a little more secure.

After I'd stretched the muscles in my back and legs, I picked up the phone and made my call.

He answered on the third ring. "Walsh here."

"Walsh, this is Monty Haaviko. I'm waiting by your car. In the carpark. I figure we got some talking to do."

Then I hung up and crushed the phone before pitching it away. And I stood there, feeling my blood singing through my veins and my lungs expanding and contracting. Feeling every fiber of muscle and bone and sinew.

The backpack went up on the vent beside the VCR and I took the opportunity to unfasten the connectors on the camera and plug in my own. Then I flipped on the machine to Record and hopped down again.

I wanted to run and hide. I wanted to get a good rifle and a good scope. I wanted to knife Walsh or blow him up or ambush him in a dark alley. I wanted for none of this to have ever happened. I wanted to turn myself inside out and vanish. I wanted a cold beer and a hot pretzel. But mostly I wanted to run. Hard and fast.

Instead, I waited.

Nearby the elevator *pinged* and I could feel Walsh approaching. I gambled with myself that he'd be alone, that he'd be ready to play his tricks, and when he came around the corner he was almost at a jog. His face split into a grin and he made a broad gesture with his hands to throw his arms open and show the butt of the Colt tucked into his belt.

"Here I am."

He walked towards me on the tips of his toes, bouncing with energy. I could imagine what was going on in his head: his life was turning to shit, none of the cops would talk to him, no one trusted him, listened to him, adored him. In fact, no one liked him anymore. And right in front of him was me, the source of all his suffering. Although he couldn't prove a thing. And even if I wasn't the source, then I was something upon which he could vent his rage. A bad man, an evil man.

So I smiled back and started the whole thing.

45

He was a yard away with his suit coat unbuttoned and his arms outstretched.

"Go for it."

So I did.

His right-hand coat pocket was heavy so I went for that with my right hand. The steel of the gun was cold as I dipped it out while I slammed my left palm into the center of his chest and drove him back.

" 'Kay. Now what?"

His face went pale with panic and fear as his hand scrabbled at the big pistol at his waist.

"Wait-wait-wait!"

"C'mon, Walsh, go for it."

The pistol in my hand was tiny, a two-shot derringer over and under pistol. Inaccurate at more than two yards, practically unrifled. A gambler's gun, a hustler's gun, an ugly gun.

"You can't shoot a cop."

My face tightened. "Not with this."

The gun broke open just before the trigger and two little shotgun shells popped into my left hand: .410 shotgun shells loaded into the .45 caliber gun, just a load of copper BBs over a wad of powder. Up close, one shot would scrape a face down to the bone like a cheese grater.

The gun went over my left shoulder and the shells went over my right to tinkle musically among the parked cars, and Walsh went for the Colt. He was good. Fast and trained, but I knew what he was going to do before he did. His right hand drew the pistol while his left pulled a loaded clip from the back of his belt; his right thumb dumped the empty magazine while his left hand turned the full one so he could seat it right. Before the hands could meet in the middle, I stepped forward and slapped the gun away under an SUV ten yards away.

"Next?"

Nothing happened and I watched Walsh carefully, focusing on his belly. Any move he'd make would show there first. As I stood there, I felt the tension leave me. Vanish. My right hand vibrated with the pain of smashing the heavy chunk of metal. I ignored that and stepped back into place. Walsh was breathing hard now.

"C'mon, you know what to do."

He didn't do anything for a second and then his left hand came up palm-first towards me while his right drew a tiny, bright orange piece of technology from somewhere. It oriented itself towards me and then there was a puff of air and I was connected to Walsh by two tiny darts trailing lengths of micro-thin copper wire from my chest to his gun. His face went slack and I dropped to one knee.

In front of me a tiny snowstorm of flecks of paper drifted to the tarmac and the Taser hummed. But I didn't feel it, the rubber shirt kept the current from me. I'd been Tasered before and knew what I was supposed to be doing, spasming slightly, immobile, helpless. Walsh jammed the trigger again and I felt a thin wash of power again, like you'd get from licking a battery. A big battery.

I braced myself on one bent leg and my hand and watched Walsh's feet less than two yards away. The flecks of paper were between us, a security feature of the latest models of Tasers, designed to be released whenever the gun fired, while an internal computer recorded time and duration of the shocks. To make it easier for a cop to convince a jury he'd been using reasonable force.

A poacher I knew once said that you can legally shoot anything that walked or crawled, flew or swam if you said the following magical words before you fire: "It was coming right for me." Cops had learned that right well. How many times had those words been uttered, *I felt threatened and, in my professional opinion, . . . ?*

Another wash of power and Walsh stepped forward and brought his foot back to field goal my lights out. And I drove my right fist up into his crotch.

While he was down I tore the wires loose and yanked the Taser out of his nerveless hand. It went over my shoulder too and I unclenched my jaw and waited for him to get up. As I watched, he puked up coffee and raisin bran cereal.

"C'mon, Walsh. Try again, you can do it."

He rolled to his knees and pulled a short length of metal from somewhere. A flick of his wrist and it was almost a yard long, a collapsible metal baton called an Asp. He swung it inelegantly, clumsily, and I danced back out of the way to give him time to get up.

"Motherfucker, motherfucker, fuckermother."

He shifted his weight as sweat soaked his collar. I spoke gently, "C'mon, swing batter, swing . . ."

His left hand was towards me again to hold me off and his right held the Asp ready over his shoulder. When the blow came, it whistled, a killing skull breaker aimed at the crown of my head. I caught it on my raised left forearm and felt the plastic and aluminum sheath break. But by then Walsh was commited and completely open and I let one perfect punch go. It started behind my hip and I threw my shoulder first and then my elbow and then my wrist and then the knuckles.

A clumsy and simple jab. Dempsey would have wept. Ali would have spanked me. Tyson would have bitten my ear off. But it worked.

I was aiming at a space six inches past his head and it hit him right on the point of his chin. He paused as I recovered balance. And he didn't look like much there on the concrete, he didn't look like much at all.

"... and the bloody Red Baron went spinning out of sight ..."

No one heard me and five minutes later I had the VCR unplugged and in the backpack. Two minutes after that, I was out of the car park and looking for a cab.

46

A camera-repair place in the North End made ten copies of the tape while I watched. The guy even took fifty dollars to let me do it myself. I kept the original, Thompson received one, Claire ended up with two, and the other seven were mailed to reporters.

And then, with Thompson beside me, I turned myself in to the police before Walsh regained consciousness.

For a while it was touch and go. Walsh's story of an unprovoked ambush made for some interesting moments as the cops tried to separate me from my lawyer in the little room they had me in. But eventually Claire reached McMillan-Fowler and Atismak and they both saw the tape.

Outside the room with Thompson, maybe thirty cops had gathered. Through the door I could hear them talking, whispering, growling. Thompson and I could both feel the rage growing and he fished out his flask and drained it without offering me anything.

"Jesus. They're going to lynch you."

"Yep. The fixes you get me in . . ."

Thompson stared at me and strangled a laugh and outside the voices went on.

"... popped his eye right out of his ..."

"... we go in there and drag the liar out and then we SHOOT the motherfucker ..."

"Walsh, man, who could believe that some little punk ..."

"... heard he ambushed him. Got him with a bat and then heel stomped his face into ..."

"Fuck that! We protect our own!"

Eventually, though, McMillan-Fowler's voice cut through.

"All of you! Watch this. Before you do anything truly stupid."

Then she led me out while the tape was still playing on a big TV/VCR combination in the front of the room.

"Do any of you see an ambush?"

None of the cops said a word.

"Do any of you see a fair fight?"

No one said anything but some of them fidgeted. White men with mustaches and testosterone, rage and indignation.

"I see a fight between an armed man and an unarmed man. If I showed this same tape to a jury, they'd have Walsh doing five years."

She watched the cops fidget some more.

"Do any of you see anything here to protect?"

No one answered that one, and she and Atismak led me out with Thompson following.

47

Time passed.

Eventually the press forgot. Eventually the public forgot. I held my tongue and waited for the flames to die down. Against Thompson's advice, I dropped the suit against the city and the city responded with an apology. We did, however, start a case against Walsh in the civic court and in time even the police union got tired of defending him and he faded away into humiliation, forced retirement, and a court-recommended psychiatric review.

In any case, he was gone and I was where I wanted to be.

"You know this isn't fair, right?"

Claire smiled and nodded and then laughed out loud. "Of course not, dear. It's not fair at all."

I stood at the edge of the living room door and glowered at her until she laughed again.

"You look adorable, though."

I was wearing a shapeless and baggy track suit. It had been clean half an hour ago and now it was already more than slightly stained. Behind me on the rug were three children aged from eleven months to two years, fighting with grim determination over possession of various toys, and I was doing my best to ignore them. My hand unconsciously became a fist and I gestured towards the children over my shoulder.

"You can't do this. Only one of those is mine."

Claire was putting on a new pair of pumps and admiring them in the mirror she'd mounted by the hall closet. "This is true. Consider it your contribution to the war effort."

She smiled and kissed me gently on the cheek. I could swear she was mocking me. Anyone else and I'd club them down and jump all over them but from her I'd take it and grin.

Outside, a car honked twice and Claire peered out through the drapes.

"She's here. Can't be late, it being my first day and all."

Over her shoulder I could see a battered Saturn sedan with the sign on the side with Rose and Haaviko Realty. Claire said it was a small lie, just until she could get her real estate licence, which might take her another month or two. Until then she could rent houses and manage them but not sell them and that was fine by her, although she'd told me that the real money was in sales.

"Wish me luck."

She stared at me until I smiled and kissed her hard. She didn't need luck because she had talent, even Vanessa had seen that when her boss had finally quit, due to stress and ulcers. She'd been at loose ends for about a day until she'd made up her mind and called. With a little help from each other, they'd both do fine.

"Good luck, doll. But I'll get you for this."

She didn't answer but pulled on her raincoat and walked out into the rain. From the window, I watched her move down the walk with a good stride, leggy and confident. I watched her get into the car, and then I let the drapes fall. The children were watching me with wide eyes. Somehow they'd managed to pull all the books off the nearest shelf and were using them as building blocks in the center of the room.

"Shit."

Renfield whimpered from the corner and I shook my head at him. "Big dog like you and you can't even control three little kids."

He whimpered again and I noticed that someone had tied a big pink bow around his neck. The ends trailed down onto the floor and I wondered where the kids had found the ribbon.

"Well. Well. Well."

The three kids looked at me. Fred, with his sparse hair all disheveled and the beginnings of a big mouse under his right eye. Beside him was a girl in a pink jumper with blond hair in two long braids. Her name was Rachel and she was the granddaughter of the next-door neighbors. Her mother was erratic, to put it kindly, and a slut, to put it unkindly, and the grandparents were raising Rachel and they'd jumped at the offer of me babysitting her for twenty dollars a day. The last child was from the Ramirezes, a beautiful, golden-skinned boy just a little older than Fred. He was the wickedest of the lot by a long shot. Unfortunately he was also the most charming and what I thought had been quiet was, in fact, a tendency to devious plotting.

The doorbell rang and, like a starting bell, the three children used it as a sign and started to fight again. I sighed and turned to open the door, where a pink-faced girl in her late teens was holding a small, black-haired baby, who peered at me myopically through his fingers, which were laced across his eyes. Over one shoulder the woman carried a bag just slightly smaller than the kind used by hockey players to carry their gear from game to game.

"Hi!" She was incredibly chipper for 7:00 a.m.

"Good morning."

I was slightly more reserved and considerably less cheerful.

"Well, Mr. Haaviko, I read in the local paper that you were available to babysit during the day . . . ?"

I started to nod and then reconsidered. "You read?"

"Yes. It was in the Work Wanted section of the *North End Sentinel*. Now, I was just wondering . . ."

Claire. It had to be Claire. Or Elena, or maybe even Frank, he'd surely find it amusing just as long as I could still make it down to his place on Wednesdays to do the hard work. When I found out who, I'd . . .

"Um, Mr. Haaviko . . . ?"

Actually, it was kind of funny.

"Mr. Haaviko?"

I mean, really. I'd killed, burned, looted, stolen, pillaged, smuggled, conned, all that and more. Considering that background, ending up as a babysitter was kind of funny.

"Ha."

"Mr. Haaviko!"

The teenybopper in front of me was really pissed now and she stomped her foot in rage.

"I'm sorry, please do come in."

I took the child and ushered the young woman into the house. The children had stopped fighting and were trying to surround the dog, who looked at me imploringly for aid. I ignored him and turned to the young woman. "Would you like some coffee?"

She did and we went into the kitchen, where she dropped her bag to the floor with a sigh of relief.

"Now, Mr. Haaviko. It says you charge twenty dollars a day per child and that includes a snack and lunch?"

I nodded and handed her a cup of coffee, and took a sip out of mine. The smell filled my nose and the heat warmed me and I smiled again. This, the children, the house, the rain, the haggling over small sums of money, these things were all nice. These things, things I'd never wanted and never had before, these things were good and important and real. I took another sip and added a little milk to cool the mixture.

"Yes."

She stared at me and took a tiny sip of her coffee and made a face. "Well, I hope it's healthy food, Mr. Haaviko?"

It was, so I nodded and she just stood there and sighed again. "I work at Perkins, Mr. Haaviko."

That just didn't make sense but I nodded anyway. I suppose it was small talk, bad small talk, but small talk nonetheless.

"So, can you take care of my son, Mr. Haaviko?"

I finished my coffee and felt it burn down into my belly. "Sure thing, call me Monty, though. Mr. Haaviko sounds awfully formal."

I'd like to acknowledge the support and aid of the Manitoba Arts Council. Also thanks to Wayne Tefs for his superb and instructive editing and to Todd Besant for his advice and support. More thanks goes to David Neufeld, William, Lois, and Alison, Sēanin, Morgan, Erik, Robert and T, and others too numerous to mention. Also, my thanks to those in the shadows. You know who you are.